KARIN FOSSUM

In the Darkness

TRANSLATED FROM THE NORWEGIAN BY
James Anderson

VINTAGE BOOKS
London

Published by Vintage 2013

2 4 6 8 10 9 7 5 3 1

First published with the title *Evas øye* in 1995
by J. W. Cappelens Forlag AS, Oslo

First published in Great Britain in 2012 by
Harvill Secker

Vintage
Random House, 20 Vauxhall Bridge Road,
London SW1V 2SA

www.vintage-books.co.uk

Addresses for companies within The Random House Group Limited
can be found at: www.randomhouse.co.uk/offices.htm

The Random House Group Limited Reg. No. 954009

A CIP catalogue record for this book
is available from the British Library

ISBN 9780099554974

The Random House Group Limited supports the Forest Stewardship
Council® (FSC®), the leading international forest-certification
organisation. Our books carrying the FSC label are printed on FSC®-
certified paper. FSC is the only forest-certification scheme supported by
the leading environmental organisations, including Greenpeace.
Our paper procurement policy can be found at
www.randomhouse.co.uk/environment

Typeset in Sabon MT by Palimpsest Book Production Limited,
Falkirk, Stirlingshire

Printed and bound in Great Britain by
CPI Group (UK) Ltd, Croydon, CR0 4YY

TO MY FATHER

It was a Wendy house.

A tiny house with red sills and lace curtains in the windows. He halted a short distance from it, listened, but heard nothing except the dog panting by his side and a gentle rustle from the old apple trees. He stood there a moment longer, feeling the dampness of the grass seep through his shoes, and listening to his heart, which had changed its pace after the chase through the garden. The dog looked up at him and waited. Condensation poured from its great jaws, it sniffed the darkness tentatively, its ears quivered, perhaps it could hear sounds from within that he couldn't detect. He turned and looked back at the detached house behind them, its lit windows, its warmth and cosiness. No one had heard them, not even when the dog barked. His car was down on the road with two wheels on the kerb and the door open.

She's frightened of the dog, he thought with surprise. Bending down, he grabbed him by the collar and approached the door with slow steps. There certainly wouldn't be a rear exit in a little house like this, or even a lock on the door. It must be plaguing her now, if it hadn't the moment she'd shut herself in, the thought that she'd fallen straight into a trap. No way out. She hadn't got a chance.

Chapter 1

The courthouse was a gently curving, grey concrete building of seven storeys, and an effective windbreak for the town's main street, taking the sting out of the driving snow from the river. The Portakabins at the rear were sheltered, a blessing in the winter, in summer they stewed in the stagnant air. The facade above the entrance was adorned with an ultra-modern Themis and her scales, which at a distance, from down by the Statoil depot for example, looked more like a witch on a broomstick. The police service and the county jail occupied the top three floors, as well as the Portakabins.

The door swung open with an ill-tempered groan. Mrs Brenningen started and placed a finger on her book, after the phrase 'the balance of probability'. Inspector Sejer came into reception with a woman. She looked as if she'd been in the wars, her chin was grazed, her coat and skirt were torn, her mouth was bleeding.

Mrs Brenningen didn't normally stare. She'd been the receptionist at the courthouse for seventeen years, she'd seen all sorts come and go, but now she gawped. She snapped the book shut, her place marked with an old bus timetable. Sejer laid a hand on the woman's arm and led her to the lift. She walked with her head down. Then the doors closed.

Sejer's face was impassive, it was impossible to tell what he was thinking. It made him look severe, though in reality he was merely reserved, and behind the stern features dwelt a soul that was kindly enough. But he wasn't given to warm smiles, employing them only as ice-breakers when he wanted to gain access to people, and his praise was reserved for a select few. He closed the door and nodded towards the only chair, pulled a handful of tissue out of the dispenser above the wash-basin, moistened it with hot water and offered it to her. She wiped her mouth and looked around. The office was rather bare, but she studied the child's draw-ings on the wall and a small plasticine figure on his desk, which bore witness to the fact that he did indeed have a life outside these spartan surroundings. The figure was supposed to represent a rather prolapsed policeman in a violet-blue uniform, with his stomach on his knees and wearing oversized boots. It didn't much resemble the original, who was now sitting looking at her with grey, earnest eyes. There was a tape recorder on the desk and a Compaq computer. The woman peered furtively at them and hid her face in the wet tissue paper. He left her in peace. He got an audio cassette from the drawer and wrote on the white label: Eva Marie Magnus.

'Are you frightened of dogs?' he asked kindly.

She glanced up. 'In the past perhaps. But not any more.' She crumpled the tissue into a ball. 'I used to be frightened of everything. Now there's nothing I'm frightened of at all.'

Chapter 2

The river cascaded through the countryside splitting the cold town into two shivering grey floes. It was April and still wintry. Just as it reached the middle of the town, somewhere about the District Hospital, it began to roar and grumble, as if the nagging traffic and noisy industry along its banks had disturbed it. It coiled and wreathed in ever stronger currents as it advanced through the town. Past the old theatre and the Labour Party headquarters, by the railway tracks and on past the square to the old Exchange, which was now a McDonald's, down to the brewery – a pretty shade of pink and also the oldest in the country – to the Cash & Carry, the motorway bridge, a huge industrial estate with several car firms and finally the old roadside inn. There, the river could heave a final sigh and tumble into the sea.

It was late afternoon, the sun was setting, and in a

short while the brewery would be transformed from a dreary colossus into a fairy-tale castle with a thousand lights that were reflected in the river. The town was only beautiful after dark.

Eva watched the little girl as she ran along the river-bank. The distance between them was ten metres, she was careful not to let it increase. It was a grey day and few people were about on the footpaths, a bitter breeze blew off the swiftly flowing river. Eva kept an eye out for dog-owners, and in that eventuality whether the dog was loose, for she couldn't breathe easily until they'd passed. She saw none. Her skirt flapped around her legs and the wind cut right through her knitted sweater, forcing her to hug herself with both arms as she walked. Emma skipped along contentedly, if not gracefully, for she was well overweight. A fat kid with a large mouth and an angular face. Her red hair whipped the back of her neck, the moisture in the air giving it an unwashed look. Certainly not a cute little girl, but as she was unaware of the fact she pranced blithely along in her artlessness, and with an appetite for life which only a child possesses. Emma was seven, five months until she began school, Eva thought. One day she'd catch herself reflected in the critical faces of the playground, see her own unlovely person for the first time. But if she were a strong child, if she were like her father, the man who'd packed up and gone to live with someone else, she wouldn't give it another thought. This was what occupied Eva Magnus as she walked. This, and the overcoat that she'd left in the hall at home.

Eva knew every inch of the footpath, they'd walked it countless times. Emma was the one who went on about it, who wouldn't relinquish the old habit of strolling by the river; Eva could have done without it. At regular intervals the child ran down to the water's edge because she'd seen something that had to be inspected more closely. Eva watched her like a hawk. If she fell in there was no one else to save her. The river was fast-flowing, the water icy and the girl heavy. She shuddered.

This time she'd found a flat stone right down by the bank, she waved, shouting to her mother to come. Eva followed. There was just enough room for both of them to sit.

'We can't sit here, it's wet. We'll get cystitis.'

'Is that dangerous?'

'No, but it's painful. It stings, and you've got to wee all the time.'

They sat down anyway, following the eddies with their eyes, and marvelled at the movements of the water.

'Why are there currents in the water?' Emma asked.

Eva had to think for a moment. 'Well, goodness, I don't know. Perhaps it's got something to do with the riverbed; there's lots of things I don't know. When you go to school, you'll learn about all that.'

'That's what you always say when you don't know the answer.'

'But it's true. In any case you can ask your teacher. Teachers know a lot more than me.'

'I don't think so.'

An empty plastic container came sailing rapidly towards them.

'I want it! You got to get it for me!'

'Yuk no, leave it alone, it's only rubbish. I'm cold, Emma, can't we go home soon?'

'In a little while.' Emma pushed her hair behind her ears and rested her chin on her knees, but the hair was coarse and unruly, it sprang forward again. 'Is it very deep?' She nodded towards the middle of the river.

'No, not particularly,' said Eva quietly, 'eight or nine metres I should think.'

'That's really, really deep.'

'No, it's not. The deepest place in the world is in the Pacific Ocean,' she said musingly. 'Some sort of hollow. It's eleven thousand metres deep. That's what I call really, really deep.'

'I wouldn't like to go swimming there. You know everything, Mum, I don't think teachers know all that. I'd like a pink school bag,' she went on.

Eva shivered. 'Mmm,' she said. 'They are pretty. But they get dirty awfully quickly. I think those brown ones are nice, those brown leather ones, have you seen them? Like the bigger children have?'

'I'm not big. I'm only just starting school.'

'Yes, but you'll get bigger, and you can't have a new bag every year.'

'But we've got more money now, haven't we?'

Eva didn't reply. The question made her shoot a quick glance over her shoulder, a habit she'd formed. Emma found a stick and poked it into the water.

'Why is there froth in the water?' she continued. 'Nasty, yellow froth.' She whipped it a bit with her stick. 'Shall I ask at school?'

Eva still didn't answer. She, too, had her chin on her knees, her thoughts had wandered away again, and Emma had receded into the corner of her eye. The river brought back memories. Now she could see a face shimmering under the dark water. A round face with narrowed eyes and black brows.

'Lie down on the bed, Eva.'

'What?'

'Just do as I say, lie down on the bed.'

'Can we go to McDonald's?' Emma asked suddenly.

'What? Yes, why not. We'll go to McDonald's, at least it's warm there.'

She rose, slightly distractedly, and took the child by the arm. Shook her head and stared down into the river. The face had vanished now, there was nothing there, but she knew it would return, perhaps to haunt her for the rest of her days. They climbed up to the path and set off slowly back towards the town. They didn't meet a soul.

Eva felt her thoughts running wild, pursuing their own course and arriving in places she'd rather forget. The roar of the river conjured up a host of images. She had waited for them to fade, to find peace at last. And time had passed. One day at a time had turned into six months.

'Can I have a Happy Meal with a present? It's thirty-seven kroner and I haven't got Aladdin.'

'Yes.'

'What'll you have, Mum? Chicken?'

'Not sure yet.' She stared at the black water again, the thought of food was nauseating. She didn't bother with food much. Now she noticed how the surface rose and fell, under the dirty yellow scum.

'Now we've got more money, we can eat whatever we want, can't we, Mum?'

Eva kept quiet. All at once she stopped and strained her eyes. Something pale had floated up just beneath the surface of the water. It rocked sluggishly as it was pushed towards the bank by the powerful eddy. Her eyes were so taken up with watching that she'd forgotten the girl, who had also halted and who could see far better than her mother.

'It's a man!' Emma gasped. She clamped herself hard on to Eva's arm, her eyes popping out of her head. For a few moments they stood transfixed, staring at the sodden, decomposed body as it floated, head first, in amongst the stones. He was lying face down. The hair on the back of his head was thin and they could make out a bald patch. Eva was oblivious to the nails digging in through her sweater, she looked at the waxen-coloured corpse with its matted blond hair and couldn't remember seeing him before. But his trainers – those blue and white striped high-top trainers.

'It's a man,' Emma repeated, more quietly now.

Eva wanted to cry out. The cry came forcing its way up her throat but never emerged. 'He's drowned. Poor man, he's drowned, Emma!'

'Why does he look so horrible? Almost like jelly!'

'Because,' she stammered, 'because it happened some time ago.' She bit her lip so hard she pierced it. The taste of blood made her sway.

'Have we got to lift him up?'

'No, don't be silly! The police do that.'

'Are you going to phone them?'

Eva put her arm round the girl's chubby shoulders and stumbled along the path. She looked back again quickly, as if waiting for some attack, yet uncertain from which direction it would come. There was a phone box on the approach to the bridge, so she hauled the child after her and searched in her skirt pockets for change. She found a five-kroner piece. The sight of the partially decomposed man flashed before her like an ill omen, an omen of all that was to come. She had managed to calm down at last, time had settled upon everything like dust and made the nightmare pale. Now her heart was hammering beneath her sweater, completely out of control. Emma was silent. She followed her mother with frightened grey eyes and halted.

'Wait here. I'll ring and tell them to come and fetch him. Don't move!'

'We'll wait for them, won't we?'

'No, we certainly won't!'

She pushed into the box trying to control her panic. An avalanche of thoughts and ideas rushed through her head, but she dismissed each of them in turn. Then she made a quick decision. Her hands were clammy, she inserted the five-kroner piece into the slot and dialled a number with swift fingers. Her father answered, groggy, as if he'd been asleep.

'It's only me, Eva,' she whispered. 'Did I wake you?'

'Yes, but it was high time. Soon I'll be sleeping all round the clock. Is something the matter?' he growled. 'You're het up. I can hear that you're het up, I know you.'

His voice was dry and hoarse, but there was still a keenness to it, a keenness which she'd always loved. A sharpness that rooted her fast to reality.

'No, nothing's wrong. Emma and I were going out to eat and we found this phone box.'

'Well, put her on then!'

'Er, well, she's down by the water.'

She watched the numbers on the display counting down, threw a quick glance at Emma who was pressed against the glass of the door. Her nose was squashed flat like a lump of marzipan. Could she hear what they were saying?

'I haven't got a lot of change. We'll come and visit you one day soon. If you'd like.'

'Why are you whispering like that?' he demanded suspiciously.

'Am I?' she said a little louder.

'Give my girl a hug. I've got something for her when she comes.'

'What's that?'

'A school bag. She needs a school bag for the autumn, eh? I thought I'd save you the expense, things aren't all that easy for you.'

If only he'd known. She said: 'That was kind of you, Dad, but she's pretty sure about what she wants. Can we change it?'

'Yes of course, but I bought the bag they said I should. A pink leather one.'

Eva forced her voice to sound normal. 'I'll have to go, Dad, the money's run out. Look after yourself!' There was a click, and he was gone. The numbers on the display had stopped.

Emma looked at her expectantly. 'Are they coming now?'

'Yes, they're sending a police car. Come on, we'll go and eat. They'll ring if they want to speak to us, but I don't think they'll need to, at least not yet, perhaps later, but then they'll get in touch. This has nothing to do with us at all, you see, not really.' She was almost breathless, talking frantically.

'Can't we just wait and see them arrive, please can we?'

Eva shook her head. She crossed the street with the girl in tow, while the red man was still showing. They were an oddly matched pair as they walked into town, Eva tall and thin with slender shoulders and long, dark hair, Emma plump and broad and knock-kneed, with a slightly waddling gait. Both of them felt cold. And the town was cold, in the miasma from the chill river. It's an inharmonious town, Eva thought, as if it could never really be happy because it was split in two. Now the two halves were struggling to gain the upper hand. The north side with the church, the cinema and the most expensive stores, the south side with the railway, the cheap shopping centres, the pubs and the state off-licence. This last was important and ensured a steady stream of cars and people across the bridge.

'Mum, why did he drown?' Emma fixed on her mother's face and waited for an answer.

'I don't know. Perhaps he was drunk and fell into the river.'

'Perhaps he was fishing and fell out of his boat. He

should have been wearing a life jacket. Was he old, Mum?'

'Not particularly. About Dad's age perhaps.'

'At least Dad can swim,' she said with relief.

They had arrived at the green door of McDonald's. Emma put her weight against it and pushed it open. The smells within, of hamburgers and French fries, drew her and her unfailing appetite further into the place. Gone was the dead man in the river, gone all life's problems. Emma's tummy was rumbling and Aladdin was within reach.

'Find a table,' Eva said, 'and I'll order.'

She made for the corner as usual and seated herself under the flowering almond tree, which was plastic, while Eva joined the queue. She tried to banish the image that lapped at her inner eye, but it forced itself on her again. Would Emma forget it, or would she tell everyone? Perhaps she'd have nightmares. They must stifle it with silence, never mention it again. In the end she'd think it had never happened.

The queue inched forward. She stared distractedly at the youngsters behind the counter; with their red caps and red short-sleeved shirts they worked at an incredible pace. The fatty haze from the cooking hung like a curtain behind the counter, the smells of fat and frying meat, melted cheese and seasonings of all kinds forced their way into her nostrils. But they seemed oblivious to the thickness of the atmosphere, running back and forth like industrious red ants, smiling optimistically at each and every order. She watched the quick fingers and the light feet that sped across the floor. This was nothing like her own day's work. She stood in the middle of her studio most of the time, arms folded, fixing a stretched canvas with a hostile stare, or possibly an imploring one. On good days she stared aggressively and went on the attack, full of audacity and aplomb. Once in a blue moon she sold a painting.

'Happy Meal, please,' she said quickly, 'and chicken nuggets and two Cokes. Would you be very kind and put an Aladdin in? She hasn't got that one.'

The girl went to work. Her hands packed and folded at lightning speed. Over in the corner, Emma raised her head and followed her mother with her eyes as she finally came weaving across with the tray. Suddenly Eva's knees began to tremble. She sank down at the table and looked in wonderment at the girl who was eagerly struggling to open the little cardboard box. She searched for the toy. The eruption was deafening.

'I got Aladdin, Mum!' She raised the figure above her head and showed it to the entire restaurant. They all stared at her. Eva buried her face in her hands and sobbed.

'Are you ill?' Emma turned deadly serious and hid Aladdin under the table.

'No, well – just not a hundred per cent. It'll soon pass.'

'Are you upset about the dead man?'

She started. 'Yes,' she said simply. 'I'm upset about the dead man. But we won't talk about him any more. Never, d'you hear, Emma! Not to anyone! It'll only make us sad.'

'But do you think he's got children?'

Eva wiped her face with her hands. She wasn't certain of the future any more. She stared at the chicken, at the doughy brown lumps fried in fat, and knew that she couldn't eat them. The images flashed past again. She saw them through the branches of the almond tree.

'Yes,' she said at length, 'he's probably got children.'

Chapter 3

An elderly woman out walking her dog suddenly caught a glimpse of the blue and white shoe amongst the stones. She phoned from the telephone box near the bridge, just as Eva had done. When the police arrived, she was standing somewhat self-consciously by the bank with her back to the corpse. One of the officers, whose name was Karlsen, was first out of the car. He smiled politely when he caught sight of the woman and glanced inquisitively at her dog.

'He's a Chinese Crested,' she said.

It really was an intriguing creature, tiny, wrinkled and very pink. It had a thick tuft of dirty yellow hair on the crown of its head, but was otherwise entirely bald.

'What's his name?' he asked amicably.

'Adam,' she replied. He nodded and smiled, diving into the car's boot for the case of equipment. The policemen struggled with the dead man for a while, but eventually got him up on the bank where they placed him on a tarpaulin. He wasn't a big man, he just looked that way after his sojourn in the water. The woman with the dog retreated a little. The team worked quietly and precisely, the photographer took pictures, a forensic pathologist knelt by the tarpaulin and made notes. Most deaths had trivial causes and they weren't expecting anything unusual. Perhaps a drunk who'd toppled into the water, there were gangs of them under the bridge and along the footpaths in the evenings. This one was somewhere between twenty and forty, slim, but with a beer belly, blond, not particularly tall. Karlsen pulled a rubber glove on to his right hand and carefully raised the dead man's clothing.

'Stab wounds,' he said tersely. 'Several of them. Let's turn him over.' They fell silent. The only sound was that of rubber gloves being put on and pulled off, the quiet click of the camera, the breath of one or other of them, and the crackling of the plastic sheeting which they spread out by the side of the body.

'I wonder,' Karlsen muttered, 'if we haven't found Einarsson at long last.'

The man's wallet had gone, if he'd ever had one. But his wristwatch was there, a gaudy affair with a lot of extras, like the time in New York and Tokyo and London. Its black strap had dug into his swollen wrist. The corpse had been in the water a long time and had presumably been carried by the current from further upstream, and so the location of the find wasn't of special interest. Even so, they inspected it a bit, searching the bank for possible footprints, but found only a plastic can which had once contained antifreeze and an empty cigarette packet. A number of people had gathered up on the path, mostly youngsters; now they were craning their necks to steal a glance at the body on the tarpaulin. Decomposition was well under way. The skin had loosened from the body, especially on the hands, as if he were wearing oversized gloves. It was very discoloured. His eyes, which had once been green, were transparent and pale, his hair was falling out in great tufts, his face had puffed up and made his features indistinct. The fauna of the river, crayfish, insects and fish, had all tucked in greedily. The stab wounds in his side were great gaping gashes in the ashen white flesh.

'I used to fish here,' said one of the boys on the path, he'd never seen a dead body in all his seventeen years. He didn't really believe in death, just as he didn't believe in God, because he'd never seen either of them. He hunched his chin into the collar of his jacket and shivered. From now on anything was possible.

The post-mortem report arrived a fortnight later. Inspector Konrad Sejer had called five people to a conference room situated in one of the Portakabins behind the courthouse. They'd been erected there in more recent times owing to lack of space, a row of offices hidden from the public and which most people had never seen, apart from the unhappy souls who came into more intimate contact with the police. Some things had already been established. They knew the man's identity, they'd got that right away because the name Jorun was engraved on his wedding ring. A file from the previous October contained all the information about the missing Egil Einarsson, aged thirty-eight, address: Rosenkrantzgate 16, last seen on 4 October at nine in the evening. He left a wife and a six-year-old son. The file was thin, but would soon get thicker. The new photographs fattened it up well, and they weren't pretty. A number of people had been interviewed when he'd disappeared. His wife, workmates and relations, friends and neighbours. None of them had much to say. He wasn't exactly whiter than white, but he had no enemies, at least, none that they knew of. He had a regular job at the brewery, went home to his dinner every day and spent most of his spare time in his garage, tinkering with his beloved car, or with his mates at a pub on the south side. The pub was called the King's Arms. Einarsson was either a poor sod who'd been the victim of some desperado wanting money – heroin had taken a firm grip, seeing the potential in this cold, windswept town – or he had a secret. Perhaps he was in debt.

Sejer peered down at the report and rubbed his neck. It always impressed him the way criminal pathologists managed to pull together a semi-rotten mass of skin and hair, bones and muscles, and turn it into a complete human being with age and weight and physical attributes, condition, previous complaints and operations, dental hygiene and hereditary disposition.

'Remnants of cheese, meat, paprika and onion in the stomach,' he said aloud. 'Sounds like pizza.'

'Can they be sure after six months?'

'Yes, of course. When the fish haven't eaten it all. That sometimes happens.'

The man called Sejer was made of solid stuff. He was in his forty-ninth year, his forearms were already reasonably tanned, he'd rolled up his shirtsleeves and the blood vessels and sinews were conspicuous beneath the skin, making them look like seasoned wood. His face was well defined and a little sharp, his shoulders straight and broad, his good overall colour gave the impression of something that was well used, but which would also endure. His hair was spiky and steel-coloured, almost metallic, and very short. His eyes were large and clear, their irises the colour of wet slate. That was how his wife Elise had once described them years before. He'd found her description charming.

Karlsen was ten years his junior and slight by comparison. At first glance he could give the impression of being a dandy, without solidity or weight, he had a waxed moustache and a high, impressively bouffant head of hair. The youngest and sprightliest of them, Gøran Soot, was struggling to open a bag of jelly babies without making too much of a rustling noise. Soot had thick, wavy hair, a compact, muscular body and a fresh complexion. Taken on its own, each part of his body was a feast for the eye, but all together they were rather too much of a good thing. He, however, was unaware of this interesting fact. Seated by the door was Chief Inspector Holthemann, taciturn and grey, and behind him a female officer with close-cropped fair hair. At the window, with one arm propped on the sill, sat Jakob Skarre.

'How are things with Mrs Einarsson?' Sejer asked. He cared about people, knew that she had a young son.

Karlsen shook his head. 'She seemed a bit bewildered. She asked if this meant she'd get the life insurance money at last, and then broke down in despair because the first thing she'd thought about was the cash.'

'Why hasn't she had anything?'

'We had no body.'

'I'll take that up with the appropriate person,' said Sejer. 'What have they been living on these past six months?'

'Social security.'

Sejer shook his head and flipped through the report. Soot stuffed a green jelly baby into his mouth, only its legs protruded.

'The car,' Sejer went on, 'was found at the municipal dump. We rooted through the rubbish for days. In fact he was killed in a completely different location, possibly by the river. Then the killer got into the car and drove it to the rubbish tip. It's extraordinary if Einarsson really has been in the water for six months and hasn't turned up until now. That's quite some time the murderer has been clinging to the hope that he would never surface again. Well, now he's had a reality check. I imagine it'll be quite a hard one, too.'

'Did he get caught up on something?' Karlsen wondered out loud.

'Don't know. It's a bit strange, that, the riverbed is pure gravel, it's not long since it was dredged. He may have been swept in towards the bank and got caught up on something there. His appearance was roughly what we'd have anticipated, anyway.'

'The car had been cleaned and hoovered inside,' said Karlsen, 'the dashboard had been polished. Wax and cleaning stuff everywhere. He left home to sell it.'

'And his wife didn't know who the prospective purchaser was,' Sejer recalled.

'She knew nothing at all, but that was par for the course in that household.'

'No one phoned asking for him?'

'No. He told her quite suddenly that he had a purchaser. She thought it was strange. He'd scraped and saved to get that car, tinkered with it for months, treated it like his baby.'

'Maybe he needed money,' said Sejer urgently, rising. He began to pace. 'We've got to find that buyer. I wonder what happened between them. According to his wife he had a hundred kroner in his wallet. We ought to go through the car again, someone sat in it and drove it several kilometres, a murderer. He must have left something behind!'

'The car's been sold,' Karlsen put in.

'Wouldn't you just know it.'

'9 p.m.'s pretty late to go showing off a car,' said Skarre, a curly-haired man with an open face. 'It's bloody dark in October at nine in the evening. If I were going to buy a car I'd want to see it in daylight. It could have been planned. A kind of trap.'

'Yes. And if you want to test drive a car, you head out of town. Away from people.' Sejer scratched his chin with well-clipped nails. 'If he was stabbed on the fourth of October, he's been in the river six months,' he said. 'Is that consistent with the state of the body?'

'The pathologists are being difficult about that,' said Karlsen. 'Impossible to date that sort of thing, they say. Snorrasson told of a woman who was found after seven years, and she was as good as new. Some lake in Ireland. Seven years! The water was freezing cold, pure preservation. But we can assume it happened on the fourth of October. It must have been quite a strong person, I should have thought, judging by the results.'

'Let's look at the stab wounds.'

He selected a photograph from the folder, went to the board and clipped it in position. The picture showed Einarsson's back and bottom; the skin had been thoroughly washed and the stab wounds left crater-like depressions.

'They do look rather strange, fifteen stab wounds, half of which are to the lower back, bottom and abdomen, and the remainder in the victim's right side, directly above the hip, delivered with great force by a right-handed person, striking from above and slicing downwards. The knife had a long, thin blade, very thin in fact. Perhaps a fishing knife. Altogether a strange way to attack a man. But you remember what the car looked like, don't you?'

All at once he strode over and hauled Soot out of his chair. His bag of goodies fell to the floor.

'I need a victim,' Sejer said. 'Come here!' He pushed the officer over to the desk, took up position behind him and grabbed the plastic ruler. 'It could have happened something like this. This is Einarsson's car,' he said, pushing the young policeman over on to the desktop. His chin just reached the far edge. 'The bonnet is up, because they're busy looking over the engine. The killer pushes the victim on to the engine and holds him down with his left arm while he stabs him fifteen times with his right. FIFTEEN TIMES.' He wielded the ruler and prodded Soot's bottom as he counted aloud: 'One, two, three, four,' he moved his hand and stabbed him in the side, Soot squirmed a bit, as if he was ticklish, 'five, six, seven – and then he stabs him in the nether regions . . .'

'No!' Soot leapt up in horror and crossed his legs.

Sejer stopped, gave his victim a small push and sent him back to his chair as he fought to suppress a smile.

'It's a lot of times to strike with a knife. Fifteen stabs and a whole lot of blood. It must have spurted out everywhere, over the killer's clothes, face and hands, over the car and the ground. It's a bugger that he moved the car.'

'At any rate, it must have been done in the heat of the moment,' Karlsen maintained. 'It's no normal execution. Must have been an argument.'

'Perhaps they couldn't agree on a price,' quipped Skarre.

'People who decide to kill using a knife often get a nasty shock,' said Sejer. 'It's a lot harder than they think. But let's assume it actually was premeditated, and at the opportune moment he pulls out his knife, for example just as Einarsson is standing with his back to him, bending over the engine.'

He narrowed his eyes as if conjuring up the scene. 'The killer had to strike from behind, so he couldn't easily get at what he wanted. It's much harder to reach vital organs from behind. And maybe it took quite a number of stabs before Einarsson finally collapsed. It must have been a terrifying experience, he's stabbing and stabbing, his victim goes on screaming, that makes him panic and he's unable to stop. That's what happens. In his imagination it'll be one or two lunges. But how often has the killer been content with that in all the many knife murders we've dealt with? Off the top of my head I can recall one instance with seventeen stab wounds, and another with thirty-three.'

'But they knew each other, do we agree on that?'

'Knew and knew. They had some kind of relationship, yes.' Sejer seated himself and put the ruler away in the drawer. 'Well, we'll have to begin at the beginning again. We must find out who wanted to buy that car. Use the list from October and begin at the top. It might be one of his workmates.'

'The same people?' Soot looked at him dubiously. 'Are we going to ask the same questions all over again?'

'What do you mean?' Sejer raised an eyebrow.

'I mean that we ought to be finding new people. The answers will be the same as last time. I mean, nothing's really changed.'

'Hasn't it? Perhaps you've not been listening all that carefully, but we've actually found the victim now. Stuck like a pig. And you say nothing's changed?'

He fought to hold back a note of arrogance. 'I mean, we're not going to get different answers because of that.'

'That,' said Sejer holding back an even larger one, 'remains to be seen, doesn't it?'

Karlsen closed the file with a little snap.

Sejer replaced Einarsson's folder in the filing cabinet. He filed it next to the Durban case, and thought that now they could keep each other company. Maja Durban and Egil Einarsson. Both were dead, but no one knew why. Then he leant back in his chair and placed his long legs on the desk, patted his backside and fished out his wallet. Jammed in between his driving and skydiving licences he found the picture of his grandson, Matteus. He had just turned four, he could recognise most makes of car and had already had his first fight, which he'd lost grievously. It had been a bit of a surprise, that time he'd gone to Fornebu Airport to pick up his daughter Ingrid and son-in-law Erik, who'd been in Somalia for three years. She as a nurse, he as a Red Cross doctor. She'd been standing at the top of the aircraft steps, tanned golden all over and with her hair bleached by the sun. For one wild second it had been like seeing Elise, that first time they'd met. She carried the little boy on her arm. He was four months old at the time, chocolate brown, with crinkly hair and the darkest eyes he'd ever seen. The Somalis were a beautiful race, he thought. And he gazed at the photo for a while before replacing it. It was quiet in the Portakabins now, and in most of the large adjacent building. He pushed two fingers into his shirtsleeve and scratched his elbow. The skin flaked off. Underneath there was new, pink skin which also flaked off. He pulled his jacket off the chair back and locked up, then he paid a lightning visit to Mrs Brenningen on the reception desk. She put down her book immediately. In any case, she'd reached a promising love scene and wanted to save it for when she was under the bedclothes. They exchanged a few words, then he nodded briefly and headed for Rosenkrantzgate and Egil Einarsson's widow.

Chapter 4

He glanced quickly in the mirror and ran his fingers through his hair. Because it was short he didn't alter its appearance at all. It was more an act of ritual than vanity.

Sejer took every opportunity to get out of the office. He drove rather slowly through the town centre; he always drove slowly, his car was old and sluggish, a large blue Peugeot 604 which he'd never had any reason to change. In snowy conditions it was like driving a sledge. Soon he was passing colourful houses, each home to four families. They were on his right, pink, yellow and green; the sun was shining on them now making them glow invitingly. They'd been built in the fifties and possessed a certain patina that newer houses didn't have. The trees were well grown, the gardens fertile, or at least they would be when the spring arrived. But it was still cold, spring was late in coming. They'd had dry weather for a long time, and blobs of dirty snow lay like rubbish in the gutters. His eyes searched for number 16 and recognised the well-maintained green house the moment he saw it. The entrance was a chaos of trikes, lorries and plastic toys of all kinds, which the children had indiscriminately brought out from cellars and attics. Bare asphalt was always tempting after a long winter. He parked and rang the bell.

After a few moments she came to the door, with a thin little boy hanging on to her skirts.

'Mrs Einarsson,' he said, bowing slightly, 'may I come in?' Jorun Einarsson nodded vaguely and a touch unwillingly, but she hadn't many people to talk to. He was standing quite close to her, and she caught the smell of him, a mixture of jacket leather and a discreet aftershave lotion.

'I don't know any more than I did last autumn,' she said uncertainly. 'Well, apart from the fact he's dead. But I was expecting that, of course. I mean, the way the car looked . . .' She put an arm around the boy as if to protect them both.

'But now we've found him, Mrs Einarsson. So things are a bit different, aren't they?' He kept quiet and waited.

'It must have been some nutcase who wanted money.' She shook her head distractedly. 'Well, his wallet had gone. You saw that his wallet had gone. Even though he had only a hundred kroner. But people kill just for loose change nowadays.'

'I promise this won't take long.'

She gave in and retreated down the corridor. Sejer stood in the doorway to the living room and looked about. He always felt a certain dismay when it struck him just how similar people were; he saw it in their living rooms, how they filled them. They were the same everywhere, arranged in the same symmetry, with the television and video as a kind of focal point for the rest of the furniture. This was where the family huddled together to get warm. Mrs Einarsson had a pink leather suite and a shaggy white carpet under the coffee table. It was a feminine room. She'd lived alone for six months, maybe she'd spent the time expunging any masculine influence, if there'd been any to begin with. Then, as now, he could see no trace of loss or love for the man they'd found in the black river water, grey and perforated like an old sponge. What anguish there had been was directed towards other things, practical things. What was she going to live on and how could she get out and find another man when she hadn't got the money for a babysitter? Such thoughts depressed him. They caused him to examine the wedding photo above the sofa, a somewhat lavish portrait of the young Jorun with bleached hair. Standing next to her was Egil Einarsson, slender and smooth-cheeked like a confirmation candidate and sporting a thin moustache. They posed to the best of their ability before a mediocre photographer, very concerned with their appearance. Not with one another.

'I've got some coffee in the pot,' she said hesitantly.

He said yes. It would be good to have something to hold on to, even if it was only the handle of a cup. The boy trotted into the kitchen after his mother, but peeped at him stealthily from behind the door. He was thin, with a few freckles on his nose and hair that was too long and fell into his eyes all the time. In a few years he'd resemble the man in the wedding photo.

'I've forgotten your name,' Sejer said, smiling encouragingly.

The boy withheld his name for a moment, twisting the sole of his trainer into the lino and smiling shyly.

'Jan Henry.'

Sejer nodded. 'Ah, Jan Henry, of course. Can I ask you something, Jan Henry – do you collect pins?'

He nodded. 'I've got twenty-four. On my cowboy hat.'

'Bring it here,' Sejer smiled, 'and I'll give you another one. One you certainly won't have.'

The boy shot round the corner and made for his bedroom. He returned with the hat on his head, it was much too large. He removed it with respect.

'They prick so much inside,' he explained, 'so I can't wear it.'

'Look here,' said Sejer, 'a police pin. I got this from Mrs Brenningen at the station. Not bad, eh?'

The boy nodded. He searched the hat for a place of honour for the small golden pin, resolutely demoted an older one, and stuck the police pin in the middle at the front. His mother entered and gave a smile.

'Go to your room,' she said briskly, 'me and the man have got to talk.'

He put the hat on his head again and vanished.

Sejer drank his coffee and watched Mrs Einarsson who dropped two lumps of sugar in her own cup, from just above the coffee, so that it wouldn't splash. Her wedding ring had gone. Her blonde hair was dark at the parting and she was wearing too much make-up round the eyes, which made her look a bit fierce. In fact she was rather sweet, a neat, fair little person. Presumably she didn't know it. She was probably dissatisfied with her own appearance, like most women. Apart from Elise, he thought.

'We're still looking for this purchaser, Mrs Einarsson, just as we were before. For some reason your husband suddenly wanted to sell the car, even though he'd never discussed it with you. He went off to show it to someone and never returned. Perhaps someone had expressed an interest in it, stopped him in the street or whatever. Perhaps someone wanted that precise model, and got in touch. Or maybe someone was out to get him, just him, not the car, but they used it to lure him out of the house. Tempted him to sell. Do you know if he was in financial straits?'

She shook her head and crunched one of the dissolving lumps of sugar.

'You asked me that before. No, not financial straits. I mean, not that bad. But everyone needs money, don't they, we weren't well off. And now it's even worse. And I can't even get a playschool place. And I get migraines,' she massaged her temples lightly as if to demonstrate that he had to treat her gently, or it might strike like lightning at any moment, 'and it isn't so easy to work with a handicap like that, alone with a kid and all.'

He nodded sympathetically. 'But you're not aware that he used money to gamble, or that he had a loan, perhaps a private loan, which he was having difficulty managing?'

'He didn't have one. He wasn't a genius, but he wasn't a fool either. We managed. He had a job and everything. And he only spent money on the car, and an occasional beer at the pub. He could mouth off sometimes, but he wasn't tough enough to get involved in anything, I mean, anything illegal. At least I don't think so. And we were married for eight years, so I think I know him fairly well. Knew him, I mean. And I can't just sit here saying things about Egil either, even if he is dead.' She drew breath at last.

'You can't remember if any of his mates ever expressed a wish to own the car?'

'Well, yes, I'm sure they did. But he wouldn't sell. Didn't even like lending it.'

'And you don't remember phone calls in the days before he disappeared that might have been about the car?'

'No.'

'What was he like that evening when he left?'

'I've told you already. Just like normal. He got home from work at three-thirty. He was on early shift. Then he had a pizza Mexicana, and coffee, and lay in the garage all evening.'

'Lay?'

'Under the car. And tinkered. He was fixated with that car. Afterwards he washed it. I was busy in the house and didn't give it a thought until he came in right in the middle of *Casino* and said he was off out to show the car to someone.'

'No name?'

'No.'

'Nothing about where they were going to meet?'

'No.'

'And you didn't ask why he wanted to sell it?'

She touched her hair and shook her head. 'I didn't get involved with the car. I haven't even got a driving licence. It didn't matter to me what car we had, so long as we had one. And he didn't say he was going to sell it, either, just that he was going to show it to someone. And that wasn't necessarily the murderer. He could have met someone, or given someone a lift, or whatever, I don't know. This town is full of loonies, it's because of all this heroin, I don't know why you lot can't put a stop to it. Think of Jan Henry who'll have to grow up here, he's not exactly got a strong character, he's like his dad for that.'

'A strong character,' said Sejer smiling, 'is something one develops over time. Perhaps we should allow him a few more years yet. But we advertised for that prospective purchaser in the newspapers and on television,' he reminded her, 'and no one came forward. No one dared. Either your husband lied when he left home that evening, perhaps he was off to do something quite different – or that purchaser was the actual killer.'

'Lied?' She gave him an offended stare. 'If you think he had dirty secrets, you're wrong. He wasn't that sort. And there was no one after him either, women didn't find him that attractive, if you must know. If he said he was going to show the car to someone, that's the truth.'

She said this in a forthright manner that convinced him. He thought a bit, saw the boy come sneaking in and seat himself gingerly on the floor behind his mother. He gave him a surreptitious wink.

'If you think further back, was there anything that was out of the ordinary in any way? Let's say from six months before he disappeared up to the time his car was found on the dump – can you recall an episode or a period when he wasn't quite himself, or he was worried or something like that? I mean, anything at all? Telephone calls? Letters? Maybe days he got home later than normal from work, or didn't sleep well?'

Jorun Einarsson munched the other sugar lump, and he saw how her thoughts were travelling back. She cocked her head slightly over some memory or other, discarded it and mused on. Einarsson junior breathed noiselessly, like most little pitchers he had big ears.

'There was some trouble at the pub one evening. I suppose there is most of the time, and anyway it wasn't anything serious, but someone had got completely legless, so the landlord rang the police to have him taken away. It was one of Egil's mates, from the brewery. Egil followed them and pleaded with them to let him out. He promised to drive him home and get him to bed. And obviously that's what they did. That night he didn't get home till half past three in the morning and I remember that he overslept the following day.'

'Yes? Did you learn what had happened?'

'No. Only that he'd been completely pissed. Not Egil, but the other man. Egil had the car, he was on the early shift. Anyway, I didn't ask, that sort of thing doesn't interest me.'

'Was he a man who cared about other people, d'you think? It was rather good of him. He could have turned his back and left him to it.'

'He wasn't especially caring,' she said, 'since you ask. He didn't notice his surroundings much normally. So I admit I was a bit surprised that he really had taken that trouble. Saved a bloke from a drunk and disorderly charge. Yes, I was a bit taken aback perhaps, but they were mates, after all. Quite honestly, I hadn't thought about it much. Not before now, I mean, when you asked about it.'

'When roughly did this happen?'

'Oh God, I can't remember. Shortly before he went missing.'

'Weeks? Months?'

'No, a few days perhaps.'

'A few days? Did you mention that episode when we spoke to you last autumn?'

'Don't think so.'

'And his drunken mate, Mrs Einarsson, do you know who he was?'

She shook her head, stole a quick glance over her shoulder and caught sight of the child.

'Jan Henry! I thought I told you to go to your room!'

He got up and slunk out of the room like an unwelcome dog. She poured more coffee.

'The name, Mrs Einarsson,' he said quietly.

'No, I can't remember,' she said. 'There's so many of them, a whole gang who hang out at that pub.'

'But he overslept the next day, didn't you say?'

'Yes.'

'And they've got a time-clock at the brewery, haven't they?'

'Mmm.'

He considered. 'And when you got the car back from our technical people, you sold it?'

'Yes, I needed the money. Besides I can't afford to drive anyway, so I sold the car to my brother, along with some tools that were in the back. A socket set and a jack. And some clutter which I hadn't got a clue what it was. Besides, there was something missing, something that wasn't there.'

'What?'

'I can't remember now. My brother asked about it, and we searched but couldn't find it. I can't remember what it was.'

'Try. It could be important.'

'No, I don't think it was important, but I can't remember what it was. We searched in the garage too.'

'Ring the station if you remember. Could you ask your brother?'

'He's off travelling. But he'll be back sometime.'

'Thanks for the coffee, Mrs Einarsson,' he said getting up.

She leapt up from her chair, slightly flustered and blushing because he was off so suddenly, and followed him to the door. He bowed and went to the car park. Just as he put the key in the door, he caught sight of the boy, he was standing with both feet in a flower bed, turning the soil with terrific energy. His trainers were filthy. Sejer waved.

'Hi. Haven't you got anyone to play with?'

'No,' he smiled bashfully. 'Why haven't you got a police car when you're at work?'

'Good question. But you see, I'm actually on my way home. I live a bit further along the road, and this way I don't have to go back to the station to change cars.' He thought for a moment. 'Have you ever been in a police car?'

'No.'

'Next time I come to see your mum I'll come in a police car. You can come for a drive with me, if you'd like.'

The boy smiled from ear to ear, but there was a shadow of doubt, perhaps it came from bitter experience.

'It's a promise,' Sejer assured him. 'And you won't have to wait long!' He slid in behind the steering wheel and rolled off slowly down the street. In the mirror he saw the thin arm waving.

He was still thinking about the boy as he passed the trotting course on the left and the Church of the Latter-day Saints on his right. 'God forgive you, Konrad,' he said to himself, 'if you forget that police car next time.'

Chapter 5

Emma was playing with a farm on the living room floor.

The animals were ranged in neat lines, pink pigs, brown and white dappled cows, hens and sheep. A Tyrannosaurus rex surveyed the scene, the head with its tiny brain just reached to the ridge of the barn.

At regular intervals she ran to the window watching eagerly for her father's car. Every other weekend she stayed with her father and she looked forward to it each time with equal fervour. Eva was expectant too. She sat tensely on the sofa and waited, needing to get the child out of the house so she could have peace to think. She usually used such free weekends for working. Now she was totally paralysed. Everything was different. They'd found him.

Emma hadn't brought up the subject of the dead man for several days. But that didn't mean she'd forgotten him. She could tell by her mother's face that he wasn't to be mentioned, and although she didn't know why, she respected it.

In the studio a canvas stood prepared on the easel. She had already primed it black, without a hint of light. She couldn't be bothered to look at it. There was so much else now that needed to be done first. She sat on the sofa listening with the same intensity as Emma for the red Volvo which would turn into the courtyard at any moment. Complete order reigned on the farm, apart from the green monster that towered behind the barn. It looked strange.

'That dinosaur doesn't quite fit in, does it Emma?'

Emma pouted.

'I know that. It's only visiting.'

'Ah, I see. I should have realised.'

She drew her legs up and pulled her long skirt over her knees. Tried to empty her head of thoughts. Emma sat down again, pushed the piglets one after the other under the sow's belly.

'There's not enough teats. This one hasn't got one.' She raised a piglet between two fingers and looked enquiringly at her mother.

'Mmm. That's what happens. Those piglets starve to death. Or you have to feed them from a bottle and farmers usually haven't got the time.'

Emma pondered this for a bit. 'I can give it to Dino. He's got to have food, too.'

'But they only eat grass and leaves and that sort of thing, don't they?'

'Not this one, he's a meat-eater,' Emma explained, and pushed the piglet between the green monster's sharp teeth.

Eva shook her head in disbelief at this practical solution. Children never ceased to amaze her. And just then there was the sound of revving in the courtyard. Emma vanished as fast as she was able, out through the hallway to greet her father.

Eva raised her head dully as he appeared in the doorway. This man had been the guiding beacon in her life. When Emma stood next to him she seemed smaller and trimmer than usual. They suited one another, both with red hair and carrying far too much weight. They loved each other, too, and she was pleased about that. She'd never been jealous, not even of the new woman in his life. Her great grief was that he'd left her, but now that he'd done it, she wished him the best of luck. It was that simple.

'Eva!' he smiled, his ginger forelock nodding. 'You look tired.'

'I've got one or two problems.' She smoothed her skirt.

'Artistic things?' he asked, without a trace of sarcasm.

'No. Tangible, worldly things.'

'Are they serious?'

'Far worse than you can imagine.'

He contemplated her answer and his brow furrowed. 'If I can help with anything, you must let me know.'

'You may have no choice in the end.'

He stood there staring at her earnestly, with Emma hanging on to his trouser leg. The child was heavy enough to make him lose his balance. He felt enormous sympathy, but she inhabited a world that was completely beyond his ken, an artistic world. He'd never felt at home there. Nevertheless, she was an important part of his life and would always remain so.

'Fetch your bag, Emma, and give Mum a hug.'

She obeyed his command with great enthusiasm. Then they disappeared through the door. Eva went to the window and looked after them, followed the car with her eyes as it slid out into the traffic, then seated herself again, with her legs up and her head on the back of the sofa. She shut her eyes. It was pleasantly dusky in the room and perfectly still. She breathed as calmly and regularly as she could and allowed the silence to settle over her. This was the sort of moment she must enjoy to the full, treasure and remember. She knew it wouldn't last.

Sejer had poured himself a generous whisky and chased the dog off the sofa. It was a five-year-old male Leonberger weighing seventy kilos, but really soppy, and his name was Kollberg. In fact, he was called something else, because the kennel put their name on the pedigree according to their own system. In his case they'd used Beatles song titles. They'd begun at the beginning of the alphabet, and by the time Kollberg had been born they'd got to L. And so he was given the name Love Me Do. His sister was called Lucy In the Sky. Sejer groaned at the mere thought of it.

The dog resigned himself with a heavy sigh and settled at his feet. His great head rested on Sejer's feet and caused him to sweat inside his tennis socks. But he hadn't the heart to move them. And anyway it was lovely, especially in the winter. He sipped his whisky and lit a roll-up. These were his vices, this one glass of whisky and a single hand-rolled cigarette. Because he smoked so little, he immediately felt his heart begin to beat a little faster. On calm days he went to the aerodrome and went parachuting, but this he didn't regard as a vice, as Elise had done. Now he was in his eighth year of widowhood and his daughter was grown up and well taken care of. In any case, Sejer wasn't a daring man, he never jumped except in ideal weather conditions and never tried any dangerous stunts. It was just that he enjoyed the tremendous rush through the air, the relinquishing of all contact, the giddying view, the perspective it gave him, the farms and fields so far below with their lovely patterns of subdued colour, the light, delicate road network in between, like the lymphatic system of some giant organism, and the buildings arranged in neat rows, red, green and white houses. Man really is a creature who needs systems, he thought, and blew smoke under the lampshade.

Egil Einarsson had a system, too, with his orderly life, a job at the brewery, a wife and son, a stable group of friends and the pub on the south side. A fixed routine year after year, home, brewery, home, pub, home. The car with all its minute parts that needed to be cleaned and oiled and tightened. Week after month after year. Nothing on his file. No drama of any sort had ruffled his life, he had toiled his way through school like every other youngster, without arousing much attention, was confirmed, went on to do an engineering apprenticeship in Gothenburg which lasted two years, and which he never actually used, and finally ended up as a brewery worker. Liked it. Earned enough. Never reached any of life's dizzying heights, but didn't fall into many of its sloughs either. A straightforward man. His wife was nice enough and had certainly done her bit. And then someone had stabbed him. Fifteen times. How could a bloke like Einarsson arouse such passions? Sejer wondered. He sipped his whisky and went on grappling with vague thoughts. Of course it was true that they ought to have some new names on their list, people they hadn't thought of, people he could interview, so that an entirely new angle might suddenly emerge and throw new light on the whole tragedy. He kept coming back to the car. An Opel Manta, '88 model. All of a sudden he'd wanted to sell it. Someone had expressed an interest in it, that was what must have happened. He hadn't advertised it in any of the papers, hadn't told a soul he wanted to sell, they'd checked that. He sucked at his roll-up and held the smoke inside him for a few seconds. Who had he bought it from? he thought suddenly. That was a question he'd never actually asked himself. Perhaps he should have done. He jumped up and went to the phone. Just as he heard the ringing tone he realised that perhaps it was a bit late to be calling people. Mrs Einarsson answered on the second ring. She listened without asking questions and pondered a bit at the other end of the line: 'Purchase agreement? Yes, I should have it in our paperwork drawer, but you'll have to wait a second.'

He waited, listening as drawers were opened and closed, and papers shuffled.

'I can hardly read it,' she complained.

'Try. I can come by and collect it tomorrow if you can't make it out.'

'Well, it's an address on Erik Børresensgate anyway. Mikkelsen, I think. Can't read the first name, nor the street number. Unless it's a 5 perhaps, could be a 5. Or a 6. Erik Børresensgate 5 or 6.'

'That'll do fine, I'm sure. Thanks very much!'

He made a note on the pad by the phone. It was important not to miss anything. If he couldn't find out who the car went to, he could find out where it came from. That was something anyway.

Chapter 6

A new day was already on the wane when Karlsen got back from the canteen with two prawn open sandwiches and a Coke. He'd just sat down and was cutting into one slice, when Sejer appeared in the doorway. The more abstemious inspector carried a couple of cheese sandwiches and a bottle of mineral water. There was a newspaper under his arm. 'May I join you?'

Karlsen nodded, dipped the sandwich into mayonnaise and took a bite.

Sejer drew up a chair, seated himself and pulled a slice of cheese out of the bread. He rolled it into a tube and bit off the end.

'I've got Maja Durban out of the file,' he said.

'Why? Surely there's no connection there.'

'Nothing obvious. But there aren't that many murders in this town, and they occurred within days of each other. Einarsson frequented the King's Arms, Durban lived three hundred metres away. We ought to check more closely. Look at this!'

He got up, went to the map on the wall and took two red mapping pins out of a tray. Accurately, and without searching, he stuck one pin in the block on Tordenskioldsgate and one in the King's Arms. Then he sat down.

'Look at that map. It's the whole of the county borough, the map is two metres by three.'

He reached for Karlsen's anglepoise reading lamp, which could be turned in all directions. He pointed the light at the map.

'Maja Durban was found dead on the first of October. On the fourth of October, Einarsson was killed, at least that's when we must assume it happened. This is hardly a metropolis, we're not overwhelmed by such incidents, but look at how close the pins are!'

Karlsen stared. The pins showed like two closely spaced red eyes on the black and white map.

'True enough. But they weren't acquainted as far as we know.'

'There's a lot we don't know. Is there anything we do know?'

'That's rather pessimistic, isn't it! But I think we ought at least to do a DNA on Einarsson and check it against Durban.'

'Well, why not? We're not paying.'

For a while they ate in silence. They were men who

had a great respect for one another, in a tacit way. They didn't make a fuss about it, but they shared a decided mutual sympathy which they exercised with patience. Karlsen was ten years younger and had a wife who needed humouring. So Sejer kept in the background, in the certainty that the man had enough with his family, something he regarded as a sacred institution. He was interrupted in his thoughts by an officer who appeared at the door.

'A couple of messages,' she said, handing him a small piece of paper. 'And Andreassen from TV 2 phoned, he wondered if you'd appear on *Eyewitness* with the Einarsson case.'

Sejer tensed and his gaze wavered uneasily.

'Er, perhaps that's one for you, Karlsen? You're slightly more photogenic than me.'

Karlsen grinned. Sejer loathed appearing in public, he had very few weak points, but this was one of them.

'Sorry. I'm just off to a conference now, don't you remember? I'm away for ten days.'

'Ask Skarre. He'll be delighted, no doubt. I'll help him, provided I don't have to sit under those studio lights. Go and tell him straight away!'

She smiled and disappeared, and he began to read the messages. He glanced at his watch. The 'oldies' were going to go parachuting at Jarlsberg that weekend, provided the weather held. And ring Jorun Einarsson.

He took his time, finished his meal and pushed the chair back in. 'I'm going out for a bit.'

'My goodness, you've been inside for almost half an hour! Moss is already growing on your shoes.'

'The problem with people is that they stay inside all day long,' Sejer replied. 'Nothing's happening here in the office, is it?'

'No, you're probably right. But you're a devil for finding things to do out of doors. You've really got a talent for it, Konrad.'

'You've got to use your imagination,' he countered.

'Hey, just a sec.'

Karlsen looked sheepish and put his hand into his shirt pocket.

'I've got a shopping list from my other half. D'you know much about women's stuff?'

'Try me.'

'Here, after shoulder of pork – it says "Pantyliners". Must be English. Got any ideas?'

'Couldn't you phone her and find out?'

'She's not answering.'

'Try Mrs Brenningen. I think it sounds like tights or something. Well, good luck!' He chuckled and went out.

He'd just seated himself in the car and run his fingers through his hair, when suddenly he remembered. He got out again, locked the car, and went to one of the police cars instead, just as he'd promised little Jan Henry. Like most other people, Mikkelsen would almost certainly be at work now, so he headed for Rosenkrantzgate first. Jorun Einarsson was on the small lawn in front of the house hanging out washing. A pair of pyjamas with a Tom & Jerry print and a tee shirt with a picture of Donald Duck on it flapped lustily in the breeze. She had just fished out a pair of lacy black panties when he arrived in front of the house, and was now standing there clutching them, not quite sure what to do.

'I didn't have far to drive,' he explained politely, trying not to look at her underwear, 'so I thought I might as well come round. Please, finish what you're doing.'

She hung up the rest of her washing quickly and put the clothes basket under her arm.

'Isn't your son at home?'

'He's in the garage.' She pointed along the road. 'He used to hang out in there with his father. Before. Watched him mucking around with the car. Sometimes he still goes in there, and just sits staring at the wall. He'll be out again in a while.'

Sejer looked at the garage, which was a double one, green, the same colour as the house. Then he followed her inside.

'What was it, Mrs Einarsson?' he asked straight out. They were standing in the entrance to the living room.

She put the basket on the floor and pushed a few wisps of bleached hair away from her face.

'I rang my brother. He's in Stavanger at a hardware trade fair. It was a boiler suit. You know, one of those green nylon ones with lots of pockets. Egil used it when he was working on the car and he always kept it in the boot. I searched for it, because I remembered it cost quite a lot. And he liked to have it handy in case the car broke down and he had to get out and start tinkering, as he used to call it. That was what my brother wanted it for, too. So when I didn't find it in the car, I searched in the garage. But it wasn't in there either. It's simply vanished. That, and a large torch.'

'Did you ask us about them?'

'No, but surely the police can't just take things from cars without saying?'

'Certainly not. But I'll check to make sure. Did he always have it with him?'

'Always. He was very organised when it came to that car. He never drove anywhere without an extra can of petrol. And engine oil and screen wash and some water. And that green boiler suit. I could have done with that torch myself really, the fuses go sometimes. The electrics are so bad here, something should be done about them. But the committee we've got now are the most useless bunch we've ever had, they put up the rent once a year and tell us they're saving up for balconies. But that won't happen in my time. Well, anyway, as I said, it was a boiler suit.'

'That's useful information,' he said, praising her. 'A good thing you remembered it.'

And it had been useful to the murderer, too, he thought, something he could pull over his own bloody clothes.

She blushed becomingly and picked the clothes basket up again. It was a large basket made of turquoise plastic, and when she balanced it on her hip as she was doing now, she assumed a somewhat strange and crooked posture.

'I promised your boy a ride in the car. May I fetch him from the garage?'

She glanced at him in surprise. 'Certainly. But we're going out later, so you mustn't be too long.'

'Just a short run.'

He went outside again and made for the garage. On a workbench against one wall Jan Henry was sitting swinging his legs. He'd got oil on his trainers. When he caught sight of Sejer, he started slightly, then brightened up.

'I've got the police car with me today. Your mum's given me permission to take you on a little run, if you'd like to come. You can try the siren out.'

He jumped down from the bench, which was quite high, and he had to take a couple of steps to regain his balance.

'Is it a Volvo?'

'No, it's a Ford.'

Jan Henry ran ahead and Sejer looked at his legs, at how pale and almost abnormally thin they were. He was nearly swallowed up by the front seat, and it was difficult to fasten the seat belt in a secure fashion, but it would have to do. He could barely see out over the dashboard, even if he craned his neck. Then Sejer started up and swung on to the road. There was silence for a while, just the even hum of the engine and the occasional swish of cars passing in the left-hand lane. The boy had stuffed his fingers between his thighs as if he was frightened of touching anything inadvertently.

'D'you miss your dad, Jan Henry?' Sejer asked quietly.

The boy stared back in surprise, as if it were the first time anyone had thought to ask him such a question. His answer was clear.

'Very much,' he said simply.

They fell silent again. Sejer headed down towards the textile mill, indicated right and drove towards the rapids.

'It's so quiet in the garage,' the boy said suddenly.

'Yes. A pity Mum can't do car repairs.'

'Mmm. Dad was always in there doing things. In his spare time.'

'And all those nice smells,' Sejer grinned, 'oil and petrol and suchlike.'

'He promised me a boiler suit,' he went on, 'just like his one. But he didn't have time before he disappeared. The boiler suit had fourteen pockets in it. I was going to wear it when I was working on my bike. It's called a mechanic's suit.'

'Yup, a mechanic's suit, that's right. I've got one myself, but mine's blue, and it's got FINA on the back. I'm not sure it's got fourteen pockets. Eight or ten perhaps.'

'The blue ones are nice, too. Do they have them in children's sizes?' he asked precociously.

'I'm not sure about that, but I'll definitely look into it.'

He made a little mental note, indicated right again and drew up. They could see down to NRK's local broadcasting centre in its idyllic setting down by the river. He pointed to the windows glinting in the sun.

'Shall we wind them up a bit? With the sirens?'

Jan Henry nodded.

'Press here,' he said pointing, 'then we'll see just how hungry they are for news down there. Perhaps they'll come rushing out with all their microphones.'

The siren started and wailed loudly in the silence, rebounded off the hillside opposite and came howling back again. Inside the car it didn't sound so piercing, but when its hundred decibels had been going for a few seconds, the first face appeared at one of the shiny windows. Then another. Then one of them opened a door and walked out on to the balcony at the end of the building. They could see him raise a hand and shade his eyes from the sun.

'They think it's at least a murder!' the boy exclaimed.

Sejer chuckled and studied the winter-wan faces that continued to emerge from the building.

'We'd better pipe down. See if you can switch it off, now.'

He could. His eyes were shining with delight and his cheeks were flecked with red.

'How does it work?' he asked with childish confidence in Sejer's abilities.

'Well,' said Sejer digging deep into his memory, 'it's like this, first they make an oscillating circuit electronically, which in turn creates a square pulse, which is amplified by an amplifier and fed into a loudspeaker.'

Jan Henry nodded.

'And then they vary it from eight hundred to sixteen hundred cycles. In other words, they alter its strength, to make it easier to hear.'

'At the siren factory?'

'Yup. At the siren factory. In America, or Spain. But now we'll go and get an ice cream, Jan Henry.'

'Yes. We deserve one, even though we haven't caught any baddies.'

They pulled out on to the main road again and turned left towards the town. When they got to the trotting course, he stopped, parked and steered the boy over to the kiosk. Once he'd got it, he needed a bit of help with the paper. They sat on a bench in the sun sucking and licking. Jan Henry had chosen an ice lolly, red and yellow and tipped with chocolate, while Sejer ate a strawberry ice cream, which had been his favourite ever since boyhood. He'd never seen any reason to change.

'Are you going back to work afterwards?' Jan Henry was wiping juice from his chin with his free hand.

'Yes, but I've got to visit a man first. In Erik Børresensgate.'

'Is he a baddie?'

'No, no,' Sejer smiled. 'Probably not.'

'But you're not completely certain? He *could* be?'

Sejer had to capitulate and chuckled a little.

'Well, yes, possibly. That's why I'm going to see him. But it's mainly to make sure that he *isn't*. Because then I can cross him off the list. That's the way we do it, you see, until there's only one person left.'

'I bet he'll be scared when you come in that car.'

'Yes, I'm sure he will. Everyone is. People are funny like that. You see, nearly everyone's got something in their past they feel guilty about. And when I suddenly turn up at their door, I can almost see them searching their memories to work out what I've discovered. I shouldn't laugh, but sometimes it's impossible not to.'

The boy nodded, and basked in the company of this

wise policeman. They finished their ice creams and returned to the car. Sejer got a serviette from the kiosk, and wiped the boy's mouth and helped him with his seat belt.

'Mum and me are going to town to hire videos. One for each of us.'

Sejer put the car in gear and checked the mirror.

'And what are you going to get? A film about baddies?'

'Yes. *Home Alone* 2. I've seen the first one twice.'

'You'll have to take the bus out and back. If you haven't got a car.'

'Yes. It takes rather a long time, but it doesn't matter, 'cause we've got lots of time, really. Before, when Dad – when we had a car, it only took a minute to drive there and back.' He poked a finger up his nose and picked it a bit. 'Dad wanted a BMW. He'd been to see it. It was white. If that woman had bought the Manta.'

Sejer almost drove off the road. His heart gave a great leap, then he controlled himself.

'What was that you were saying, Jan Henry – I wasn't quite paying attention.'

'A woman. Wanted to buy our car.'

'Did Dad talk about it?'

'Yes. In the garage. It was that day – the last day he was at home.'

'A woman?' Sejer felt a shiver run down his spine.

'Did he say what she was called?' He glanced in the mirror, changed lanes and held his breath.

'Yes, because he had her name on a bit of paper.'

'Oh, really?'

'But I can't remember it now, it's such a long time ago.'

'On a piece of paper? Did you see it?'

'Yes, he had it in the pocket of his boiler suit. He was lying on his back under the car, and I was sitting on the bench as usual. Well, it wasn't a piece of paper exactly, more a bit of paper. Sort of half of a sheet of paper.'

'But you say you saw it – did he take it out of his pocket?'

'Yes, from his chest pocket. He read the name, and then . . .'

'He put it back in his pocket?'

'No.'

'Did he throw it away?'

'I can't remember what he did with it,' he said wistfully.

'If you were to think very hard, do you think you could remember what he did with it?'

'Don't know.' The boy looked earnestly at the policeman, he was beginning to realise that it was important. 'But if I remember about it I'll say,' he whispered.

'Jan Henry,' Sejer said softly, 'this is very, very important.'

They'd arrived at the green house.

'I know it is.'

'So if you should remember anything about this woman, anything at all, you must let Mum know, so that she can phone me.'

'All right then. If I remember. But it is a long time ago.'

'It certainly is. But it is possible, if you try very hard and think about something for a long time, day after day, to remember something you thought you'd forgotten.'

'Bye.'

'See you,' Sejer said.

He turned the car and watched him in the mirror as he ran to the house.

'I ought to have realised,' he said to himself, 'that the boy would know something. He was always hanging round the garage with his father. Will I never learn?'

Chapter 7

A woman.

He thought about it as he parked at the courthouse and walked the few metres to Mikkelsen's address. There could have been two of them. The woman might have been there to entice him out, while the man lurked in the background and did the dirty work. But why?

Erik Børresensgate 6 was a shop that sold bathroom fittings, so he entered the lobby of number 5 and saw there was a J. Mikkelsen on the first floor. He was unemployed and therefore at home, a man in his mid-twenties with both knees sticking out of his denim jeans.

'Do you know Egil Einarsson?' Sejer asked, studying the man's reaction. They were seated on opposite sides of the kitchen table. Mikkelsen pushed a pile of lottery tickets, the salt and pepper cellars and the latest edition of *Esquire* out of the way.

'Einarsson? Well, it's got a familiar ring, but I don't know why. Einarsson. Sounds like someone from Iceland.'

He didn't seem to be hiding anything. In that case it was clearly a waste of time sitting here leaning on this checked oilcloth, in the middle of the day, investigating a blind alley.

'He's dead. He was found in the river a couple of weeks ago.'

'Aaah, yes!' He nodded energetically and massaged the thin gold ring he wore in his ear. 'I saw it in the paper. Killed with a knife and stuff. Yes, now I'm with you, Einarsson, yes. Soon it'll be like America here, it's all these drugs if you ask me.'

He didn't ask him. He kept quiet and waited, inquisitively watching the young face under the perfectly straight hairline which made his ponytail suit him so well. Some people were lucky enough to look good wearing one, Sejer thought. But there weren't many of them.

'Well, I didn't know him.'

'So you don't know what sort of car he had?'

'Car? Well no, why should I know that?'

'He had an Opel Manta. Eighty-eight model. Exceptionally well maintained. He bought it from you, two years ago.'

'Oh Christ, was that him?'

Mikkelsen nodded to himself. 'Of course, that was why he seemed familiar. Bloody hell.' He reached for a packet of nicotine gum on the table, stood it on end, gave it a little flick, and stood it up again. 'How d'you find that out?'

'Well, the two of you wrote out a purchase agreement, just like people do. Did you advertise in the paper?'

'No, I drove around with a card in the window. Saved the money. It took a couple of days, and then he rang. He was a funny bloke. He'd been saving up since the year dot, and paid cash.'

'Why did you want to sell it?'

'I didn't want to. I lost my job and couldn't afford to keep it any longer.'

'So now you haven't got a car?'

'Yes I have. I've got an Escort which I bought at a car auction, an old one. But it just sits there most of the time, I haven't got the money for petrol while I'm on social security.'

'Well, that's fine.' Sejer rose.

'No, it's not at all fine, if you ask me!'

They both chuckled.

'Do they work?' Sejer asked, pointing at the packet of chewing gum.

The younger man thought a bit: 'Yeah, they do, but you get totally hooked on them. They're expensive as well. And they taste disgusting, like chewing a fag.'

Sejer left, crossed Mikkelsen from the top of the list and put him at the bottom instead. He cut across the street and felt the sun warming him gently through the leather of his jacket. This was the best time, when the anticipation of summer still lay some way in the future, a dream of the cabin on Sandøya, of sun and sea and salt water, the essence of all previous summers, the good holidays. Occasionally he felt a slight uneasiness, the bitter experience of summers that had been rainy and windy, there had been a number of those, too. But during sunny summers he found peace, he didn't itch so much then.

He jogged up the shallow steps and pushed open the door, nodded briefly to Mrs Brenningen in reception. She really was a good-looking woman, Mrs Brenningen, cheerful and friendly. Not that he chased women, perhaps he ought to, but that would have to wait. For the moment he contented himself with just looking at them.

'Is it exciting?' he enquired, nodding at the book she was reading in between busy periods.

'Not too bad,' she smiled. 'Power, lust and intrigue.'

'Sounds just like the police.'

He chose the stairs, closed the door and sank down in the chair from Kinnarps, which he'd paid for out of his own pocket. Then he got up again, pulled Maja Durban's folder from the file and sat reading. He gazed at the pictures of her, first the one taken while she was alive, a pretty, slightly rounded woman with a chubby face and black eyebrows. Small eyes. Rather close-cropped hair. It suited her well. An attractive woman favoured by fortune, the way she was smiling said a lot about who she was, a mischievous, teasing smile that brought small wrinkles to her cheeks. In the other photograph she was stretched out on a bed staring at the ceiling with eyes wide open. The face expressed neither fear nor astonishment. It expressed nothing whatsoever, it resembled a colourless mask.

The folder also contained a number of photos of the flat. Its rooms were neat, pretty spaces full of beautiful things, feminine, but without frills or pastels, the furniture and carpets were in vivid colours, reds, greens, yellows, colours a strong woman would choose, he thought. Nothing bore any mark of what had happened, nothing had been broken or upset, it was as if everything had happened silently and unobtrusively. And totally unexpectedly. She had known him. Opened the door to him and removed her clothes herself. First they'd made love, and nothing indicated that it had occurred against her will. Then something had happened. A breakdown, a short-circuit. And a strong man could squeeze the life out of a small woman in mere seconds, he knew that, just a few kicks and it would be over. No one can hear your screams if you've got a muffler of duck down over your mouth, he thought.

Remnants of sperm which had been found inside the victim had been DNA tested, but as they hadn't yet got a database, he had nothing to check it against. The submission was with Parliament and would come up this spring. And after that, he thought, anyone who got into trouble would have to take great care with any bodily function. Every kind of human trace could be scraped up and DNA tested, with an error of one in seventeen billion. For a while they had toyed with the idea of getting government permission to summon and test every man in the county borough between the ages of eighteen and fifty, but this would have meant calling in thousands of men. The project would have cost several million kroner and taken as long as two years. The Minister of Justice considered the project, such as it was, in all seriousness, until she began to understand the details of the case and learn a little more about the victim. Maja Durban wasn't considered worth all that money. He could understand that to some extent.

Occasionally he would fantasise about a future system in which all Norwegian nationals were automatically tested at birth and put on file. This thought conjured up a mind-boggling vista. For a while he sat reading through the interviews, there weren't many of them regrettably, three colleagues, five neighbours from the block where she lived and two male acquaintances who claimed to know her only slightly. And finally, that childhood friend, with her hazy account. Maybe she'd got off too lightly, maybe she knew more than she was saying. A vaguely neurotic sort, but decent enough, at any event he'd never had reason to bring her in. And why would she have killed Durban? A woman doesn't kill her friend, he thought. Besides, she'd made rather an impression on him, that leggy painter with the lovely hair, Eva Marie Magnus.

Chapter 8

None of the crime-scene officers could recall a green boiler suit.

Neither had they seen a torch or a note with a name and telephone number. The glove compartment had been emptied and sifted, there were the usual things people keep in glove compartments, a driver's licence, an instruction manual, a city map, a packet of cigarettes, a chocolate wrapper. Two empty disposable lighters. And, despite his wife's hint at his lack of allure – a packet of condoms. It had all been diligently noted down.

Afterwards he phoned the brewery. He asked for the personnel department, and an obliging man with the remnants of a Finnmark brogue answered.

'Einarsson? Certainly I remember him. It was a really dreadful story, and he had a family as well, I believe. But in fact he was one of our most punctual people.

Almost no absences at all in seven years, as far as I can see. And that's some going. But as regards September and October last, let's see . . .' Sejer could hear him leafing through papers. 'This could take a little time, we've got 150 men here. Would you like me to call you back?'

'I'd prefer to wait.'

'All right then.'

His voice was replaced with a drinking song that reverberated down the line. Sejer thought it was rather amusing, at least it was better than muzak. It was a Danish recording with an accordion. Really lively.

'Well, now.' He cleared his throat. 'Are you there? He clocked in fairly late here, I see, one day in October. The second of October. He didn't arrive until nine-thirty. Presumably he'd overslept. They go to the pub sometimes, the lads here.'

Sejer drummed his fingers. 'Well, I'm grateful for that. One small thing while I remember. Mrs Einarsson's alone with a six-year-old boy, and she appears not to have received any payment from you yet, is that possible?'

'Yes, hmm, that's right.'

'How so? Einarsson had a company insurance policy, didn't he?'

'Oh yes, yes, but we didn't know for certain what had happened. And the rules are quite explicit. People do run off sometimes. For one reason or another, you just don't know, people do such strange things nowadays.'

'Well at least he went to the trouble of slaughtering a chicken or something,' Sejer said dryly, 'and spilling its blood over the car. I assume you've been given some details?'

'Yes, that's right. But I can promise we'll expedite the matter, we've got all we need now.' He sounded uneasy. The Finnmark accent had got steadily more pronounced.

'That's good enough for me,' Sejer said lightly.

Then he nodded to himself. It was rather odd, although it might just be coincidence. That Einarsson overslept on that of all days. The day after Maja Durban was murdered.

To get to the King's Arms he had to cross the bridge. He drove slowly, admiring the sculptures on each parapet, a few metres apart. They depicted women at work, women balancing water vessels on their heads, with babies in their arms, or women dancing. A fantastic sight high above the dirty river water. Thereafter he turned right, past the old hotel, and cruised slowly up the one-way street.

He parked and locked the car. It was dark inside the bar, the air was stale, the walls and furniture and all the other fittings were well saturated with tobacco smoke and sweat, it had impregnated the woodwork and given the pub the patina its regulars wanted. And the King's Arms really did hang on the burlap-covered walls in the guise of old swords, revolvers and rifles, and even a fine old crossbow. He halted at the counter, letting his eyes accustom themselves to the gloom. At the end of the room he saw a double swing-door. Just then it opened, and a short man in a white cook's jacket and checked trousers hove into view.

'Are you the manager?'

Sejer looked enquiringly at him. He liked the old-fashioned cook's costume, the way he liked traditions generally.

'That's me. But I don't buy on the premises.'

'Police,' he replied.

'That's different. Just let me shut up the freezer.'

He darted back in again. Sejer looked about him. The pub had twelve tables arranged in horseshoe fashion, and each table had room for six. At that moment there wasn't a soul there, the ashtrays were empty and there were no candles in the candlesticks.

The cook, who was also the manager, came through the swing-doors and nodded obligingly. In place of a cook's hat he had grease or gel or some other stuff in his hair, it lay black and shiny across his scalp like the carapace of a dung beetle. It would take a hurricane to lift a hair off that and blow it into the soup. Practical, Sejer thought.

'Are you here every evening?'

'That's me, every single evening. Apart from Mondays, when we're closed.'

'Pretty unsociable hours I'd imagine? Up until two every morning?'

'Most definitely, if you've got a wife and kids and a dog and a boat and a cabin in the mountains. I haven't got any of them.' He grinned. 'This suits me just fine. And anyway I like it, and the boys who come here. You know, one big family!'

He embraced a cubic metre of air with his arms and gave a little hop to land on the bar stool.

'Good.' Sejer had to smile at this little man in his checked trousers. He was somewhere in his forties, his white jacket was scrupulously clean, just like his nails.

'You know the gang from the brewery, don't you, who come in here?'

'Came in here. It's pretty well fallen apart now. I don't quite know why. But Primus has gone of course, that's part of the reason.'

'Primus?'

'Egil Einarsson. The Primus Motor of the gang. He kept the whole thing together, really. Isn't that why you've come?'

'Did they really call him that?'

The manager smiled, picked a couple of peanuts from a dish and pushed them over towards Sejer. They reminded him of small, fat maggots, and he left them alone.

'But were there many of them?'

'Ten or twelve altogether – the hard core comprised four or five blokes who were in here almost every day. I could really count on those boys, that they'd be in. No idea what happened, apart from Primus getting stabbed by someone. I don't know why the others kept away. A sad business. They really were a source of income those boys. Enjoyed themselves, too. Decent people.'

'Tell me what they did when they were here. What they talked about.'

He ran his hand back across his hair, a totally unnecessary adjustment. 'Played a lot of darts.' He indicated a large dartboard at the back of the premises. 'Played tournaments and suchlike. Talked and laughed and argued. Drank and laughed and messed about. Basically, they behaved like most lads. They could relax here, never brought their wives along. This is a man's bar.'

'What did they talk about?'

'Cars, women, football. And work, if something special had happened. And women, or have I already said that?'

'Did they argue sometimes?'

'Oh yes, but nothing serious. I mean, they always parted friends.'

'Did you know them by name?'

'Well, yes, if you call Primus and Peddik and Graffen names – I hadn't a clue what they were really called.

Apart from Arvesen, the youngest of them. Nico Arvesen.'

'Who was Graffen?'

'A graphic artist. Worked on posters and advertising material for the brewery, very good stuff, too. I don't know his name.'

'Could any of them have knifed Einarsson?'

'No, no way. Must be someone else. They were friends.'

'Did they know Maja Durban?'

'Everyone did. Didn't you?'

He ignored the question. 'The evening Durban was killed you had a disturbance here, didn't you?'

'That's right. And the only reason I remember it is because of the flashing blue lights. That sort of thing isn't normally a problem. But no one gets off scot-free.'

'Did the trouble start before or after you saw the emergency vehicles?'

'Oh God, I'll have to think.' He munched peanuts and licked his lips. 'Before, I think.'

'Do you know what caused the disturbance?'

'Drink, of course. Peddik had too much. I had to ring for the Black Maria, even though I hate doing it. I pride myself on dealing with things myself, but that evening it didn't work. He went completely off the rails in here, I'm no doctor, but I think it was something akin to the DTs.'

'But was he usually boisterous?'

'A bit excitable, no doubt about it. But several of them were. They were pretty loud the whole lot of them. Primus was one of the quieter ones in fact, occasionally he would rumble a bit, like one of those small earthquakes in San Francisco, the ones that make glasses in cocktail cabinets tinkle. It was rare that anything came of it. He came in his car too, drank Coke or Seven Up. Always did the paperwork when they were playing tournaments.'

'So our people took this Peddik in?'

'Yup. But afterwards I found out they changed their minds.'

'Einarsson pleaded his case.'

'Hey, can you really do that?'

'Well, even we are open to reason. There's nothing better than social networks, you know. We've got too few of them. You didn't catch anything? During the trouble?'

'Oh yes, I couldn't help it. "Fucking women", and that sort of thing.'

'Problems with women?'

'Doubt it. Just a lot of alcohol, and then they go for the most obvious thing. His marriage probably wasn't of the best, well, that's why they come here after all, isn't it?' He pulled a toothpick from a little barrel on the bar and scraped his pristine nails. 'Do you think there's a connection between the two killings?'

'I've no idea,' Sejer said. 'But I can't help wondering, because as I sit here looking down the street, I can almost see the block of flats Maja lived in. Almost.'

'I know what you mean. A gorgeous woman she was. Just how girls should look.'

'Did she come here often?'

'Nope. She was too refined for that. She popped in occasionally, just to down a quick cognac in record time and rush out again. I doubt she had much leisure. Hard-working girl. Kept going all the time.'

'The men who come here must have talked about it a bit?'

'Maja's murder was like a fresh cowpat in here and they buzzed around it for weeks. People always indulge themselves.'

Sejer slipped down off the barstool. 'And now they don't come any more?'

'Oh yes, they drop in, but there's no system now. They don't come together. They just have a couple of halves and leave again. I'm sorry,' he said suddenly, 'I really should have offered you a drink.'

'I'll save it till later. Perhaps I'll pop in sometime for a beer. Are you a good cook?'

'Come along one evening and try our Schnitzel Cordon Bleu.'

Sejer went through the door and was brought up short by the bright daylight. The cook was at his heels.

'There was a copper here before, after Durban was

killed. A sort of English dandy with a handlebar moustache.'

'Karlsen,' said Sejer smiling. 'He's from Hokksund.'

'Oh well, I shan't hold that against him.'

'Did you notice if any of them disappeared during the evening and came back again?'

'I knew you'd ask that,' he grinned. 'But I can't remember the details now. They were always shooting in and out, and it was six months ago. Sometimes they'd nip out to the seven o'clock film showing and come back again, sometimes they'd eat at the Peking, but have most of their drinks here. Occasionally Einarsson would go out and get some coffee, which I don't sell. But that precise evening, I've no idea. I trust you'll understand.'

'Thanks for the chat. It was pleasant anyway.'

On his way home he pulled up at the Fina service station. He went into the shop and took a *Dagbladet* out of the rack. A pretty girl with fair, curly hair was behind the counter. A plumpish face, with cheeks that were round and golden, like freshly baked buns. But as she wasn't more than seventeen, he held all but his paternal feelings in check.

'That nice suit you're wearing,' he said, pointing, 'is just like the one I've got at home in my garage.'

'Oh?'

'Have you any idea if they come in children's sizes?'

'Er, no, I haven't got a clue.'

'Is there anyone you could ask?'

'Yes, but I'll have to make a phone call.'

He nodded and opened his newspaper while she dialled a number. He liked the smell in the Fina shop, a mixture of oil and chocolate, tobacco and petrol.

'The smallest size is for ten-year-olds. They cost 225 kroner.'

'Could you order me one? Smallest size? It'll be a bit large perhaps, but he'll grow into it.'

She nodded, he placed his card on the counter and thanked her, paid for his paper and left. When he got home he took a packet of ready-made soup out of the freezer. He wasn't very good at cooking, Elise was always the one who'd done that. It was as if he couldn't be bothered any more. In the old days, hunger had been a stimulating pang in his stomach, which sometimes grew into a wild anticipation of what Elise might have waiting in her saucepans. Now it was more of a growling dog which he threw a biscuit to, when it got really noisy. But he was good at washing up. Every day without fail throughout more than twenty years of married life, he'd washed up. He sank down at the kitchen table and ate the soup slowly with a glass of fruit juice. His thoughts wandered and ended up at Eva Magnus. He searched for something he could use as an excuse for visiting her again, but found nothing. Her daughter was about the same age as Jan Henry. Her husband had left her, and had certainly never met Maja Durban. But there was nothing wrong with having a talk to him anyway, because he would undoubtedly have heard of her. Sejer knew that the daughter spent every other weekend with her father, so he probably lived locally. He tried to recollect his name, but couldn't. However, he could find that out. Just to be on the safe side; you could never tell. A new name on the list. And he had plenty of time.

He finished his meal, rinsed his soup bowl under the tap and went to the phone. He rang the club and booked a jump that Saturday, unless it was too windy, he stipulated, because he couldn't abide wind. After that, he looked up the name Magnus in the phone book, allowing his finger to run slowly down the list of names. Just as he'd known it would, the name jumped out at him as soon as he saw it: Jostein Magnus. Civil engineer. Address: Lille Frydenlund. He went back to the kitchen, filtered a large cup of coffee and made for his chair in the living room. Immediately Kollberg came and laid his head on Sejer's feet. He opened the newspaper, and halfway through a glowing report on the EU, he fell asleep.

Chapter 9

Emma was back home again. It was a relief. Eva had no more thoughts to think, she'd merely gone over the same ones again and again, so it was better to have the girl around, with all the hurry and fretting that entailed. Now it was just a case of waiting. She took her daughter's hand, her plump, soft hand, and led her out to the car. She hadn't said a word about the pink school bag that was waiting at her father's; it was to be a surprise. She wouldn't rob him of those shrieks of delight, his life had few enough of those already. Emma got into the back of the car and did up the seat belt herself, she was wearing a brown trouser suit which suited her quite well, and Eva had helped her with her hair. Her father lived some distance off, well over half an hour's journey in the car, but after only five minutes Emma began to whine. Eva became irritated. Her nerves were at full stretch, she couldn't take much more.

'Can I have an ice cream?'

'We've just got into the car. Can't we drive to Grandad's just *once* without buying anything?'

'Just an ice lolly?'

You're too fat, Eva thought, you shouldn't eat anything for a long time.

She'd never told Emma she was fat. She had the idea that Emma didn't realise it herself, and that were she to say it out loud, her obesity would become a real problem for the first time. Become visible to Emma herself.

'Can we at least get out of town first?' she said shortly. 'Anyway, Grandad's waiting. Perhaps he's made dinner, and we mustn't ruin our appetites.'

'You can't ruin an appetite,' came Emma's uncomprehending retort. She wasn't acquainted with the phenomenon, she always had an appetite.

Eva made no answer. She was thinking that school would begin soon, and then Emma would have to see the school doctor. Hopefully, there'd be several pupils with the same problem; it was a possibility as there were twenty-six in the class. It was strange, here she sat thinking about the future, a future she might not even have a share in. Perhaps it would be Jostein who'd take her to school. Manage her unruly hair, hold her chubby hand.

The traffic flowed evenly, and she stuck rigidly to the speed limit. It had become a sort of mania with her not to give anyone the excuse to stop her for anything, not to attract any attention. As soon as they were out of the town centre they passed a twenty-four-hour Esso service station on the left.

'It's easy to stop, Mum, if we want to get an ice cream!'

'That's enough now, Emma!' Her voice was sharp. She relented and added in a milder tone: 'Perhaps on the way back.'

There was silence. Eva saw the girl's face in the mirror, with her round cheeks and the wide jaw she'd got from her father. It was a serious face, which had no inkling of the future, and all the things she might have to endure, if . . .

'I can see right down to the road,' Emma said suddenly. She leant forward in her seat and stared down at the floor of the car.

'I know, it's rust. We're going to buy a new car, I just haven't got round to it.'

'But we can afford it, can't we? Can we afford it, Mum?'

She checked the mirror. No cars following. 'Yes,' she said tersely.

The rest of the journey passed in silence.

Her father had been to the door and unlocked it. He'd seen her old Ascona from a long way off, so they gave a quick ring and walked straight in. His legs were bad and he was slow on his feet. Eva put her arms around him and embraced him hard as she always did, he smelt of Player's cigarettes and aftershave. Emma had to wait her turn.

'The women in my life!' he cried joyously. And then: 'You mustn't get any thinner, Eva. You look like a black beanpole in that costume.'

'Thanks for the compliment,' she said, 'but you're hardly roly-poly yourself. So you see where I get it from.'

'Well, well. It's good there's someone who knows how to look after herself,' he said, and grasped Emma round the waist with a skinny arm. 'Go out to my workroom, and you might find a present there.'

Emma tore herself loose and dashed off. Shortly after they heard her ecstatic glee all through the house.

'Pink!' she screamed, and came tramping out. It clashed horribly with her red hair, Eva thought sadly, brown would have been better. She tried to stifle the sombre thoughts that assailed her from every direction.

Her father had ordered chicken from the shop and Eva helped him with the food.

'You'll stay, won't you,' he cajoled, 'then we can have a bit of red wine. Like in the old days. Soon I'll forget how to behave in civilised society, you're the only one who comes.'

'Doesn't Jostein ever come?'

'Yes, yes occasionally. There's nothing wrong with Jostein,' he said quickly. 'He phones as well, and sends cards. I like Jostein a lot, he really was a terrific son-in-law. Your mother always said so, too.'

Emma drank ginger ale and ate her chicken with reverence. Eva's father needed some help cutting up his food. When alone he lived mainly on porridge, but he didn't advertise the fact. Eva dealt with the meat for him, got rid of the bones and poured the wine. It was a Canepa, which was the only thing his stomach could take, but by way of compensation he drank a lot of it. Now and then she loaded her food on to Emma's plate. It was terrible, but all the time Emma was eating there was little chance that she'd remember the corpse in the river.

'Have you got anyone to share your bed with at the moment, young Eva?' he asked suddenly.

Eva's eyes opened wide. 'Well, what do you know, I haven't.'

'Ah well,' he said. 'Someone will turn up.'

'It is possible to live without all that,' she said flatly.

'You're telling me,' he said. 'I've been a widower for fourteen years!'

'And don't try to tell me it's been fourteen years since you were last in action!' she protested. 'I know you.'

He chortled and sipped his wine. 'But it's not healthy, you know.'

'I can't just pick someone off the street,' she said, sinking her teeth into a fried chicken leg.

'Of course you can. You just invite him to dinner. Most men would say yes, I'm sure of that. You're a nice-looking girl, Eva. A bit thin, but pretty. You're like your mother.'

'No, I'm like you.'

'Have you sold any pictures? Are you working hard?'

'The answer is no. And yes.'

'You must let me know if you need money.'

'I don't need any. What I mean is, we've got good at managing without much.'

'Before, we never used to have the money to go to McDonald's,' Emma put in loudly, 'but we have now!'

Eva felt herself reddening. It was irritating, her father knew her only too well and was quick on the uptake.

'Are you keeping secrets from me?'

'I'm nearly forty, of course I'm keeping secrets from you.'

'Well, all right then, I won't say any more now. But heaven help you if there's anything I can give you and you don't ask for it. I'll get grumpy, you've been warned.'

'I know you will,' she smiled.

They finished the meal in silence. Then she emptied the bottle into her father's glass and cleared the table. She worked slowly. She was thinking that this might be the last time she would potter about in her father's house. From now on she'd always think like that.

'Lie down on the sofa. I'll make us some coffee.'

'I've got some liqueur,' he said hoarsely.

'Don't worry, I'm sure I'll find it. Go and lie down now, I'll wash up and read to Emma in the meantime. Then we'll have another bottle of wine later.'

He stood up with difficulty, and she put a steadying hand under his arm. Emma decided she'd sing to him, to send him off to sleep more quickly, and he was all for it. Eva went back into the kitchen, stuffed some money into the jam jar that held his savings, and filled the sink with water. Soon Emma's voice rang through the house. She sang 'Morningtown Ride', until Eva was left bending over the washing-up, her tears of mirth and misery dripping into the suds.

In the evening she spread a rug over him and propped him up on a couple of pillows. They'd switched off most of the lights and sat in the semi-darkness. Emma's bedroom door was open, they could hear her snoring softly.

'D'you miss Mum?' she asked, stroking his hand.

'Every hour of the day.'

'I think she's here now.'

'Of course she is, in some way or other. But I don't know just how, I can't work it out.' His hand fumbled over the table towards his cigarettes, and she lit one for him. 'Why was she unhappy, d'you think?'

'I don't know. Do you believe in God?' she continued.

'Don't be silly!'

They fell silent again for a long while. He drank the red wine steadily, and she knew he'd fall asleep on the sofa and wake up with a backache, as he always did.

'When I'm grown up I'm going to marry you,' she said wearily. She closed her eyes and knew that she would drop off too, sitting with her head on the back of the sofa. She couldn't be bothered to fight it. While she was here in her father's living room, she felt safe. As she had when she'd been little and he could protect her. He couldn't protect her any more, but it was a good feeling all the same.

Chapter 10

Sejer awoke with a stiff neck. As usual he'd fallen asleep in his armchair after dinner and, added to this, his feet were soaking. The dog had slobbered on them. He headed for the shower. Slowly he undressed without looking in the mirror; once under the spray he stretched himself gingerly and grimaced each time he touched the wall tiles. They were vinyl, a kind of imitation marble. They'd yellowed with the years. When he thought about it, he couldn't imagine anything more ugly to put on a bathroom wall. Elise had nagged him for ages, begged him to put up something different, she thought they were hideous too. Yes, yes, he'd said, I'm working on it. We'll do it in the spring, Elise. And so the years had passed. And later, when she was lying there hairless, ill and as emaciated as an old, old woman, and he, in his despair, wanted to tackle the bloody bathroom, she had shaken her head. She'd rather he sat by her bedside. You'll have plenty of time for the bathroom later, Konrad, she'd said feebly.

A huge sorrow overwhelmed him, and he had to blink hard to stop it gaining the upper hand. He hadn't time for that, not now at any rate. When he'd dried and dressed himself he went into the living room and phoned his daughter, Ingrid, she was the only child they'd had. They talked about this and that for a long while, and before he rang off he said goodnight to Matteus. After this he felt better. Before going out, he stopped in front of the photograph of Elise which hung above the sofa, she smiled at him, a brilliant smile with perfect teeth and without a care in the world. Not then. He'd always liked this picture. But just recently it had begun to irritate him, he wanted a different expression now, perhaps a portrait in which she was looking serious, something that more closely matched his own mood. Like the one Ingrid had hanging above her piano. Perhaps they could do a swap. He thought about it vaguely as he let Kollberg jump into the back seat and drove in the direction of Frydenlund. He wasn't quite sure what he was going to talk about when he got there, but as usual he relied on his talent for improvisation, which was considerable. People usually felt duty-bound to fill in the gaps that cropped up during a conversation, they always thought silences were painful. It was this kind of febrile talk he encouraged, because occasionally they would blurt out things he found useful. And Jostein

Magnus didn't know he was coming. He couldn't confer with his ex-wife beforehand. He could, of course, refuse to open his mouth at all, but they never thought of that. The notion made him smile.

Magnus had let Eva keep their old detached home at Engelstad and had moved into a flat in Frydenlund. These were far from the ugliest blocks of flats he'd ever seen, they were certainly nicer than the one he lived in himself. Surrounded by a large, park-like area, the five-storey blocks stood in a semicircle, like inverted dominoes, white, with black spots. If an outer one fell, the whole row would come crashing down. The occupants were a creative lot. There was a profusion of beds and bushes along the walls and in front of the entrances, and they would soon be flowering. The outside was tidy, the asphalt up to the doors had been hosed clear of all gravel and dust. The door to each flat was tastefully decorated with a pretty nameplate or dried flowers.

It was his partner who answered. He studied her with curiosity, trying to form an opinion about this woman who had supplanted Eva Magnus. She was a buxom, feminine type with a figure that burgeoned out everywhere; Sejer hardly knew where to look. Eva Marie, with all her lean, dark earnestness, wouldn't have stood a chance against this curly cherub.

'Sejer,' he said mildly, 'police.'

She flung open the door immediately. Because he was

smiling as broadly as he could she didn't ask if anything was wrong, the way people often did if he wore a different expression, the serious mask, as he did sometimes. But she had a questioning look. 'I've only come to have a chat,' he went on, 'with Mr Magnus.'

'Oh yes! He's inside.'

He followed her in. A red-haired giant got up from the sofa. On the table in front of him, on top of a newspaper, lay a tube of glue and a dinosaur made of wood. It had lost one of its legs.

They shook hands, the giant hadn't learnt to control his strength, but anyway, he probably considered it unnecessary to hold back with Sejer. Even so, the policeman was slight by comparison and his hand got some rough treatment.

'Please sit down,' he said. 'Have we got anything to drink, Sofie?'

'This is just an informal visit,' he commenced, 'I'm just being inquisitive.' He settled comfortably in his seat and continued. 'I've come simply and solely because you were married to Eva Magnus and must, I'm sure, recall the murder of Maja Durban.'

Magnus nodded. 'Yes, I remember that of course. It was a grisly business. Haven't you caught anyone yet? It's a long time ago. Well, I didn't keep up with it in the papers, and Eva never spoke about it any more, you see – but I thought this was about something else, I'd almost forgotten that stuff about Durban. But you ask away. If I know the answer, I'll tell you.' He opened his arms wide. A sympathetic man, warm and generous.

'What did you think I came about?' Sejer asked enquiringly.

'Er – could we talk about that later?'

'OK.'

He was handed a glass of fizzy orange and expressed his thanks.

'Did you know Maja Durban?'

'No, not at all. But I'd heard about her. Eva and Maja went their separate ways when they were girls. But they'd obviously been pretty close friends while it lasted. You know what girls are, it's like life and death to them. She read about Maja's killing quite by chance in the newspaper. They hadn't seen each other since '69. Or maybe it was '70?'

'Exactly. Apart from the day she was killed, that is.'

'The day before she was killed.'

'That was when they met each other in town. The following day she visited Durban in her flat.'

Magnus glanced up.

'Didn't you know that?'

'No,' he said slowly. 'She – well, fine. I suppose I wasn't meant to know it.'

Sejer was slightly taken aback. 'Do you happen to know the name Egil Einarsson?' He drank his orange and felt easy and relaxed, this was a house of innocence after all and that was quite liberating.

'No, I don't think so. Unless that's the name of the man who was found floating in the river here some weeks ago.'

'It is.'

'Ah? Ah, I see. Yes, I've heard the whole story.'

He pulled out a mahogany-coloured pipe from his shirt pocket and searched for matches on the table.

The buxom Sofie had been bustling about, now she stood with a bag of peanuts in one hand while she rooted in a cupboard for something to put them in. Sejer couldn't abide peanuts.

'But I haven't a clue who he was. There was a picture in the paper' – he struck a match, puffed hard a couple of times and exhaled – 'but even though we live in a small town, I didn't know him. Nor did Eva.'

'Eva?'

'She saw him close up, in a manner of speaking. Even though he wasn't particularly recognisable just then, well, I thought that was why you'd come. Because she found the corpse, she and Emma. It was rather scary, but we've talked it over. My daughter and I,' he added. 'She's here every other weekend. I believe she's finally forgotten it now. But you never know with youngsters. Sometimes they hold things in out of consideration for us grown-ups.'

He'd got his pipe alight at last. Sejer stared into his effervescing drink and for once was at a loss for words.

'Your ex-wife – found Einarsson's body?'

'Yes. I thought you knew that. After all, it was she who rang and notified you. Isn't that why you're here?' he said in surprise.

'No,' said Sejer. 'It was an elderly lady who phoned us. Her name was Markestad, I think. Erna Markestad.'

'Oh? Then there were probably several people who phoned, in the confusion. But it *was* definitely Eva and Emma who found him first. They phoned the police from a phone box, Emma told me the whole story. They were out walking, on the path by the river. They often go there, Emma loves it.'

'Emma told you about it – but did Eva?'

'Er, no. She didn't actually mention it straight away. But we've talked about it since.'

'Isn't that a bit strange? Of course, I don't know how much you talk, but . . .'

'Yes,' he said quietly, 'I suppose it was strange. That she didn't mention it herself. We talk quite a lot. Emma told me about it in the car coming here. That they'd gone on a walk by the river, just as that poor man came drifting into the bank. So they rushed off and rang from a phone box. Afterwards they had a meal at McDonald's. That, by the way, is Emma's idea of paradise on earth,' he chuckled.

'Didn't they wait for the police?'

'No, seems not. But . . .' There was silence for a moment round the table, and for the first time Jostein Magnus looked as if he was doubtful. 'But it's not right of me to sit here giving things away about Eva. And talking about what she says and doesn't say. She'll certainly have her reasons. Perhaps you had several phone calls, and only one was recorded. Or something.'

Sejer nodded. He'd managed to think things through a bit now, and his face had resumed its normal expression. 'Yes, he *was* drifting in the middle of town. There must have been several people who saw him. And it can be pretty hectic at the station now and again, especially just before the weekend. I must admit it can become a bit confused.'

He lied as plausibly as he could and wondered about the strange coincidence. Or was it a coincidence?

He carried on a polite conversation with Magnus for as long as he thought necessary. He took small sips of his drink, but didn't touch the peanuts.

'So now you've got two unsolved murders?' He squeezed out a drop of glue, and stood by with a knee-joint of thin plywood.

'Yes, that's right. Sometimes it happens that no one has seen or heard a thing. Or they don't think it's important. People are either so keen on publicity that they bombard us with every kind of suspicious circumstance, or they're so frightened of making a fool of themselves that they decide to keep quiet. The serious informants in between are really quite few. Unfortunately.'

'This is an Anatosaurus,' he said suddenly and with a smile, lifting the dinosaur. 'Twelve metres long. Two thousand teeth, and a brain the size of an orange. It could swim, too. What a thing to meet in the forest!'

Sejer smiled.

'You know,' Magnus continued, 'these prehistoric monsters have invaded our society to such an extent, I wouldn't be surprised if one of them suddenly bit off our chimney.'

'I know what you mean. I've got a grandson of four.'

'Well,' Magnus concluded, 'I imagine Eva has given all the help she could. They were close friends after all. They would have killed for each other.'

Maybe they would, Sejer thought. Maybe they just would.

By the time he got into his car and Kollberg had finished his extravagant greeting – as if he'd been to the South Pole and back since last they'd met – he knew that Magnus would have already dialled his ex-wife. This was a nuisance, he thought. He would rather arrive unexpectedly. Even so, she wouldn't have much time, it would take him fifteen minutes to drive from Frydenlund to Engelstad. He ought really to have checked with the desk sergeant first, to see if she actually had phoned but for some reason it hadn't been logged. But he didn't think such an error could have occurred. Every police officer worth his salt knew that it wasn't uncommon for the culprit themselves to tele-phone, so they always asked for a name and address. If it was withheld, the conversation was entered into the duty register as anonymous, with the date, time and sex. He drove on relentlessly and didn't even momentarily succumb to the temptation to ease down a bit. Perhaps even now he could reach her in the middle of her conversation with Jostein Magnus, while she was still floundering, trying to work out a service-able explanation. After all, he thought, who finds a corpse in the river, shrugs their shoulders and goes to McDonald's for a meal?

For interest's sake, he picked up his mobile and dialled the number of the household he'd just left. He got the engaged tone.

As he turned into the street he saw the darkened house and the empty drive. The car wasn't there. He sat at the wheel for a while swallowing his disappointment. Well, he registered with relief, the curtains were still up, so she hadn't moved at any rate. He put the car in gear and drove out on to the main road again, glanced at the time and decided on a lightning trip to the cemetery. He often liked to stroll there, see how the patches of snow were shrinking, and begin to plan what he would plant in the spring. Maybe alpine primulas, he thought, they'd go well with the violet crocuses which were just about to come out, if only they could get the tiniest bit of warmth.

The church was large, ostentatious and brick red, confidently lording it over its surroundings on a hill above the town. He'd never liked it particularly, it was a bit too strutting for his taste, but there was nowhere else to bury her. The headstone was of red thulite, and the only inscription was her name, Elise. In somewhat large letters. Dates had been omitted. That would have made her one of many, he felt, and she wasn't. By pushing gently into the earth with one finger, he caught sight of the first yellowish-green shoots, and that cheered him. He stood for a moment and peered down the slope; at least she had company. The most lonely thing in the whole world, he thought suddenly, was a churchyard with only one stone.

'What do you think it's like lying here, Kollberg? D'you think it's cold?'

The dog stared at him with black eyes and pricked up his ears.

'There are cemeteries for dogs now, too. I used to laugh at them, but all things considered I've gradually changed my mind. Because now you're all I have.'

He stroked the dog's great head and sighed heavily.

He walked back to the car. On the way he passed Maja Durban's grave, which was completely bare, apart from a bunch of dry, brown heather. It should have been removed. He bent down quickly, gathered the dried remains in his hands and scratched the ground before the headstone so that dark, damp earth was visible.

He threw the heather in the compost bin near the water pump. Then he drove off again, and on a sudden impulse he headed towards the station.

Skarre was on duty. He sat reading a paperback with his feet on the table. The cover looked gory.

'In the early hours of the second of October,' Sejer announced tersely, 'there was some trouble at the King's Arms, and we nearly arrested a man for drunkenness.'

'Nearly?'

'Yes. Apparently he got off at the last moment. I want to have his name.'

'If it was entered!'

'He was saved by a mate. More precisely by Egil Einarsson. But that could be in the report. They call him Peddik. Try it!'

'I remember him,' Skarre said. He bent over the keyboard and began searching while Sejer waited. Now it was evening at last, his whisky was within reach and the darkness was falling outside the window, as if the courthouse was a great parrot cage and somebody had thrown a cover over it. Everything went quiet. Skarre clicked away, cast his eyes over break-ins and domestics and stolen bikes, he used all ten digits on the keyboard.

'Have you been on a course?' Sejer asked.

'Ahron,' he answered. 'Peter Fredrik Ahron. Tollbugata number 4.'

Sejer took in the name, pulled the bottom desk drawer out with the toe of his boot and put his foot on it.

'Of course. The one we had dealings with when Einarsson went missing. Peter Fredrik. You interviewed him, is that right?'

'Yes, that's right. I spoke to several of them. One of them was called Arvesen, I think.'

'Can you remember anything? About Ahron?'

'Certainly. I remember that I didn't like the bloke. And that he was pretty nervous. I remember I was taken aback slightly, he was supposed to have had a violent quarrel with Einarsson, I learnt that afterwards when I talked to Arvesen, but it didn't stand up to further scrutiny. He spoke very nicely about Einarsson. Said he wouldn't have harmed a fly, and if anything had happened to him it must have been a big mistake.'

'Did you do a routine check on their records?'

'I did. Arvesen had fines for speeding, Einarsson was clean and Ahron had a conviction for drink-driving.'

'You've got a very retentive memory, Skarre.'

'Yes, I have.'

'What are you reading?'

'A crime novel.'

Sejer raised his eyebrows.

'Don't you read crime, Konrad?'

'Christ, no, at least not any longer. I used to sometimes. When I was younger.'

'This one here,' said Skarre, waving the book, 'is just brilliant. In a different league, you can't put it down.'

'I find that hard to believe.'

'You ought to try it, you can borrow it when I've finished.'

'No thanks, I'd rather not. But at home I've got a whole heap of really good crime novels, which you can borrow. If you like that sort of thing.'

'Er, are they very old?'

'About as old as you,' he said smiling, and gave the drawer a gentle kick. It closed with a snap.

Chapter 11

Saturday dawned calm and clear. As he turned into Jarlsberg Aerodrome he looked at the windsock. Nodding there against its post it resembled some huge discarded condom hurled down by one of the gods. He parked, locked up and lifted his parachute out of the boot. His suit was in a carrier bag. The weather was ideal, two jumps perhaps, he thought, and caught sight of part of the younger contingent busy over at the packing table. They looked as if they'd been poured into their mauve and red and turquoise jumpsuits, and once packed their parachutes looked like small daysacks.

'Do you spray those things on?' he said looking at the thin boyish bodies, where every muscle, or lack of it, was visible beneath the gossamer-thin fabric.

'That's right,' said a fair-haired youth. 'You can't get any speed up in that six-man tent you're carrying there, you know.' He was referring to the boiler suit. 'But maybe it's hectic enough at work?'

'You could say that. This'll slow me down a bit.'

He dropped the suit and the parachute on the ground, and stared up at the sky, shading his eyes with a hand.

'What are we flying in?'

'The Cessna. Five at a time, and the older ones jump first. Hauger and Bjørneberg are coming down later, so you could make up a little three-man formation. You're all about the same weight I should imagine. Otherwise you'll lose those old skills, you know.'

'I'll think about it,' he said dryly. 'But I can hold hands on the ground. One of the things I like up there,' he said nodding skywards, 'is the loneliness. And up there it's really immense. You'll understand that kind of thing when you're older.'

Formation jumping was about as popular with Sejer as synchronised swimming. He bought a Coke from the machine and sat near the packing table for a while. He drank slowly and watched the jumpers who'd begun to descend. First there was a drop of beginners. They looked like wounded crows as they came to earth in the strangest ways. The first ended up in the ploughed field, chin first, the second struck the wing of an aggressive model plane which was buzzing in the grass. They had to share their drop zone with the aeromodelling club, a cause of constant friction which sometimes almost boiled over into hostilities. Now there were the sounds of oaths and curses. There wasn't a perfect landing roll to be seen. It seemed so easy when you did it from a kitchen chair, he thought, that was how they practised, jumping ten or fifteen times off a kitchen chair, rolling and springing up again as easy as winking. The reality was different. He'd broken his ankle the first time, and Elise had smiled as he limped into the flat with his foot in plaster, not unkindly, but she had warned him in advance. That apart, he'd got off lightly, almost too lightly. After 2,017 jumps he'd never had to use his reserve parachute, and that in itself was disturbing. Everyone did eventually, sooner or later it would be his turn. Perhaps it'll be today, he thought, as he always did each time he put it on the packing table getting ready for his first jump. He must never forget that sooner or later he would pull the cord, glance up at the blue sky and realise that there was no parachute above him. The blue and green parachute which he'd had for fifteen years and which he'd never had any reason to replace.

He got up again and put the bottle in the car. He looked at the lazy landscape, which was dull and flat here on the ground, but became a lovely pastel-tinted panorama at ten thousand feet. The air was crystal clear, the sun flashed brightly in the car windows. He pulled on his blue boiler suit, buckled up his parachute and ambled towards the red and white plane that was slowly coming in to land. Two youths and a girl of about sixteen clambered in first. He was sitting by the door, they were all closely packed like sardines in a tin with their knees drawn up under their chins and their arms folded around their legs. He tightened his bootlaces and pulled his leather helmet over his head, nodded to the fifth man who scrambled in and squeezed down facing him. The pilot turned, gave a thumbs-up and started the engine. There wasn't much noise, but there was a bit of bumping as they began to move. At such moments he always tried to empty his head of thoughts, he watched the parked cars flashing past and felt the wheels leave the ground. He followed the needle on the altimeter as they rose to check that it was working. They were approaching five thousand feet. He saw the fjord twinkling blue, and the traffic on the motorway. From this altitude the cars moved slowly, as if in slow motion, although they were doing ninety or a hundred kilometres per hour. A throat was cleared, the three youngsters went through their formation with their hands, they looked like little children in brightly coloured playsuits, in the middle of a singing game. He heard the engine revs drop and tightened his chinstrap, glanced yet again at his bootlaces and at the altimeter which was still going up, and smiled a little at the stickers on the aircraft door, white clouds containing various epithets: Blue sky forever. Chickens, turn back! And: Give my regards to Mum. Then they were up, and he nodded again to Trondsen opposite to signify that he'd jump first. He turned to face the inside of the plane with his back to the door and stared right into the young faces which were so strangely smooth, they really did look like small kids, he couldn't ever remember being *so* sleek himself, but it was a long time ago, more than thirty years, he thought, and Trondsen opened the door, so that the noise from outside and the pressure of the wind pushed him into the small plane and prevented him from falling out until he was ready. Your parachute may not work, Konrad, he said to himself. He always said this as he sat waiting, so that he wouldn't forget it. He gave a thumbs-up, stared unsmilingly one last time at the young faces. They didn't smile either. Then he tipped over backwards and fell.

Chapter 12

The following day he put Kollberg into the car again and drove to the nursing home where his mother had lived for four years. He parked in the visitors' car park, gave the dog a quick pep talk and walked to the main entrance. He always had to psych himself up before he went, needed that extra bit of energy. It was lacking now, but a fortnight had passed since his last visit. He straightened up and nodded to the caretaker who was just coming along with a stepladder on his shoulder, he had a relaxed swing to his walk and a contented smile on his face, the sort of man who loved his job, who lacked nothing in life and who perhaps never understood what everyone else was making such a fuss about. Extraordinary. There aren't many expressions like that, Sejer thought, and suddenly caught sight of his own gloomy face in the glass door facing him. I'm not especially happy, he thought suddenly, but then I've never been very concerned about it either. He took the stairs to the first floor, nodded briefly to a couple of members of staff and walked straight to her door. She had a single room. He knocked loudly three times and went in. Inside, he stopped a moment, so that the sounds could register with her, it always took a little time. There, she was turning her head. He smiled and went to her bed, pulled up the chair and encompassed her thin hand in his.

'Hello, Mum,' he said. Her eyes had become paler and they were very shiny. 'It's only me. Come to see how you're doing.' He squeezed her hand, but she didn't squeeze back.

'I was in the vicinity,' he lied.

He felt no sense of guilt. He had to talk about something, and it wasn't always easy.

'I hope you've got all you need here.'

He looked around, as if he were checking.

'I hope they take the time to pop in and sit on your bed now and again – the staff here. They say they do. I hope they're telling the truth.'

She didn't reply. She stared at him with her light eyes as if waiting for something more.

'I haven't brought anything with me. It's a bit difficult, they tell me flowers aren't very good for you, and there's not a lot else to choose from. So I've just brought myself. Kollberg's in the car,' he added.

Her eyes relinquished him and turned towards the window.

'It's overcast,' he said quickly. 'But nice and bright.

Not too cold. Hope you'll be able to lie out on the veranda when summer comes. You always did like to get out as soon as you had the chance, just like me.'

He took her other hand as well, they were lost in his own.

'Your nails are too long,' he said suddenly. 'They should be clipped.'

He felt them with his finger, they were thick and yellow.

'It would only take a couple of minutes, I could do it, but I'm a bit clumsy I'm afraid. Haven't they got people here who take care of that kind of thing?'

She looked at him again, with her mouth half open. Her false teeth had been removed, they claimed that they only got in her way. It made her look older than she really was. But her hair was combed and she was clean, the sheets were clean, the room was clean. He gave a small sigh. He looked at her again searching hard for the least sign of recognition, but found none. She shifted her gaze once more. When at last he got up and went to the door, she was still staring out of the window, as if she'd already forgotten him. Out in the corridor he met one of the nurses. She smiled invitingly at the tall figure, he gave a quick smile back.

'Her nails are too long,' he said quietly. 'Would it be possible to do something about that?'

Then he left to struggle with the depression which

always came over him after his visits to his mother. These depressions lasted a couple of hours, and then lifted.

Later, he drove out to Engelstad, but first he made a couple of phone calls. A question had arisen in his mind, and the answers he received gave him something to think about. Even people's tiniest movements create ripples, he thought, just as the fall of a minute pebble could be registered in a totally different place on a totally different shore, a place you hadn't even dreamt of.

Eva Magnus opened the door, dressed in a voluminous shirt which was covered in black and white paint. A block of wood wrapped in sandpaper was in her hand. He could see from her face that he was expected, and that she'd already made up her mind what she was going to say. It infuriated him.

'Nice to see you again, Mrs Magnus. It's been some time.'

She gave a small nod.

'The last time it was Maja Durban – and now it's Egil Einarsson. Strange, isn't it?'

His comment caused her to take a deep breath.

'I've only got one small question.' He spoke politely, but not diffidently. He was never diffident. He exuded authority and, if he wanted to, could make people a trifle nervous – as he was doing now.

'Yes, I've already heard about it,' she said, and

retreated a little way into the hall. She shook her long hair back over her shoulder and closed the door behind him. 'Jostein phoned. But I've got nothing to add. Just that I saw that poor man float in, and that I rang you. At around five in the afternoon. Emma was with me. I can't remember who I spoke to, if that's what you're wondering, but if you've neglected to register a call, that isn't my problem. I did my duty if you can call it that. I haven't got anything more to say.'

She'd rattled off her speech. She'd clearly practised it several times.

'Help me a little with the voice anyway, so I can deal with this neglect of duty. It's really quite serious if this sort of thing occurs. All incoming calls should be logged. It's something we really do have to crack down on, if you know what I mean.'

She was standing with her back to him at the door of the living room, and he glimpsed the large black and white paintings which had made such an impression on him the first time. He couldn't see her face but, like a hedgehog, all her spines were up. She knew he was bluffing, but she couldn't say so.

'Well, goodness, he had a perfectly normal voice. I didn't think anything about it.'

'East Norwegian dialect?'

'Er, yes, I mean no, I can't remember if there was any special dialect, I don't notice things like that.

Anyway, I was a bit stressed, with Emma and every-thing. And he wasn't exactly a pleasant sight.'

She went into the living room now, still with her back towards him. He followed.

'Old or young?'

'No idea.'

'In fact, it was a female officer on the desk that afternoon,' he lied.

Eva halted in the living room. 'Oh? Then she must have gone to the loo or something,' she said quickly. 'I spoke to a man, I'm sure of that at least.'

'With a southern dialect?'

'For God's sake, I don't know. It was a man, I can't remember any more. I *did* phone, and there's nothing more to say.'

'And – what did he say?'

'Say? Well, not much, but he asked where I was phoning from.'

'And after that?'

'Nothing really.'

'But he asked you to wait at the scene?'

'No. I just explained where it was.'

'What?'

'Yes. And I said it was near the Labour Party head-quarters. Where the statue of the log-driver is.'

'And then you both left?'

'Yes, we went and ate. Emma was hungry.'

'My dear Mrs Magnus,' he said slowly, 'are you

seriously telling me that you phoned and reported finding a body, and you weren't even asked to wait there?'

'But for God's sake, I can't be answerable for the mistakes your people make when they're at work! He might have been young and inexperienced for all I know, but it wasn't my fault!'

'So you thought he sounded young?'

'No, I don't know, I don't notice things like that.'

'Artists always notice things like that,' he said briskly. 'They're observant, they take in everything, every detail. Isn't that right?'

She didn't answer. Her mouth was pursed into a tight line.

'I'm going to tell you something,' he said quietly. 'I don't believe you.'

'That's your problem.'

'Shall I tell you why?' he asked.

'I'm not interested.'

'Because,' he went on, lowering his voice even more, 'yours was the call that they all dream of getting. On the long, dull afternoon shift. A corpse is discovered. Nothing gets an officer more excited, more involved, than a dead man in the river on a humdrum afternoon, in amongst the domestic disturbances and the car thefts and all the swearing from the drunks in the holding cells. You see?'

'This one must have been an exception, then.'

'I've seen quite a lot of things in the service,' he confessed, and shuddered at the thought, 'but never that.'

Now she'd dug right in, just stared at him defiantly.

'Are you working on a picture?' he asked suddenly.

'Yes, of course. That's how I earn my living, as you know.'

She still hadn't sat down, and so he couldn't sit down either.

'It can't be easy. To make a living from, I mean.'

'No. Like I said before, it isn't easy. But we manage.'

She was getting impatient, but she didn't dare hurry him. Nobody did. She waited, tensing her slender shoulders, hoping he would go so that she could breathe freely once again, as freely as she could with all she knew.

'"Necessity is the mother of invention",' he said sharply. 'You're unusually punctual paying your bills at the moment. Compared to the time *before* Ms Durban died. You were late with everything then. It's really quite admirable.'

'What on earth do you know about that?'

'I only had to make a phone call. To the council, to the power and phone companies. It's funny, you know, when you ring from the police, information simply pours out.'

She wavered for a second, made a great effort to pull

herself together and met his gaze. Her eyes flickered like torches in a strong wind.

'Was your daughter in the phone box with you?' he asked mildly.

'No she waited outside. It was so cramped in there. She takes up quite a lot of room.'

He nodded to himself. She'd turned again, away from him. 'But you knew that Durban and Einarsson were acquainted, didn't you?'

The question was a shot in the dark, and hung there in the room. She opened her mouth to reply, closed it again and opened it once more, while he waited patiently with his gaze fixed on her golden eyes. He felt like a bully. But she knew something, he had to get it out of her.

She continued to struggle a little with her thoughts, then she mumbled: 'I don't know anything about it.'

'Lies,' he said slowly, 'are like sand. Have you ever considered that? The first is just a minute grain, but sooner or later you've got to go a bit further and add another to the first, so that they're growing all the time and getting bigger and bigger. In the end they're so heavy you can't bear the weight.'

She was silent. Her eyes filled, and she blinked rapidly a couple of times. And then he smiled. She stared at him a little confused, he was so different when he smiled.

'Aren't you ever going to paint with colours?'

'Why should I?'

'Because reality isn't black and white.'

'Well, then it probably isn't reality I'm painting,' she said sullenly.

'So what is it?'

'I don't know really. Emotions, perhaps.'

'Aren't emotions real?'

There was no answer. She stood at the door a long time watching him as he went to the car, as if she wanted to hold him back with her eyes. And really wanted him to turn and come back.

Afterwards he drove to his daughter's house. He reached it just as Matteus had finished his bath. Warm and wet and with a thousand small glittering drops of water in his curly hair. He got into a pair of yellow pyjamas and looked just like a chocolate wrapped in gold paper.

He smelt of soap and toothpaste, and the bath water still contained a shark, a crocodile, a whale and a water-melon-shaped sponge.

'It's high time,' his daughter said with a smile, and embraced him, slightly embarrassed, because it was so long between visits.

'It's busy at work. But I'm here now. Don't make anything extra, I'll just have a sandwich if you've got one, Ingrid. And a coffee. Isn't Erik at home?'

'He's playing bridge. I've got a pizza in the freezer, and cold beer.'

'And I've got the car,' he smiled.

'And I've got the number of the taxi,' she parried.

'The way you twist things about!'

'No,' she laughed, 'but I'll twist this!' She pinched his nose.

He seated himself in the living room with Matteus and a gaudy children's book of dinosaurs. The small, freshly bathed body was so warm in his lap that sweat began to prickle on his scalp. He read a few lines and ran his hand through the coal-black hair; he never ceased to be amazed at how crinkly it was, at how unimaginably small each individual curl was, and the feel of it against his hand. Not soft and silky like Norwegian children's hair, but coarse, almost like steel wool.

'Grandad going to sleep here?' the boy said hopefully.

'I'll sleep here if Mum lets me,' he promised, 'and I'm going to buy you a Fina suit which you can wear when you're mending your trike.'

Later he sat on the edge of Matteus's bed for a while, and his daughter could hear indecipherable mumblings from within. There were growlings and rumblings, probably supposed to be a rendering of some nursery rhyme or other. His musical abilities weren't much to boast about, but it achieved the desired effect for all that. Soon Matteus had fallen asleep with his mouth half open, his small teeth shining like chalky-white pearls in his mouth. Sejer sighed, rose and sat down to eat with his daughter, who'd begun to be seriously grown up, and who was almost as beautiful as her mother had been, but only almost. He ate slowly and drank beer with the meal, registering all the while that his daughter's house smelt exactly like his own had done while Elise was alive. She used the same detergents and the same toiletries, he'd recognised them on the bathroom shelf. She seasoned food in the same way her mother had done. And each time she rose to fetch more beer, he followed her movements clandestinely, and saw that she had the same walk, the same small feet and the same mannerisms when she spoke and laughed. Long after he'd gone to bed in what they called the guest room, which in reality was a tiny child's bedroom that they hadn't yet managed to fill, he lay thinking about it. He felt at home. As if time had stood still. And when he closed his eyes and shut out the strange curtains, everything was almost as it had been long ago. And perhaps, in the morning, it would be Elise who would come to wake him.

Eva Magnus sat shivering in a thin nightie. She wanted to go to bed, but couldn't seem to leave her chair. It was getting harder and harder to do the things she needed to, as if she felt the whole time that it was a wasted effort. She jumped when the phone rang, the clock told her it must be her father, nobody else phoned this late.

'Yes?' She got into a more comfortable position. She had to treasure the talks with her father, and they could be lengthy.

'Eva Marie Magnus?'

'Yes?'

An unknown voice. She'd never heard it before, at least she didn't think so. Who would ring so late in the evening, if they didn't even know her?

There was a small click. He'd hung up. Suddenly she began to tremble violently, she looked fearfully out of the windows and listened. All was quiet.

Chapter 13

Ingrid had given him a tube of tar ointment. He sniffed it tentatively, wrinkled his nose and put it in the drawer. Then he stared at the pictures on the desk in front of him, of the beautiful Maja Durban and the somewhat more prosaic Einarsson, who was as bereft of force and manliness as she was bereft of innocence. He couldn't imagine them knowing each other, moving in the same circles. Or even that they'd had acquaintances in common. But Eva Magnus was a link. She'd found Einarsson in the river, and for some reason she'd said nothing about it. She'd been friends with Durban and was one of the last people to see her alive. Only days separated their killings, and both frequented the south side, although that meant nothing, it was a small town.

Two unsolved murders didn't disturb his equilibrium, and he wasn't capable of becoming stressed. Rather, he became dogged, even more attentive, as he organised and reorganised his thoughts in logical sequences, tried various juxtapositions and played the resulting possibilities to himself like short film clips. He made deeper inroads into what was really his leisure time, although he had enough of that for his own needs anyway. His whole intuition told him there was a connection between the two victims, although he lacked most of the hard facts. Could Einarsson have had an affair, even though the idea made his wife smile? Certainly, wives didn't know everything. Apart from Elise, he thought, and realised all at once that he was blushing at the thought. He should have hauled Eva Magnus in and really piled on the pressure, but he couldn't do that without reasonable grounds. She should have been in here on the other side of his desk, off balance and insecure, not as she was in her own home, but alone and anxious within this great edifice, this grey giant of a building which could break anybody. Easy enough to stick to a story at home. My home is my castle. He should have had one of those old-fashioned mangles, and put her through it to see what got squeezed out. Probably black and white paint, he thought. Yet he had no grounds for bringing her in, that was the problem. She had done absolutely nothing illegal, she'd made a statement after Durban's murder, and he'd believed her. She lived as most people did, took her daughter to playschool, painted, shopped for food, didn't keep company of any sort, not even that of other artists.

And it wasn't a crime to pay your bills before they fell due. He cursed the fact that she'd been given such an easy ride from the start. He had believed her, that she knew absolutely nothing at all. And perhaps it was true that she'd met Durban quite accidentally. The fact that someone killed her the following evening must have been a shock. It might explain her strained manner when he'd visited her the first time. An almost quivering nervousness. But who, he thought again, finds a body in the river, shrugs their shoulders and goes for a meal at McDonald's? And also, she had more money than she had before. Where had she got it from?

He sat there sifting for a while, continually gazing out of the window, but seeing nothing except roofs and the tops of the tallest trees. It was a paltry view, but at least there was a bit of sky, and that was the most important thing. That was what the prisoners looked at, he thought, sitting in their cells. That was what they missed. The various colours, the changing light. The constant motion of the clouds. Sejer grunted, opened his desk drawer and took out a bag of Fisherman's Friends. The phone rang just as he'd stuck two fingers in the bag. It was Mrs Brenningen down below in reception, she said she had a small boy with her who absolutely had to speak to him.

'You'll have to be quick,' she said, 'he wants a pee!'

'A small boy?'

'A skinny little lad. Jan Henry.'

Sejer leapt to his feet and sprinted to the lift. It descended through the building almost noiselessly. He didn't like the way it made so little sound, it would have made a solider impression if it had been more raucous. It wasn't that lifts made him nervous or anything, it was just a thought.

Jan Henry stood quietly in the wide space watching out for him. Sejer was moved when he saw the thin little figure; here in this large lobby he seemed even more lost. He took him by the hand and led him over to the toilets. He waited outside until he'd finished. Afterwards he looked very relieved.

'Mum's at the hairdresser,' he explained.

'Is she? So she knows you're here?'

'No, not that I'm here exactly, but she said I could go for a walk. It takes such a long time. She's going to have curls.'

'A perm? Yes, that's no joke, takes about two hours,' Sejer said knowledgeably. 'Come up to the office with me and I'll show you where I work.'

He took the boy's hand again and shepherded him into the lift, while Mrs Brenningen sent him a long, appreciative look. She'd witnessed the power play and got through most of her book's intrigues. Now only the lust remained.

'You probably don't like Farris mineral water, Jan Henry,' he said, looking round the office for something to offer him. Farris and Fisherman's Friends were hardly the things to offer a small boy with all his taste buds unsullied and intact.

'Yes, I like Farris. Dad used to give me some,' he said contentedly.

'That's lucky then.' He tugged a plastic cup loose from the stack above the sink, filled it and placed it on the desk in front of him. The boy took a long drink and burped gently. 'How have you been keeping?' he asked amicably and noticed that his freckles had multiplied.

'Not too bad,' he mumbled. And then added, as if in explanation for why he'd come: 'Mum's got a boyfriend.'

'Oh, my goodness,' he exclaimed, 'so that's the reason for the curls.'

'I don't know. But he's got a motorbike.'

'Has he? A Japanese one?'

'BMW.'

'No! Been on it?'

'Only backwards and forwards between the clothes lines.'

'That's not too bad, perhaps the trips will gradually get longer. You wear a helmet, don't you?'

'Oh yes.'

'And your mum, does she go on it?'

'No, she'd rather die. But he's trying to change her mind.'

Sejer drank from the bottle and smiled. 'It was nice of you to come, I don't often get visits at work.'

'Don't you?'

'No, I mean, not visits like this one. Which are just nice. Which haven't got anything to do with work, if you see what I mean.'

'Oh yes. But actually I've come with that note,' he said quickly. 'You said I should say if I remembered anything. About the note, that Dad had.'

Sejer snapped his mouth shut and clamped himself to the edge of the desk. 'The note?' he stammered.

'I found it in the garage. I sat on the bench for a few days and thought, just like you said. And when I closed my eyes I imagined Dad just as he was on that day – the day when he didn't come back. And he'd got the note out of his pocket. And suddenly I remembered that he was lying under the car and pulled the note out of his pocket. He read it, and wriggled out a bit, and then he just stretched back, like this' – he stretched one arm above his head and seemed to relinquish something in the air – 'and put it down on a little shelf under the bench, right near the ground. I jumped down and looked, and there it was.'

Sejer felt his blood pressure rising, but as it was low to begin with, his well-trained body experienced no strong physical effect. The boy had put his hand in his pocket. Now he held it out and in his fingers was a crumpled piece of paper.

Sejer's hands trembled, he flattened it out and read. There was the name Liland, and a phone number.

The sheet of paper had been torn in two, as if there had perhaps been more writing. Liland?

'Well done, young man!' he said firmly, and poured more Farris. It was a local number and didn't necessarily prove anything. He knew that much, after almost thirty years in the force. Despite everything, most people were honest, and there was nothing illegal about showing interest in a car. Especially not in an Opel Manta, which was an attractive proposition for anyone who liked German cars, he thought. If Einarsson really had expressed an interest in selling it. But he nodded contentedly and itched to snatch up the phone, he almost felt like having a roll-up, but he never brought the pouch with him to work, he only had a few nasty, dry cigarettes that he offered to others. Jan Henry deserved a little tour of the station, perhaps a quick look at one of the remand cells and an interview room. Einarsson's killer had been on the loose for more than six months, an hour here or there made little difference. He took the boy's hand and led him along the corridors. His hand was thinner than the strong, podgy fists that Matteus owned. I mustn't forget that mechanic's suit, he said to himself again, as he struggled to take small steps. He halted at the furthest cell and unlocked the door. Jan Henry peeked in.

'Is that the toilet?' he asked, pointing to a hole in the floor.

'Yes.'

'I wouldn't want to sleep here.'

'You won't have to. Just do what your mum tells you.'

'But the floor's hot.' He wiggled his toes inside his trainers.

'Yes, that's right. We don't want them freezing to death.'

'D'you look at them through the window?'

'Yes we do. Come on, we'll go out again. I'll lift you up and you can take a look yourself.'

The small body jumped up between his arms.

'It looks just like what I thought it would look like,' he said simply.

'Yes. It looks like a prison, doesn't it?'

'Are there lots of prisoners here?'

'We haven't got many at the moment. There's room for thirty-nine, but just now we've got twenty-eight. Mostly men, and a few women.'

'Women as well?'

'Yup.'

'I didn't know women went to prison.'

'Didn't you? Did you think they were nicer than us?'

'Yes.'

'I'll tell you a secret,' he whispered. 'They are.'

'But they must be allowed radios. Someone's got music on.'

'That's coming from in there.' Sejer pointed to a grey door. 'There's a cinema in there. And at the moment they're watching a film called *Schindler's List*.'

'Cinema?'

'They've got all they need here. Library, school, doctor, workshop. Most of them work while they're inside, just at the moment they're having a break. And they've all got to wash their own clothes, and they cook their own meals, in the kitchen upstairs. And then there's an exercise room and an activities room. And when they need fresh air, we take them up on to the roof where there's a roof garden.'

'They've got everything, then!'

'Well, I don't know about that. They can't take a stroll into town on a fine day and buy an ice cream. We can.'

'Do they escape sometimes?'

'Yes, but not very often.'

'Do they shoot the guards and take their keys?'

'No, it's not as exciting as that. They break a window and climb down the side of the building, where they've usually got an accomplice waiting in a car. And we've had broken bones and concussion here, too. It's a long way down.'

'Do they tear the bedclothes into strips like in the films?'

'No, no. They steal nylon rope from the workshop. They're not in their cells most of the time, you see, they're mainly moving around the building.'

He took his hand once more, passed the security centre and pointed so that the boy could see himself on the monitor. He stopped and waved into the camera.

Then they made their way to the lift. Afterwards he accompanied Jan Henry the two blocks to the hairdresser's and saw him safely inside and ensconced on a flower-patterned Manila sofa. He strode back as fast as he could.

In his office, he immediately looked up the name Liland in the phone book. He found six entries for the name, including a firm. He went through the numbers with his finger, but couldn't find the one he had on the piece of paper. That was strange. And none of them were women. Somewhat nonplussed he lifted the receiver and dialled the number on the paper. It rang once, twice, three times, he glanced quickly at the time and counted the rings, on the sixth it was answered. A male voice.

'Larsgård,' he heard.

'Larsgård?'

There was silence for a moment while he thought about the name, whether he'd heard it before. He didn't think he had. He glanced out of the window, down at the square and gazed thoughtfully at the big fountain, it was dry now, waiting for spring, like everything else.

'Yes, Larsgård.'

'Is there someone there called Liland?' he asked expectantly.

'Liland?' The man on the line was silent for a second, then he cleared his voice. 'No, my friend, there is not. Not any longer.'

'Not any longer? Has Liland gone away?'

'Well, yes, you could say that. Quite a long way away in fact, right over to eternity. I mean she's dead, that was my wife. Her maiden name was Liland. Kristine Liland.'

'I'm terribly sorry.'

'I'm sure you are, but that word hardly describes my feelings.'

'Did she die recently?'

'Good lord, no, she died years ago.'

'Really? No one else of that name at your number either?'

'No, there's only me here, no one else. I've lived on my own ever since. Who is this? What's this about?'

He'd become suspicious now, his voice had assumed a harder edge.

'It's the police. We're investigating a murder and there's a small detail I really need to check. Could I pop by and have a talk?'

'Certainly, just come along. I don't get many visitors.'

Sejer wrote down the address and reckoned it would take half an hour to drive there. He moved the magnet on the board, allowing himself a couple of hours, grabbed his jacket by the collar and left the office. A waste of time, he thought to himself. But at least it was an opportunity to get out of the building. He hated sitting still, he hated looking out over the roofs and treetops through dusty windowpanes.

He drove slowly, as he always did, through the town, which had finally begun to take on some colour. The Parks and Recreation Service was in full swing, they'd planted petunias and marigolds everywhere, presumably they'd get nipped by the frost. Personally, he always waited until after Independence Day on 17 May. It had taken him twenty years to find a place in his heart for this town, but now it was there, small parts of it had stirred him one after the other, first the old fire station, then the wooded hillsides high above the town, covered on this side by stately old buildings and formerly genteel homes, several of which had been turned into exclusive little galleries and offices, whereas the hillsides on the south side were mainly occupied by high-rise blocks, where all the town's immigrants and asylum seekers had congregated, with all that that implied of stifling prejudice and the attendant unrest. Eventually, a new police team was set up, and that worked reasonably well.

He also loved the town bridge with its beautiful sculptures and the big square, the town's pride, with its ingeniously patterned cobblestones. In summer it was transformed into a cornucopia of fruit and vegetables and flowers. Just at the moment the little train was rattling about as it always did when summer was in the offing, he'd taken Matteus on it once, but it had been torture squeezing his long legs into the tiny carriage. Now it was full of perspiring mothers and small pink faces with dummies and bonnets, it bumped about quite a lot on the uneven surface. He left the town centre behind and drove to his own flat. He considered that Kollberg would benefit from a little airing in the car, he was alone so much of the time. He got the lead, attached it and ran down the stairs.

Larsgård sounded like a bit of an old fogey. Why didn't the name and number correspond? He puzzled over this as he drove south, as sedately as a clergyman, past the power station and the campsite, watching the traffic behind him in the mirror and allowing drivers to pass when they got impatient; everyone who found themselves behind Sejer on the road became impatient, a fact he accepted with perfect equanimity. When he got to the flatbread factory he turned to the left, drove for a couple of minutes through fields and meadows and ended up at a cluster of four or five houses. There was also a diminutive smallholding on the periphery. Larsgård lived in the yellow house, which was rather pretty, very small with brick-red bargeboards and a little lean-to adjoining it. He parked and ambled over to the steps. But before he reached them, the door opened, and a thin, lanky man appeared. He was wearing a knitted jacket and checked slippers and he supported himself on the door frame. He had a stick in his hand. Sejer ransacked his memory, something about the old man seemed familiar. But he couldn't think why.

'Did it take you long to find me?'

'No, no, not at all. This isn't exactly Chicago, and we've got the road atlas.'

They shook hands. He pressed the bony hand with a certain caution, in case the man had arthritis or some other painful accompaniment to old age. Then he followed him into the house. It was untidy and comfortable at the same time, and pleasantly dusky. The air was fresh, there was no dust lying in the corners here.

'So you live alone here?' he asked lowering himself into an old armchair of fifties vintage, the sort he found so good to sit in.

'Completely alone.' The man sank on to the sofa with great difficulty. 'And it's not always easy. My legs are rotting away, you know. They're filling up with water, can you imagine anything worse? And my heart's on the wrong side too, but at least it's still ticking. Touch wood,' he said suddenly and rapped his knuckles on the woodwork.

'Really? Is that possible? To have your heart on the wrong side?'

'Oh yes. I can see you don't believe me. You're wearing the same expression as everyone else when I tell them. But I had to have my left lung removed when I was younger. I had tuberculosis, was up at Vardåsen for a couple of years. It was all right there, it wasn't that, but when they took out my lung it left so much bloody room that the whole damned thing began to move to the right. Well, anyway, it's ticking away as I said, I manage just about. I've got a carer who comes once a week. She cleans the entire house for me and does all the washing, and throws out the rubbish and the food that's turned mouldy in the fridge over the past week, and gives the house plants a bit of attention. And each time she brings along three or four bottles of wine. She's not supposed to do it, apparently. Buying wine for me, I mean, only if I'm with her. So she swears me to secrecy. But I don't suppose you'll tell. Will you?'

'Of course not.' Sejer smiled. 'I always have a whisky myself before I go to bed, have done for years. And heaven help the carer who refuses to go to the off-licence for me, when the time comes. I thought that was what they were for,' he said naively.

'*One* whisky?'

'Just one. But it's pretty generous.'

'Ah, yes. D'you know, there's actually room for four shots in a glass. I've worked it out. Ballantine's?'

'Famous Grouse. The one with the grouse on the label.'

'Never heard of it. But what brings you here? Did my wife have some guilty secrets?'

'I'm sure she didn't, but I want to show you something.' Sejer brought out the note from his inner pocket. 'Do you recognise that handwriting?'

Larsgård held the paper close up to his face, it shook

violently between his trembling fingers. 'No-oh,' he said uncertainly, 'should I?'

'I don't know. Perhaps. There's quite a lot I don't know. I'm investigating the murder of a thirty-eight-year-old man who was found floating in the river. And he didn't exactly fall in while he was fishing. The evening he disappeared, which was about six months ago now, he told his wife that he was going out to show his car to someone who'd expressed an interest in it. The man must have made a note of this person's name and phone number on a piece of paper which, quite by chance, I've managed to get hold of. This piece of paper. With the name Liland and your phone number, Mr Larsgård. Can you explain it?'

The old man shook his head, Sejer could see his brow furrowing. 'I won't even try,' he replied, his voice slightly brusque, 'because I don't understand a thing about it.' Somewhere at the back of his mind he recalled a wrong number. Something about a car. How long ago had that been? Maybe six months, maybe he ought to mention it. He let it go.

'But are there people you know on your late wife's side with that name?'

'No. My wife was an only child. Her family name has gone now.'

'But someone used it. Presumably a woman.'

'A woman? There are lots of people called Liland.'

'No, only six in this town. None with this number.'

The old man took a cigarette from the packet on the table and Sejer lit it for him.

'I've no more to add. It must be a mistake. And the dead don't go around buying second-hand cars. And anyway she couldn't even drive. My wife, I mean. I suppose he hadn't even sold his car, if you found him dead. Doubtless because he had the wrong number.'

Sejer said nothing. He was looking at the old man as he was speaking, then his eyes wandered thoughtfully over the walls. Suddenly, his grip tensed on the arms of his chair and he felt the hairs on his neck rising. Above Larsgård's head was a small painting. It was black and white with a little grey, an abstract painting, the style seemed strangely familiar. He closed his eyes for an instant then opened them again.

'That's rather a nice picture you have there, above the sofa,' he said quietly.

'Do you know about art?' he asked quickly. 'D'you think it's good? I told my girl she ought to paint with colours, then she might be able to sell them. She tries to make a living from it. My daughter. I don't know much about art, so I can't say if it's good or not, but she's done it for years and it hasn't made her rich.'

'Eva Marie,' Sejer said softly.

'Yes, Eva. What? D'you know my Eva? Is it possible?' He was rocking slightly, as if he were anxious about something.

'Yes, a little bit, by chance. Her pictures are good,'

Sejer added quickly. 'People are a bit slow on the uptake. Just wait, she'll come into her own, you'll see.' He rubbed his jaw in disbelief. 'So, you're Eva Magnus's father?'

'Is there anything wrong with that?'

'Certainly not,' Sejer said. 'Tell me, Liland wouldn't be her middle name or anything like that?'

'No. She's just called Magnus. And she certainly hasn't the money to buy another car. She's divorced now, lives alone with little roly-poly Emma. My only grandchild.'

Sejer rose, ignoring the old man's astonished look, and pushed his face right up to the painting on the wall. He examined the signature. E. M. MAGNUS. The letters were sharp and inclined, they were a bit like old-fashioned runes, he thought, and looked down at the note. LILAND. Precisely the same letters. One didn't even need a handwriting expert to see that. He drew breath.

'You've every reason to be proud of your daughter. I just had to look into this note. So you don't know the handwriting?' he asked again.

The old man didn't answer. He pursed his lips as if suddenly afraid.

Sejer put the note back into his pocket. 'I won't disturb you any longer. I can see this is a mistake.'

'Disturb? You must be mad, how often do you think someone like me gets a visitor?'

'It's quite possible I may pop round again,' he said as lightly as he could. He walked slowly to the front door so that the old man could follow him out. He halted at the top of the steps and stared across the fields. He could hardly believe that he'd run across the name Eva Magnus yet again. As if she had a finger in every pie. It was strange.

'Your name's Sejer,' the old man said suddenly. 'It's Danish, isn't it?'

'That's right.'

'Did you grow up in Haukervika?'

'I did,' he said, surprised.

'I think I remember you. A thin little lad forever scratching himself.'

'I still do. Where did you live?'

'In that rambling green place behind the sports ground. Eva loved that house. You've grown since I last saw you!'

Sejer nodded slowly. 'I suppose I must have.'

'But what have we got here?' He peered at the back seat and caught sight of the dog.

'My dog.'

'Good lord, quite a size.'

'Yes, he certainly is a big boy.'

'What's his name?'

'Kollberg.'

'Huh? What a name! Well well, you've got your reasons, no doubt. But I think you could have brought him in.'

'I don't as a rule. Not everybody likes it.'

'But I do. I had one myself, years ago. A Dobermann. She was a bitch, and I called her Dibah. But her real name was Kyrkjebakkens Farah Dibah. Have you ever heard anything so ridiculous?'

'Yes.'

He got into the Peugeot and turned on the engine. Things will be heating up for you now, Eva, he thought, because in a couple of minutes you'll have your old dad on the line, and that'll give you something to think about. He was annoyed that there was always someone around who could phone and warn her!

'Drive slowly through the fields,' Larsgård admonished, 'lots of animals running back and forth across the road.'

'I always drive slowly. She's an old car.'

'Not as old as me.'

Larsgård waved after him as he drove off.

Chapter 14

Eva stood with the phone in her hand.

He'd found the note. After six months he'd found the note.

The police had handwriting experts, they could find out who'd written it, but first they had to have something to compare it with, and then they could study each little loop, the joins and circles, dots and dashes, a unique pattern which revealed the writer, with every characteristic and neurotic tendency, perhaps even sex and age. They went to college and studied all this, it was a science.

It wouldn't take Sejer many minutes to drive from her father's place to her own house. She hadn't much time. She dropped the receiver with a clatter and steadied herself a moment against the wall. Then as if in a daze she went to the hall and took her coat from the peg. She laid it on the dining table with her bag and a packet of cigarettes. She sprinted to the bathroom, packed her toothbrush and some toothpaste in a bag, threw in a hairbrush and the packet of paracetamol. She ran into the bedroom and grabbed some clothes out of the wardrobe, underwear, tee shirts and socks. Every now and again she checked the time; she made her way into the kitchen and opened the freezer, found a packet marked 'Bacon' and dropped it in her bag, ran back into the living room and switched off the lights, checked that the windows were properly fastened. It had only taken a few minutes, so she stood in the middle of the room and looked round one last time. She didn't know where she'd go, only that she had to get away. Emma could live with Jostein. She liked it there, perhaps she'd really prefer to be there anyway. This realisation almost paralysed her completely. But she couldn't give way to sobs now; she went into the hall, put on her coat, slung the bag on her shoulder and opened the door. There was a man outside on the steps, staring at her. She'd never seen him before in her life.

Sejer drove out of the tunnel, his brow deeply furrowed.

'Kollberg,' he said, 'this is really odd.'

He put on his sunglasses. 'I wonder why we always come back to this woman. What an earth is she up to?'

He stared down at the town, which was dirty and grey after the winter. 'The old chap certainly hasn't got anything to do with it, he must be eighty if he's a day, possibly more. But what the hell would an erudite artist like her want with a clod of a brewery worker? He certainly had no money. By the way, are you hungry?'

'Woof!'

'Yes, me too. But we must get to Engelstad first. Afterwards we'll enjoy ourselves, stop at 7-Eleven on our way home. A pork chop for me and some dry biscuits for you.'

Kollberg whined.

'Only pulling your leg! Two pork chops and a beer for each of us.'

The dog lay down again, happy. He didn't understand a word of the conversation, but he liked the sound of his master's voice when he said the final bit.

Chapter 15

Eva stared open-mouthed at the stranger. Behind him was a blue Saab, she didn't recognise that either.

'Sorry,' she stammered, 'I thought you were someone else.'

'Oh yes? Why did you think that, Eva?'

She blinked uncertainly. Then she was filled with a horrible suspicion. It struck her mind like lightning, her face stiffened and felt like thick paper. After six months the note had turned up, she didn't know where from. After six months he was at her door, the man she'd been waiting for. She thought he'd given up. He mounted the last couple of steps and leant with one arm on the door frame. She could feel his breath.

'Know what I found recently? When I was clearing out Maja's things? I found a painting. Quite an exciting painting as a matter of fact, with your name in one corner. I hadn't thought of that. She mentioned you the evening she rang, that she'd met you in town. It was that evening, you know – the evening before she died. An old childhood friend, she said. The kind you swap all your secrets with.'

His voice sounded as if it emanated from a reptile, it was rough and hoarse.

'You shouldn't leave your paintings around like that with a signature and everything. I cleared out some furniture to sell, and there it was. I've been looking for you, I've been looking for six months. It wasn't easy, there are so many Evas. What happened, Eva, was the temptation too great? She told you about the money, eh, and then you killed her?'

Eva had to steady herself on the wall. 'I did not kill her!'

He looked at her through narrowed eyes. 'I don't give a fuck about that! The money's mine!'

She backed into the hallway and slammed the door shut. It had a night latch. She stumbled through the living room, hearing him begin to work on the lock, quietly at first, as if he had a picklock. She wasted no time. She shot down the cellar steps, ran through it, squeezing past the old carpenter's bench, and found the main electricity switch. Everything went black. Now, from up above, she heard him attacking the door with heavier tools, there was banging and scraping. She fumbled her way to the cellar door, ran her hands over the woodwork, her temples pounding. The door hadn't been used for years, perhaps it was locked, perhaps with a padlock, she couldn't remember, but it led out into a wilderness of garden, and just behind the hedge was her neighbour's garden and a side street she could escape into. More violent blows upstairs: the sound of metal splintering woodwork, perhaps he was wielding an axe. She found the bar that ran across the door and hoped it wasn't padlocked, she couldn't feel anything, but it wouldn't budge, it had probably rusted fast. Quickly, she removed a shoe and used the heel to hit it from below, she struck it again and again while the man upstairs smashed his way through the door and tramped into the living room, and at last it gave. She lifted it carefully, because now he'd halted, he stood still listening, at any moment he'd see the stairs down to the cellar and realise that she was standing down here in the dark, that perhaps there was a way out, she couldn't open it now that he was so silent. She waited for him to move again, and he did, he approached the stairs, the soles of his shoes sighing on the parquet flooring, she popped her shoe back on and pushed the door open with one shoulder, she hoped it wouldn't creak, but it gave a squeal that reverberated in the cellar's space. Now there was only the cellar hatch above her. She thought it was open, she'd never normally locked it, so she ascended the four steps and had begun to push at it with her shoulder when she heard his footfall on the stairs, he'd realised now that she'd fled this way, so he began to hurry, while Eva used her shoulder as a battering ram and drove it up against the hatch again and again. It opened a crack, then closed again, through the gap she saw that someone had put a peg through the steel catch outside, perhaps it had been Jostein, he'd always been so practical. But if it were a wooden peg it would break, sooner or later it would break, so she continued to attack the hatch with her shoulder, the chink got larger, it felt as if her shoulder would break before the peg, it was numb, almost without feeling, so she continued, and suddenly she saw his foot on the bottom step of the cellar stairs, a light-coloured moccasin, and his white teeth in the dark. He moved a few paces and stretched out an arm, and Eva battered her shoulder into the hatch with all her might. Just then the peg broke and the hatch flew up with a crash. She fell down the four steps, got up them again, shot out of the opening and was making for the hedge when she felt his hands round her ankle, he had a firm hold, he yanked her towards him, her chin bumped down the steps. The cement floor was icy. She couldn't feel her shoulder any more. The inside of her mouth was bleeding. He dropped her foot with a little thud.

Eva lay on her stomach. He stood astride her and she caught the scent of his aftershave, a strangely alien smell in the musty cellar. Her thoughts swam for an instant, then she thought: he isn't particularly large, he's quite slender, and the cellar hatch is open. I've got longer legs, if I could only surprise him . . .

'Lie still,' he snarled.

She tried to make a plan. She had to think of something, ruin his concentration, catch him off balance. There were four steps up to the garden, if she took two at a time . . .

'Tell me where you've hidden the money, and nothing will happen to you.' His voice was almost comforting. 'But if you don't, things will heat up, in lots of places.'

He struck a match. She gulped back the beginnings of nausea and tried to think, how many seconds would she need to stand up and dash out, get through the hedge and cross her neighbour's lawn? She went through the movement in her mind, drawing her arms and legs under her, leaping up, two steps, into the hedge, across the lawn, down the street, traffic, people . . .

'I can't hear you,' he said huskily.

'I don't keep it here,' she groaned. 'You didn't really think I would, did you?'

He laughed softly. 'It doesn't matter to me where it is. Provided you show me the way.'

What would surprise him, she thought, some unexpected action, perhaps a loud scream, the scream that never materialises from the throat when you're truly frightened, but sticks there blocking the breath? A scream. Perhaps that would paralyse him for a couple of seconds, just long enough to get halfway up from the floor.

She raised her head.

'Yes?' he said.

She drew air into her lungs, filled them to capacity and got ready.

'Which will it be?'

The match went out. And then she screamed. Her scream reverberated, bouncing off the cellar walls in piercing waves from room to room, she jumped up, drew in more air and screamed again, and now he collected himself, sprang after her just as she took the four steps in two bounds, she crossed the garden and dived into the hedge, felt it catching and tearing at her skin and hair, and heard her coat ripping and his panting right behind her, as she pushed her way through and suddenly was out again, picking up speed, went on round her neighbour's house and out through the gate, down the street, which was silent now, cut in through another gate, she was covering the distance with her long legs, the pain and the fear gave her strength, she heard his feet a little way behind, ran round the house, found a further hedge, she could go through it and continue across another property, but she decided against it, ran instead round the house and stopped at the opposite corner, just in time to see him in pursuit. He thought she'd carried on through the next hedge, but she ran out on to the road again, following the ditch so that her shoes wouldn't make a noise on the asphalt, caught a glimpse of the main road far ahead, and the first car lights, then she put on speed, no longer looking back, but drove on, with lungs bursting and gasping for breath, and at last caught sight of a car, it was moving slowly, she leapt out into the road and heard the screeching of brakes. She collapsed on to the bonnet like a sack. Sejer stared at her in alarm through the windscreen. It was several seconds before she recognised him. Then she spun round, cut across the road and turned into a drive on the other side, she heard his car make a U-turn to that side of the road. It halted, a car door opened, she heard his feet on the pavement. Eva's strength was exhausted, but still she ran, with her skirt flapping round her legs, Sejer followed her into the garden, he was running on gravel, she could hear him clearly although her ears were ringing, and then another sound, a well-known sound that made her throat tighten. A dog. Kollberg wanted to join in the game. He watched lovingly as his master sped off, it took the dog a few seconds to catch him up, he wagged his tail eagerly, jumping up and tugging at his jacket, then he suddenly noticed the woman running a little way ahead and the flapping of her long skirt in the twilit garden. He forgot Sejer and bounded after her. Eva turned and saw the huge dog and its red jaws, steam was coming from its mouth, its tongue was lolling from side to side like a pendulum as it tore through the garden. She had no thought of Sejer now, she was just running from the dog, from those yellow teeth and big canine paws which cut through the long grass in huge strides, ate up the distance in great bites. There was a small Wendy house amongst the old apple trees. She careered towards it with the very last of her strength, yanked open the door and slammed it shut behind her. Inside here she was safe from the dog. At least she was safe from the dog.

Sejer eased off and walked slowly towards the diminutive house. He patted the dog, when it came back disappointed, then bent down, took it by the collar and walked towards the door. He opened it warily. She was sitting on the floor with her knees drawn up under her chin, next to a laid table. A tiny coffee pot and two china cups graced the white tablecloth. Beside her on the floor lay a discarded doll with her hair cut off.

'Eva Magnus,' he said quietly, 'I think you'd better accompany me to the station.'

Chapter 16

Eva returned to reality.

She glanced up at Sejer, amazed that he was still sitting there.

He could have told her to start talking now, but he didn't. He could take a break, it was worse for her. She was still wearing her coat, now she put her hand in her pocket and fumbled for something.

'Cigarette?' he asked, and found the packet in his desk, the packet he never touched.

He lit one for her, still keeping quiet; he could see she was trying to gather herself, find the beginning, a good place to start. The blood had begun to congeal around her mouth, and her lower lip was swollen. She couldn't go back to the house. So, finally, she began at the beginning. With the day Emma had gone on holiday, and she'd taken the bus into town. She'd been standing in Nedre Storgate feeling cold, with her back to the

Glassmagasinet department store and thirty-nine kroner in her pocket. A carrier bag in one hand. With the other, she clasped the top of her coat together under her chin. It was the last day of September, and cold.

She should have been at home working, it was eleven in the morning, but she'd fled from the house. Before that she'd phoned her electricity supplier and phone company; she'd asked them for a breathing space, for just a few more days, then she'd pay. And she was allowed to keep her electricity supply as she had a young child, but the telephone would be cut off in the course of the day. If the house burnt down, they'd have to live in the ruins as she hadn't paid her insurance. Every week a new debt-recovery threat came in the post. Her Arts Council grant was late. The fridge was empty. The thirty-nine kroner was all she had. In her studio she had great piles of paintings, the work of several years which no one wanted to buy. She glanced to her left, across to the square, to where she could make out the illuminated Sparebank sign. A few months before the bank had been robbed. The man in the tracksuit had taken less than two minutes to make off with four hundred thousand kroner. About one hundred seconds, she thought. The case remained unsolved.

She shook her head in despair and looked furtively across at the paint shop, peered down into her bag where the acrosol can of fixative lay. It had cost 102 kroner and was faulty. Something was wrong with the nozzle so that nothing came out, or worse, it would suddenly deliver a great flood of the stuff at her pictures and ruin them. Like the sketch of her father that she'd been so lucky with. She hadn't the money to buy another one, she'd have to exchange it. The few kroner she had left would buy her milk, bread and coffee and that was all. The problem was that Emma ate like a horse, a loaf didn't last long. She'd phoned the Arts Council, who'd said that her grant would be sent out 'any day now', so it could take another week. She had no idea what she would eat tomorrow. It didn't take her breath away or make her panic, she was used to living from hand to mouth, they'd done it for years. Ever since she and Emma had been left alone, and there was no longer a man bringing in money. Something would turn up, it always did. But the worry was like a barb in her breast, over the years she'd become empty inside. Sometimes reality began to quiver, and rumble quietly as if there were an earthquake in the making. The only thing that held her fast was the overarching task of satisfying Emma's hunger. While she had Emma she had a sheet anchor. Today she'd gone to her father's, and Eva searched for something to hold on to. All she had was the carrier bag.

Eva was tall and truculent, pale and frightened all at once, but the years with little money had taught her to use her imagination. Maybe she could demand her money back instead of a new aerosol, she thought, then she'd have another 102 kroner to buy food with. It was just a bit awkward asking. She was an artist, after all, she needed fixative and the man in the paint shop knew it. Perhaps she should sweep into the shop and make a real scene, act the difficult customer and mouth off and complain and threaten them with the Consumer Council; then he'd understand how the land lay, that actually she was broke and upset, and he'd refund her money. He was a nice man. Just as Père Tanguy had been when, for payment, he'd cut a pink prawn out of a van Gogh picture. Provided he could buy a tube of paint, he didn't care if he ate or not. Nor did Eva for that matter, but she had a child with a ravenous appetite. The Dutchman hadn't had to contend with that. She psyched herself up, crossed the street and went into the shop. It was warmer inside, quite cosy, and had the same smell as her studio at home. A young girl was behind the counter in the perfume section, flicking through a hair-tone chart. The paint man himself was nowhere to be seen.

'I want to return this,' Eva said with determination, 'the spray mechanism doesn't work. I want my money back.'

The girl assumed a pouting expression and took the bag. 'You couldn't have bought that here,' she said sullenly. 'We don't stock that hairspray.'

Eva rolled her eyes. 'It's not hairspray, it's fixative,'

she said wearily. 'I ruined a rather good sketch on account of that aerosol.'

The girl blushed, lifted the can out and sprayed above Eva's head. Nothing came out. 'You can have a replacement,' she said tersely.

'The money,' Eva persisted doggedly. 'I know the owner, he'd give me my money back.'

'Why?' she asked.

'Because I'm asking for it. It's called service,' she said curtly.

The girl sighed, she hadn't been in the shop long and she was twenty years Eva's junior. She opened the till and took out a hundred-kroner note and two kroner pieces.

'Just sign here.'

Eva signed her name, took the money and left. She tried to relax. Now perhaps she could manage for a couple of days more. She did some mental arithmetic and worked out she had 141 kroner, almost enough to treat herself to a cup of coffee at Glassmagasinet's in-store café. You could get a coffee there without having to eat as well. She crossed the street and went through the double glass doors which parted invitingly. She took a quick look in the book and stationery department and was just about to make for the escalator, when she caught sight of a woman standing at one of the shelves. A buxom brunette with closely cropped hair and dark eyebrows. She was leafing through a book. Many years had passed, but it wasn't a face you could forget. Eva stopped dead, she couldn't believe her eyes. Suddenly the years fell away and she was transported all the way back to that day when, as a fifteen-year-old, she'd been sitting on the stone steps at home. Everything they possessed had been packed in boxes and put on a lorry. She sat staring at it, unable to believe that everything had really fitted into one small lorry, when the house and garage and cellar had been so full of stuff. They were moving. Just then it was as if they didn't live anywhere, it was horrible. Eva didn't want to leave. Her father went about with restless eyes as if afraid they'd forget something. He'd got a job at last. But he couldn't meet Eva's gaze.

Then there was a crunch of gravel and a familiar figure rounded the corner.

'I had to come and say goodbye,' she said.

Eva nodded.

'We can write to each other, can't we? I've never had anyone to write letters to before. Will you come back in the summer holidays?'

'Don't know,' Eva mumbled.

She'd never find another friend, she was certain of it. They'd grown up together, they'd shared everything. No one else knew how she felt. The future was a dreary grey landscape, she wanted to cry. There was a quick, shy hug, and then she'd gone. That was almost twenty-five years ago, and since then they'd never set eyes on one another. Not until now.

'Maja?' she queried and waited expectantly. The woman turned and tried to pinpoint the call, and caught sight of Eva. Her eyes opened wide and grew large, then she rushed towards her.

'Well, of all things! I can't believe my eyes. Eva Marie! My God, how tall you've grown!'

'And you're even smaller than I remember you!'

Then they were silent for a moment, suddenly bashful, as they scrutinised one another to pick out everything, the changes, all the traces left by the inter-vening years, recognising their own decay in the other's wrinkles and lines, and after that they searched for everything they knew so well and which still was there. Maja said: 'We'll go to the café. Come along, we must talk, Eva. So, you're still living here? You really do still live here?'

She placed an arm around Eva's waist and shep-herded her along, full of amazement, but soon the same person Eva remembered: bright, chatty, determined and always bubbly, in other words the opposite of Eva. They had complemented one another. Oh God, how they'd needed each other!

'I never got any further,' Eva replied. 'This is a bad place to live, I should never have come with that removal lorry.'

'You're just like you were when we were girls,' Maja

giggled. 'Downcast. Come on, let's grab that window table!'

They rushed over to claim it before anyone else, and plonked themselves down on the chairs. Maja got to her feet again.

'Sit here and keep our places, I'll go and get us something. What would you like?'

'Just coffee.'

'You need a piece of cake,' Maja objected, 'you're thinner than ever.'

'I haven't got the money.' She'd blurted it out before she'd had time to think.

'Oh? Well I have.'

She went off, and Eva watched the way she helped herself greedily at the cake counter. It was awful having to say that she couldn't afford a piece of cake, but she wasn't used to lying to Maja. The truth popped out all of its own accord. She could hardly believe it was true, that she really was over there pouring out their coffee. It was as if those twenty-five years had just rolled away, and as she looked at Maja from a distance she still seemed like a young girl. You get sleeker if you're a bit chubby, Eva thought enviously, and pulled off her coat. She didn't bother much about food. She ate only when hunger became a physical discomfort and ruined her concentration. Apart from that she lived on coffee, cigarettes and wine.

Maja returned. She placed the tray on the table and

pushed the plate across to Eva. A Danish pastry and a slice of cake covered in icing.

'I can't eat all that,' she complained.

'Then you'll have to make a special effort,' said Maja emphatically. 'It's only a matter of training. The more you eat, the bigger your stomach gets and the more food it needs to fill it. It only takes a couple of days. You're not twenty any more, you know, and it pays to put on a bit of weight when you're pushing forty. Oh God, we'll soon be forty!'

She stuck the fork into her cake so that the cream filling bulged out at the sides. Eva stared at her, watching how Maja took control, so that she herself could rest and relax and merely do as she was told. Just like when they were girls. At the same time she noticed her fingers with all their gold rings, and the bracelets that jingled round her wrists. She looked well-heeled.

'I've lived here for eighteen months,' said Maja. 'It's crazy we haven't bumped into each other before!'

'I'm hardly ever in town. Haven't much business here. I live at Engelstad.'

'Married?' asked Maja cautiously.

'Was. I've got a small girl, Emma. She's not actually all that small. She's at her father's at the moment.'

'So, a single mother with a child, then.'

Maja was trying to make sense of things. Eva felt herself dwindling. When she said it like that it sounded so pathetic. And the hard times probably showed. She bought her clothes at charity shops, whereas Maja was really quite smart. Leather jacket and boots and Levi's. Clothes like that cost a small fortune.

'Haven't you got any children?' Eva asked, holding a hand beneath her Danish pastry as it was shedding so many crumbs.

'No. What would I want one of them for?'

'They'll look after you when you're old,' Eva said simply, 'and be your comfort and joy when you're nearing your end.'

'Eva Marie, isn't that just like you. Deep into old age already. Well, you don't say, is that why people have kids?'

Eva had to laugh. She felt like a girl again, transported to the time when they were together every single day, every single free moment, for that was how it had been. Apart from the summer holidays, when she was sent to her uncle's in the country. Those holidays had been unbearable, she thought, unbearable without Maja.

'You'll regret it one day. Just wait.'

'I never regret things.'

'No, you probably don't. I regret almost everything in life.'

'You've got to stop doing that, Eva Marie. It's bad for your health.'

'But I don't regret Emma, though.'

'No, I suppose people don't regret their kids, do they. Why aren't you married any more?'

'He found someone else and left.'

Maja shook her head. 'And if I know you, you even helped him pack, didn't you?'

'Yes I did, actually. He's so impractical. Anyway, it was better than sitting doing nothing and watching all that furniture disappear.'

'I'd have gone over to a girlfriend's and cracked open a bottle.'

'I haven't got any girlfriends.'

They ate cake in silence. Now and then they shook their heads gently, as if they still couldn't believe that fate had really brought them together again. They had so much to talk about they didn't know where to begin. In her mind, Eva was still sitting on those cold stone steps staring at the green lorry.

'You never answered my letters,' said Maja suddenly. She sounded indignant.

'No. My father went on at me about writing, but I refused. I was bitter and cross about having to leave. I probably wanted to pay him back.'

'I was the one who suffered.'

'Yes, I'm a bit clumsy like that. D'you still smoke?' She rummaged in her bag for cigarettes.

'Like a chimney. But not those factory sweepings of yours.'

Maja took a pouch of tobacco from her jacket pocket and began rolling. 'What d'you do for a living?'

The despair showed on her cheeks. It was an innocent

question, but she hated it. She was suddenly tempted to tell a white lie, but it was difficult to fool Maja. She'd never managed to before.

'I've often asked myself the same question. Nothing very lucrative, is one way of putting it. I paint.'

Maja raised her eyebrows.

'So you're an artist?'

'Yes, yes I am, even though most people wouldn't agree with me. What I mean is, I don't sell a lot, but I regard that as a passing phase. Otherwise I'd probably have given up.'

'But don't you work at all?'

'Work?' Eva looked at her open-mouthed. 'D'you think pictures paint themselves or something? Of course I work! And it's not exactly an eight-hour day, either, I can tell you. Work follows me to bed at night. You never get any peace. You want to get up and start making alterations all the time.'

Maja smiled wryly. 'Forgive my silly question. I just wondered if you had a little job on the side, with a regular wage.'

'Then I wouldn't have time to paint,' Eva said sullenly.

'No, I can see that. It probably takes a fair time, painting a picture.'

'About six months.'

'What? Are they *that* big?'

Eva sighed and lit her cigarette. Maja had blood-red nail varnish and well-manicured hands, her own were a sorry sight. 'People don't understand how difficult it is,' she said despairingly. 'They think it just goes on to the canvas ready-formed from some secret muse.'

'I don't know anything about it,' Maja said softly. 'It just amazes me that people choose a life like that if it's so difficult. And when you've got a child and everything.'

'I didn't choose it.'

'Surely you did?'

'No, not really. You become an artist because you have to. Because there aren't any alternatives.'

'I don't understand that either. Hasn't everyone got alternatives?'

Eva gave up trying to explain. She'd eaten both cakes just to please Maja, and now she was feeling queasy. 'Tell me what *you* do instead. Whatever it is, you earn more than me.'

Maja lit her roll-up. 'I almost certainly do. I'm self-employed just like you. I run a small one-woman firm. I work hard and single-mindedly to save up some money, and I'm actually contemplating hanging up my hat in the New Year. Then I'll head off to northern France and open a small hotel. Perhaps in Normandy. It's an old dream of mine.'

'Wow!' Eva smoked and waited for more.

'It's hard work and it needs quite a lot of self-discipline, but it's worth it. It's simply a means to an end, and I won't give up until I've got what I want.'

'No, I can well believe that.'

'If you were a different type of person, Eva, I'd have offered you a partnership.' She leant across the table. 'No capital. Full training. And you'd have made a fortune in record time. You really would. Then you could have saved for your own small gallery. You would have been able to do that in, let's say a couple of years. Every other route is just the long way round, if you ask me.'

'But – what exactly do you *do*?' Eva stared in wonder at her friend.

Maja had folded her napkin into a hard lump while she talked, now she looked right at Eva. 'Let's call it customer service of a sort. People ring and make an appointment, and I receive them. There are so many needs out there, you know, and this niche in the market is really deep. About as deep as the Mariana Trench in the Pacific, I should think. But in plain terms I'm a call girl. Or, if you prefer, a good, old-fashioned whore.'

Eva turned bright red. She must have misheard. Or was Maja simply teasing her, she'd always been a terrible tease. 'What?'

Maja gave a sardonic smile and flicked the ash off her roll-up.

And Eva couldn't help staring, she looked with quite different eyes now at the gold jewellery, the costly clothes, the wristwatch and the wallet that bulged opulently on the table by the side of her coffee cup.

And up at her face again, as if she were seeing it for the first time.

'You've always been easy to shock,' said Maja dryly.

'Yes, it's true, you'll have to forgive me, but you did rather catch me off guard.' She tried to compose herself. The conversation was moving towards an unknown hinterland, and she was trying to get her bearings. 'Well, you don't exactly walk the streets do you, I mean, you don't look like it.' She felt inept.

'No, Eva Marie, I don't. I'm not on drugs, either. I work hard, like other people. Apart from the fact I don't pay income tax.'

'Have you – do many people know about it?'

'Only my clients, and there are lots of them. But most are regulars. It's really pretty good, the jungle telegraph does its work and business flourishes. I'm not bursting with pride, but I'm not ashamed either.' She stopped for a moment. 'Well, what do you think, Eva,' she said, pulling at her cigarette, 'do you think I should be ashamed?'

Eva shook her head. But the mere thought, the first dim flickering pictures that came when she thought of Maja and her occupation, or when she thought of herself in the same situation, made her stomach turn.

'No, goodness, I don't know. It's just so – unexpected. I can't see why you need to.'

'I don't *need* to. I've chosen to.'

'But how can you choose something like that?'

'It was simple. Loads of money as fast as possible. Tax free.'

'Well, but your health! I mean, what does it do to your self-respect? When you go giving yourself away to just anyone?'

'I don't give anything away at all, I sell it. In any case, we all have to make a distinction between professional and private life, and I don't find that at all difficult.' She smiled, and Eva saw that her dimples had got deeper with the years.

'But what would a man say if he found out about it?'

'He'd have to accept it or walk away,' she said curtly.

'But isn't it a heavy burden to carry year after year? Surely, there must be lots of people you *can't* tell?'

'Haven't you got secrets? Everyone has. This is so like you, isn't it,' she added, 'you make everything so difficult, you ask too many questions. I'd like a little bed-and-breakfast place, on the coast if possible, maybe Normandy. An old house preferably, one I could do up myself. I need a couple of million kroner. By New Year I'll have it, and then I'm off.'

'A couple of million?' Eva felt quite weak.

'And besides, I've learnt a lot.'

'What can you learn from that?'

'Oh, lots of things. If you only knew. Much more than you learn when you're painting, I'll bet. And if you do learn anything, it'll probably only be about yourself. I think being a painter's a bit egoistic. You're really exploring yourself. Instead of the people round you.'

'You sound just like my father.'

'How's he keeping?'

'Not all that well. He's on his own now.'

'Oh? I didn't know. What happened to your mother?'

'I'll tell you about it another time.'

They fell silent a while and let their thoughts roam. To a stranger they didn't seem to belong together at all, it needed a sharp eye to perceive the bonds that existed.

'In work terms we're both outsiders,' Maja said, 'but at least I'm making money, and that's why we work after all, isn't it? If I didn't have enough for a slice of cake in a café I couldn't survive. I mean, what does it do to your self-respect?'

Eva had to smile at her own line being thrown back at her. 'It makes me feel lousy,' she said suddenly. She couldn't be bothered to pretend any more. 'I've got 140 kroner in my wallet and unpaid bills amounting to ten thousand in the drawer at home. They're cutting off the phone today, and I haven't paid the house insurance. But I'm expecting some money, any day now. I get a grant,' she said proudly, 'from the Arts Council.'

'So you're on handouts?'

'No! Good God, of course I'm not!' Eva's composure evaporated. 'It's money I get because my work is considered to be important and promising! It gives me the chance to carry on and develop so that sooner or later I'll be able to stand on my own artistic legs!'

That hit home.

'Sorry,' Maja said lamely. 'I'm just not very familiar with the terminology here. So really it's something positive, this grant?'

'Of course! It's what everyone hopes for.'

'Well, I don't get a state subsidy.'

'That *would* look good,' said Eva grinning.

'I'll get some more coffee.'

Eva fished out another cigarette and followed the full figure with her eyes. She couldn't take in the fact that Maja had done this. The Maja she thought she knew so well. But earning a couple of million, that wasn't exactly peanuts – could it really be true? Was it that easy? She thought of all the things she could do with two million. She could pay all her debts. Buy a small gallery. No, two million couldn't be right, she was probably laying it on a bit thick. But she didn't usually tell tall stories. They never used to lie to each other.

'There you are! I hope your coffee won't go down the wrong way, now that you know where the money's coming from.'

Eva had to laugh. 'No, it tastes just as good,' she said smiling.

'That's just what I thought. It's strange isn't it, Eva? To put the whole thing in a nutshell: we're driven on by the things we need, the things we want. And when we achieve our aims we're satisfied for a short while, and then we set ourselves new objectives. At least, I do. And in that way I feel I'm alive, that something's happening and that I'm getting on. I mean, how long have you been stuck in the same rut? Artistically and financially?'

'Ah, quite a long time. At least ten years.'

'And you're not getting any younger. I don't think that sounds too good. What is it you paint? Landscapes?'

Eva drank some coffee and prepared herself for a long defence. 'Abstracts. And I paint in black and white, and the shades in between.'

Maja nodded patiently.

'I've got a special technique that I've developed over the years,' Eva said. 'I stretch a canvas of the size I want, paint it with a white foundation, and add a coat of light grey, quite a thick coat, and when it's dry I continue with a darker grey. And when that's dry, I add an even darker layer, and I go on like this until I end up with pure black. Then I let it dry. Really thoroughly. Eventually, I'm standing in front of a large, black surface, and now I have to delve into it to bring out the light.'

Maja was listening with a polite expression.

'Then I get to work,' Eva went on, and now her enthusiasm began to show, it was so rare for anyone to sit and listen like this, it was glorious, she had to make the most of it. 'I scrape out the picture. I work with an old-fashioned paint-scraper, and with a steel brush, or possibly with sandpaper or a knife. When I scrape gently I find shades of grey, and if I scrape hard, I get right down to the white and bring out a lot of light.'

'But what's it supposed to represent?'

'Well, I don't know if I can answer that. The viewer must decide what they see. It kind of forms by itself. It's simply light and shadow, light and shadow. I like them, I think they're good. I know I'm a great artist,' she said defiantly.

'Well, that certainly wasn't particularly modest.'

'No. It was "the productive egoist's essential brutality". As Charles Morice called it.'

'I'm not quite with you. It all sounds very exciting, but it's not much good if no one wants to buy them.'

'I can't paint the pictures people want,' Eva said despairingly. 'I have to paint the pictures *I* want. Otherwise it wouldn't be art. It would just be doing things to order. Illustrations that people wanted to hang over their sofas.'

'I've got some pictures in my flat,' Maja said with a smile, 'I'd love to know what you think of them.'

'Hmm. If I know you, they'll be pretty, colourful paintings of birds and flowers and things.'

'They arc. Should I be embarrassed about them, d'you think?'

'Maybe, especially if you paid a lot for them.'

'I did.'

Eva chuckled.

'I thought artists used paintbrushes,' Maja said suddenly. 'Don't you ever use a brush?'

'Never. The way I do it, it's all there ready when I begin to scrape. All the light, all the darkness. I just have to reveal it, seek it out. It's thrilling, I never quite know what I'm going to find. I've tried painting with a brush, but it didn't work, it was like an artificial extension of my arm, I couldn't get close enough. Everyone finds their own technique, and I've found mine. And they don't look like anyone else's pictures. I've got to go on with it. Sooner or later I'll break through with somebody. Some art dealer who's excited by what I do and who'll give me a chance. And lets me have a one-woman exhibition. I need a couple of good reviews in the papers and perhaps an interview, and then the ball will be rolling. I'm sure of it, I'm not going to give up. Not on your life!'

Her own stubbornness grew as she talked, it made her feel good.

'Can't you work a bit, I mean, at an ordinary job, so that you'd get a regular income, and then paint in the evenings or something?'

'Two jobs? And looking after Emma alone? I'm not someone with a vast amount of surplus energy, Maja.'

'I've got two jobs. I have to put something on my tax return.'

'What do you do?'

'Work at the Women's Refuge.'

The absurdity of the situation made Eva laugh.

'There's no clash of interests in that. I do a good job,' Maja said stoutly.

'I don't doubt it. I bet it's right up your street. But I don't suppose your colleagues have an inkling about what you do.'

'Of course not. But I'm better equipped than most girls. I understand men, and I understand their motives.'

They carried on drinking coffee and took no notice of what was going on around them, the people that came and went, the tables that were cleared and retaken, the traffic that hummed outside. It was the way it had always been when the two of them were together, they forgot everything else.

'D'you remember when we sprayed hairspray into Mr Strande's beehives?' said Maja. 'And you got stung seventeen times?'

'Yes, thank you,' Eva said smiling. 'And you pushed me all the way home in a wheelbarrow, shouting and telling me off because I was howling so loudly. Those were the days. I got a temperature of forty-one. It was about that time that Dad contemplated keeping us apart. Anyway, I don't know how you managed to put up with me, why you didn't get fed up towing me around. I couldn't even manage to get my own boys.'

'No, you made do with the ones I managed to find. Maybe they weren't all of the best quality.'

'Course not. You took the best-looking one yourself, and I got his friend. But if it hadn't been for you, I'd probably still be a virgin.'

Maja gave her an appraising glance. 'You're really pretty good-looking, Eva. Perhaps you should be an artist's model, instead of painting yourself?'

'Ha! Have you any idea what they get paid?'

'At least it would be a regular income. You certainly wouldn't have any problems getting customers, if you were to succumb to the temptation of joining forces with me. I've never seen a girl with such long legs before. How do you find trousers long enough?'

'I only wear skirts.' Suddenly Eva began to giggle hysterically.

'What is it?'

'Do you remember Mrs Skollenborg?'

'Talk about something else!'

There was complete silence.

'Must you do this hotel thing in Normandy?'

'Yes, there's no point in doing anything here in this narrow-minded country.'

'Then I'm going to lose you again. Just now, when I've found you.'

'You could come along too, you know. France is the right place for an artist like you, isn't it?'

'You know I can't.'

'I know no such thing.'

'I've got Emma. She's six, nearly seven. She's at playschool now.'

'Don't you think children can grow up in France too?'

'Of course, but she's got a father as well.'

'But aren't you the one with custody?'

'Yes, yes,' Eva gave a little sigh.

'You make everything so difficult,' Maja said quietly, 'you've always done that. Of course you can come to France if you want to. You can work at the hotel. Five minutes every night, padding down the corridor in a white nightie and holding a five-branched candelabra. I want to have my own ghost. Then you could paint the rest of the day.'

Eva drained her coffee cup. For a while she'd forgotten about reality, but now it came surging back.

'Have you got any dinner plans today?'

'I never have dinner. I eat bread and cheese, I'm not that bothered about food.'

'I've never heard anything like it. It's hardly surprising you're in such poor shape. How can you ever produce anything decent if you're not getting the nourishment you need? You need meat! We're going to get some dinner, we'll go to Hannah's Kitchen.'

'But that's the most expensive place in town.'

'Is it really? I don't need to worry about that kind of thing, I only know they've got the best food.'

'I'm so full of cake.'

'By the time the food is on the table it will have gone down a bit.'

Eva surrendered and followed Maja. It was the way it had always been. Maja had all the ideas, Maja made the decisions and led the way and Eva trotted after her.

Chapter 17

They left Glassmagasinet arm in arm and crossed the paved square, each feeling the other's warmth, that it was the same warmth as it had been in the past. The door to Hannah's Kitchen was something Eva had seen many times, but it had always been beyond her reach. Now, it was opened for them, and Maja entered with a poised smile, while Eva searched for some passably self-confident mien. The head waiter gave a smile of recognition, a courteous smile. If he was aware of the sort of business which paid Maja's bills, he hid it well; his smile gave away nothing at all. He touched her arm very lightly and steered them across to a vacant table. Eva had to relinquish her coat in the cloakroom. Beneath it she was wearing a faded, mustard-yellow tee shirt, and it made her feel ill at ease.

'The usual, Robert,' said Maja, 'for two.'

He nodded and left.

Eva sank back in her chair and looked about her wide-eyed. The restaurant had an exclusive hush that she'd never before experienced. Maja spread herself across the table, totally indifferent to her surroundings.

'Tell me a bit about what it's like,' Eva said inquisitively, 'working the way – the way you do.'

Maja cocked her head. 'Ah, so you are curious. I thought you'd ask. People can never resist.'

Eva assumed a hurt expression.

'Well, it's all pretty trivial really. I mean, it just becomes a matter of routine.'

Suddenly she was staring at the tablecloth as if she were embarrassed.

'Men's sexual desires never cease to amaze me. How powerful they are, how very important it is to have them satiated and how quickly they finish. Maybe they think that's the best kind of sex there is,' she mused, 'the intense, crude kind without foreplay or other refinements. No ifs or buts. It just takes ten minutes, then it's over. There isn't even time to think. In fact, I make strenuous efforts not to think. I just smile as prettily as I can when they pay the bill. But actually . . .'

'Yes?'

'I'm giving up soon. I've been at it a long time.'

'And the bill?'

'A thousand, give or take. Money first, goodies after. I lie still with my eyes closed and a becoming smile and

I don't give even the tiniest moan. No kissing or necking, I can't be bothered to treat them like babies. Clothes off and condoms on. It's like working a one-armed bandit, the money comes pouring out.'

'A thousand kroner? And how many are there each day?'

'Four or five, occasionally more. Five times a week. Four weeks a month. Well, you work it out.'

'At home in your flat?'

'Yes.'

A waiter placed prawn cocktails and white wine on the table.

'So where do you live?'

'In the flats in Tordenskioldsgate.'

'Don't any of your neighbours suspect?'

'They don't suspect, they know. Several of them are regular customers.'

Eva sighed faintly and chewed a prawn reverently. They were as large as crayfish tails.

'I've got an extra bedroom,' Maja said suddenly.

Eva snorted. 'I can just see myself. Like some terrified twelve-year-old virgin.'

'Only for the first week, then it becomes a job. You could do a few hours while Emma was at playschool. Think of all the nice food you could bring home for her.'

'She's way overweight.'

'Fresh fruit then, chicken and salad,' Maja said.

'I expect it sounds unbelievable, but I am tempted,' Eva admitted. 'I'm just too scared. I'm not made that way.' For a mad second it irritated her. 'We'll see.'

The waiter cleared the table and returned immediately with fillet steak, baby carrots, broccoli and Hasselback potatoes. Now he filled their glasses with red wine.

'But you're not working tonight?'

'I've got a day off today, but I'll do a bit tomorrow. Bottoms up!'

Eva felt the tender steak melt on her tongue. The red wine was at room temperature, and had little resemblance to her father's Canepa. The first bottle was soon emptied, and Maja ordered another.

'But I can't quite get over it,' Eva said in wonderment, 'that you really sell your body.'

'It's better than selling your soul,' she replied flatly. 'Isn't that what you artists do? If there's one thing we ought to keep to ourselves and hide from others, it's our souls. The body is merely a container we lug around with us, I can't see anything so terribly venerable about it. Why not share it around and be generous if people can enjoy it? But the soul – displaying your dreams and desires, your own anxiety and despair in a gallery to all the world and his wife – and then taking money for it – *that's* what I call real prostitution.'

Eva tensed, a baby carrot protruding between her lips. 'It's not quite like that.'

'Isn't it? Isn't it what all artists say? That you've got to have the courage to stand there completely naked?'

'Where exactly did you pick that up from?'

'I'm not a fool just because I'm a whore. It's a common misconception.' She wiped the corners of her mouth with her napkin. 'Another misconception is that prostitutes are unhappy women who've lost all self-respect, who shiver on street corners in thin stockings and whose only reward is a drubbing from some brutal pimp, after which they spend most of the day lying there mumbling in some kind of drug-induced state. All that,' she said chewing her fillet steak, 'is only a small part of the business. The prostitutes I know are hard-working, intelligent girls who know what they want. But then, I've got a soft spot for prostitutes. They're the most decent bunch of women you could find.' She motioned to the waiter to fill their glasses again.

Eva was already tipsy. 'I'm not right for it even so,' she mumbled. 'You said I was too thin.'

'Hah! You're absolutely fantastic. A bit different, perhaps, even a little unusual. But what you've got between your legs, Eva, is a gold mine. A real gold mine. And that's where they want to go. Men are straightforward like that, at least the ones who come to me are.'

Eventually the pudding arrived. A mixture of ice-cold strawberries and blackberries on a base of hot vanilla sauce. Eva pulled off the leaves. 'Greenery in the dessert,' she muttered, 'I don't see the point of it. Anyway, I've never understood men,' she continued, 'I mean, what do they want exactly?'

'Well-rounded, warm-hearted women with a zest for life. And there certainly aren't many of those about. Women have quite impossible ideals in my opinion, I don't understand them at all. They don't seem to want to have a good time. I was looking at the autumn fashions just recently on TV, where the supermodels were parading the latest thing. Naomi Campbell – you've seen her, haven't you – she appeared in something thigh-length and minced out on to the catwalk on the skinniest legs I've ever seen. The woman looks as if she's made entirely of PVC. When I look at those kind of girls, I wonder if they ever go to the toilet and shit like normal people.'

Eva exploded with laughter and sprayed vanilla sauce over the tablecloth.

'You shouldn't take yourself so seriously,' she went on earnestly. 'We're all going to die anyway. In a hundred years everything will be forgotten. A bit of money would help things along. You're dreaming of becoming a great artist, aren't you?'

'I *am* great,' she slurred. 'It's just that no one realises.' She snuffled a bit, she was becoming very drunk. 'And I'm thoroughly sloshed as well.'

'Good for you. The coffee and cognac will be here soon. And stop that whining, it's time you grew up.'

'D'you believe in God?' Eva asked.

'Oh, come on.' Maja wiped vanilla sauce from her mouth. 'But now and then I save people from despair and do a good deed, that's the way I like to look at it. Not every man finds a woman. I was once visited by a young boy whose thing was decorating his body with rings and pearls. They were all over him, in every conceivable place, he sparkled and glittered like an American Christmas tree. The girls wouldn't have any more to do with him.'

'So what did you do?'

'Gave him a really good time and charged a bit extra.'

Eva sipped the cognac and lit the wrong end of a cigarette.

'Come back with me and see the flat,' Maja said. 'Give yourself a chance to get out of the rut. It's only an episode in your life. Look on it as a new experience.'

Eva made no answer. She seemed paralysed by something completely unreal, something that scared her rigid. But there could be no doubt: Maja's suggestion was in the process of taking root within her, and now it was up for assessment.

They were lying on Maja's double bed and Eva had got a bad attack of hiccups.

'Maja,' she said, 'what exactly is the Mariana Trench?'

'The deepest bit of ocean in the world. Eleven

thousand metres deep. Just try imagining it, *eleven thousand metres*.'

'How do you know about it?'

'No idea. I probably read it somewhere. By comparison, our mucky river flowing through town here is only eight point eight metres deep under the bridge.'

'Goodness, the things you know.'

'What little spare time I have isn't spent reading *Cocktail*, if that's what you think.'

'It used to be.'

'That was twenty-five years ago, and you were quite keen on it, too.'

They both cackled.

'Maja, the paintings on your walls are simply ghastly. That's what *real* prostitution is, let me tell you, painting just to sell. With only that in view.'

'Do we need food or don't we?'

'A bit of food, I don't really need all that much.'

'But electricity and telephones are useful, aren't they?'

'Hmm.'

'I'm going to give you ten thousand kroner when you go.'

'What?' She propped herself up on her elbow swaying with alarm.

'And you bring along a picture when you come tomorrow. A good one, which you'd price at ten thousand. I'll buy a picture from you. I'm curious. Perhaps you'll be famous one day, perhaps I'll make a killing.'

'One can always hope.'

Maja smiled contentedly. 'We'll get things going for you, Eva, just you wait. When is Emma coming home?'

'I don't know yet. She usually rings when she's had enough.'

'In that case you might as well begin tomorrow. Only a try-out, of course. I'll help you get going, there are a few little things you'll need to know about. I'll send a taxi for you, what, about six? Tomorrow evening? I take care of the clothes and stuff.'

'Clothes?'

'You can't work in what you've got on. I'm not being rude, but the clothes you wear aren't the slightest bit sexy.'

'And why should I go round looking sexy?'

Maja sat up and looked at her in astonishment. 'You're not all that different to other women. I dare say you want a man, too, don't you?'

'Yes,' said Eva wearily, 'I suppose I do.'

'Then you ought to stop dressing like a scarecrow.'

'You really know how to dish out the compliments.'

'Oh, I'm just jealous. You're elegant, I'm nothing but a chubby bitch with a set of spare tyres and a double chin.'

'No, you're a well-rounded, warm-hearted woman with a zest for life. Have you any self-respect?' Eva enquired suddenly.

'About twice as much as you, I should think.'

'I only wondered.'

'I can envisage it already. The rumours about the leggy artist will run like wildfire through the town. Perhaps you'll steal my clients from me, perhaps I'm just about to give away my entire livelihood.'

'If you've got almost two million, I don't feel sorry for you.'

Eva went home in a taxi paid for by Maja. At the same time she took the opportunity to order a cab for the following evening at six. She fumbled with the key and staggered into her studio, and began scrutinising her paintings with a critical eye. Because she was pretty drunk, they made a huge impression on her and, feeling content, she lay down on the sofa and fell asleep with her clothes on.

Chapter 18

Just as she awoke, in the instant before the hangover made itself felt, she recalled her dream. She had dreamt about Maja. Only when she opened her eyes did reality return clearly, and she got up alarmed. She found to her amazement that she'd slept in her studio, and fully dressed at that.

She tottered into the bathroom and approached the mirror with some misgiving. Her mascara was water-resistant, it hadn't run, but her lashes stuck out from the rims of her red eyes like singed straws. The pores of her skin were large as snakebites. She groaned into the basin and turned on the cold water tap. What had they been talking about? It came back to her slowly, and her heart gradually beat faster as she dredged up more of the conversation. Maja, the Maja of her childhood, her very best friend whom she hadn't seen for twenty-five years, was a prostitute. A rich prostitute, she thought with horror, as she vaguely recalled how they'd discussed her own prospects for getting out of financial straits. It was incredible that she'd even contemplated the possibility! She splashed cold water on her face and groaned again, opened the door of the medicine cabinet and took out a packet of paracetamol. She washed a couple of tablets down with some water and pulled off her tee shirt and underwear. Maybe I've got a beer in the fridge, she thought. Then it struck her that she was feeling far too fragile to work and that yet another day would pass without any progress. She showered and scrubbed herself for as long as she could bear, felt the tablets working slowly and got into a dressing gown, black with Chinese dragons on the back. Then she went out into the living room to search her bag for a cigarette. She opened it and found herself staring down at a bundle of notes. For an instant she gawped at them in surprise, then she remembered. She counted them. Ten thousand kroner. Enough to pay off all the bills in the drawer. She shook her head in disbelief, then went into her studio and looked at her pictures again. One of them had been pulled out on to the floor, when had she done that?

But it was probably the best one she had. An almost completely black picture with a very bright stripe slanting across the canvas. As if it had been torn in two. She couldn't help smiling a little at the thought of Maja's face when she entered carrying this. Then she continued searching in her bag, discovered a packet containing just one cigarette, lit it and peered in the fridge. It was nearly empty. Butter, ketchup and a bottle of soya oil were all that was left. She sighed, then suddenly remembered the wad of money and smiled once more. What she needed now was an ice-cold beer. So, she threw on some clothes, heaved her coat on to her shoulders and trudged purposefully off to the small shop on the corner. Omar's opened at eight in the morning, what a blessing he was. Nor did he look askance, even when people were buying beer before anyone else was up. His shop stood in that venerable district of detached houses like some strange bird, to the considerable consternation of many, but to Eva's delight.

His teeth showed chalky white with enthusiasm when she entered his shop. She pulled a couple of half-litre bottles of beer from a crate, grabbed a newspaper and forty Prince Mild.

'A very good day today!' he smiled encouragingly.

'Perhaps it will be in a while,' Eva groaned, 'but not just at the moment.'

'Well, I know it will be a good day. But two bottles is not a lot if the day turns out bad.'

'You know, I think you're right,' Eva said. She fetched another bottle, and paid.

'Ah, I think I've got an account here, too,' she remembered, 'I'll pay that as well.'

'A very good day for me also!'

He rifled through the shoebox where he kept all his credit records. 'Seven hundred and fifty-two.'

Eva was moved. He'd never mentioned it. She handed him a thousand-kroner note and glanced down at the mail order catalogue he'd been leafing through. 'Anything exciting there?'

'Oh yes, this here, I'm buying for my wife. Coming in the post in two weeks.'

Eva peered down. 'What is it?'

'Burl remover. Good for jumpers and sofa cushions and furniture. There are no burls in my country. You have strange materials here.'

'I like burls,' Eva said. 'They make me think of old teddy bears. The teddy I had when I was young had lots of burls.'

'Yes, yes,' he sparkled. 'Happy memory. But in my country there are no teddy bears also.'

The beer was tepid. She laid one bottle under running cold water, then searched the telephone book for Maja's number. Just to mention that she must forget all the drunken talk from the previous evening, she hadn't been in full possession of her faculties. The phone was dead. Of course, they'd disconnected it. She cursed softly, went to the bathroom and sat on the loo with her skirt pulled up round her waist. Well, today I certainly look like a whore, she thought, perhaps that's what I am really, perhaps it's a good day to begin. She finished, stepped out of her skirt and got into her dressing gown again. She went out into the passage and stood in front of the hall mirror, where she could see herself from top to toe. Just for a look, she thought.

Eva was 1.83 metres tall and most of it was leg. Her face was thin and pale, her eyes golden, not dark enough to be considered brown. Her shoulders were narrow, she possessed an unusually long neck and long arms with slender wrists. Her feet were large, size forty-one, it was enough to make one weep. Her body was thin, a bit angular and not especially feminine, but her eyes were fine, at least Jostein had always said so. Large and a little slanted, they were set well apart. A judicious makeover would have worked wonders, but she'd never understood that kind of thing. Her hair just hung there, long and dark with a slight hint of red in it. She bent closer. The hair on her upper lip had begun to grow. Perhaps her oestrogen level had begun to sink, she thought. The dressing gown slid open, she pulled it aside so that she could see her small breasts, her long lithe abdomen and thighs, which were as pale as her face. She gave a trial wiggle and tossed her head slightly making her hair fan out. If Maja can become a million-aire with that round little body, I certainly can with this! she thought wickedly. And she pictured the bundle of notes once more, thought about where they'd come from and shook her head, as if she couldn't properly grasp what had happened, just last night. She did up her dressing gown again and retrieved the bottle from the sink. She wouldn't think about it at all, she'd do it. Nobody needed to know anything. Just for a while, perhaps until Christmas, just to build up her finances. She drank some beer and felt her nerves subside. I haven't really changed, she mused, merely discovered a new side to myself. She drank and smoked and daydreamed about her own small gallery which would be down by the river, preferably on the north side. Gallery Magnus. That sounded rather good. A sudden inspiration made her consider whether she ought to introduce a colour into her pictures. Deep red. Quite a thin line in the first picture, almost invisible, and gradually a bit more. She felt enormously inspired. Afterwards, she opened another bottle and thought that this was what had been missing from her life. Maja had been missing! But now she'd returned. Everything's going to work out, she thought content-edly, this is a turning point. When all the bottles were empty, she fell asleep.

The taxi tooted outside at six o'clock.

Eva had wrapped the picture in an old blanket and the driver laid it carefully in the boot. 'Drive carefully, please,' she begged, 'it's worth ten thousand kroner.'

She gave the address in Tordenskioldsgate and all at once she had the feeling that he was staring at her in the mirror. Perhaps he knew Maja. Perhaps every other man in the street had been in her bed. She brushed a bit of fluff off her skirt and realised she was nervous, the high from the beer was almost all gone, and reality was returning. But it was strange how, when Emma was away so long, she almost seemed to pack away her whole maternal role in some drawer and just revert to being Eva. That's who I am now, she thought, I'm Eva. I'm not taking any notice of what others think, I'll do what I like. She smiled to herself. The driver noticed it and smiled back in the mirror. Don't get any ideas, she thought, I don't come gratis, you know.

Chapter 19

Maja opened her arms wide and led her in. The previous day's excesses hadn't left a mark on the round face.

'Come in, Eva. You've brought the picture!'

'You'll probably faint.'

'I never faint.'

They unwrapped the picture and leant it up against the wall.

'Crikey!' Maja was dumbstruck. She studied the picture minutely. 'Well, I'll say this, it is a bit different. Has it got a title?'

'No, you must be joking.'

'Why?'

'Because I'd be dictating what you should see, and I don't want to do that. You must look at it yourself, and tell me what *you* see. Then I'll respond.'

Maja had a good think, and finally decided. 'It's a lightning strike. That's what it is.'

'Well, not bad. I see what you mean, but I see other things as well. The ground opening during an earthquake. Or the river flowing through the town at night, in moonlight. Or glowing lava pouring down a charred slope. Tomorrow you might see something else. Anyway, that was what I was aiming for. You must try to rid yourself of your preconceptions about art, Maja.'

'I'm sticking to the lightning strike. I don't like things changing and turning into something else. And now it's you who's got to rid yourself of preconceptions, my girl. I've got the spare room ready, you must come and see. Have you eaten?'

'Only drunk.'

'You're worse than a baby, you've got to be fed. Could you manage to chew on your own if I make you a sandwich?'

She drew Eva into the flat, into the spare room. It was a dark room with lots of reds, plushes and velvets and thick curtains. The bed was huge. It was adorned with a gold-fringed counterpane. The floor was covered in thick red and black carpet which felt springy under their feet as they walked.

'These are your colours,' Maja said emphatically. 'And I've a red dressing gown for you that's easy to open. Made of thin velvet. In here' – she went to the far end of the room and pulled a curtain aside – 'is a small bathroom with a basin and shower.'

Eva peered inside.

'You can work here while I'm at the refuge. I've had another key made. Come on, you've got to eat.'

'Have you done all this today?'

'Yes. What have you done?'

'Slept.'

'Then you'll be able to work late.'

'Oh, God, I'm just not sure – if I really do dare, I thought one might be enough, the first time. Maja,' she said fretfully, 'are there lots of ghastly types?'

'No, no.'

'But occasionally someone says something disgusting, or does something nasty . . .?'

'No.'

'But aren't you afraid? Alone with strange men, night after night?'

'They're the ones who are afraid, who've got bad consciences. In the first place, they've had to tell a whopping great lie to get away, then they've had to take money from the housekeeping to pay the bill. Going to a prostitute nowadays is terribly daunting. In the old days you weren't a real man if you didn't visit a brothel. Oh no, I'm never afraid. I'm a professional.'

Eva bit into the sandwich and chewed slowly. Tuna with lemon and mayonnaise. 'Do they sometimes ask you to do special things?'

'No, very rarely. They get the information they need from the jungle telegraph before their first visit.' She opened a Coke and took a long drink. 'They know I'm a proper prostitute and that certain sexual kinks are off limits. Almost everyone who comes here is a regular, and they know me. They know the rules and how far they can stretch them. If they start being silly, they won't be allowed back, and that's not a chance they're willing to take.' She finished with a small belch.

'Are they drunk?'

'Oh yes, but only slightly. They've often had a couple. Many of them come straight from the pub down the road, the King's Arms. But others come at lunchtime, in suits and carrying attaché cases.'

'Do they ever refuse to pay?'

'Never known it happen.'

'Has anyone ever hit you?'

'Nope.'

'I don't know if I dare.'

'Why should it be something you need to dare?'

'Well, I don't know – you hear so many tales.'

'It's when a man *doesn't* get what he wants that he gets angry, isn't it?'

'Yes.'

'They come here to buy something they need, and they get it. They have no reason to kick up a fuss. Is there anything wrong with going to bed with someone?'

'Nothing. Apart from the fact that many of them must be married, with children and all that.'

'Naturally, they're the ones who come, they're the

ones who get too little. Married people don't have sex with each other that often.'

'Jostein and I did.'

'Yes, to begin with perhaps. But how was it after ten years?'

Eva blushed.

'Or,' Maja continued, 'do you think we girls ought to kind of save ourselves up for the love of our lives, that sort of thing? Do you believe in the love of your life, Eva?'

'Of course not.' She drank some Coke. 'Have any of them fallen in love with you?'

'Oh yes. Especially the young ones. I think it's really sweet, and I make a bit of an extra effort for them. Last spring for example quite a young man came along, he had a really fantastic name, he was of Spanish and French extraction. Jean Lucas Cordoba. Have you ever heard anything with such a ring to it? Just imagine being called that,' she said pensively. 'Almost worth marrying just for the name, isn't it? And then there was Gøran of course, I'll never forget him. He was a virgin, so I had to give him some guidance about certain things. Afterwards he was very moved and grateful. It's not easy being a virgin when you're twenty-five and a police officer to boot. It must have needed a huge amount of courage to come here.'

Eva had finished her sandwich. She emptied her glass

and brushed the hair away from her face. 'Do you talk about anything?'

'We exchange a few words. They're the same clichés every time, roughly what I think they want to hear. They really aren't very demanding, Eva, you'll soon find that out.'

She put down the bottle.

'It's now ten to seven, and the first one is due at eight. He's been here before, he's actually rather a surly type, but he'll be finished quickly. I'll attend to him and say that there are two of us who'll share the clients. And that we're in the same line of business. Then they'll know what to expect, and you'll get the same kind of customers as me.'

'I wish I could hide in the wardrobe and watch you secretly,' Eva sighed. 'See how you go about it. The most difficult thing is finding something to say.'

'There's not much room in the wardrobe. You'd see better through a door that was slightly ajar.'

'What?'

'Well, you couldn't exactly stand at the foot of the bed, but you could watch from the other room. We'll turn off the light and open the door a fraction, then you can sit in there and look in. Then you'll get some idea. You know me, I've never been shy.'

'God, I could do with a drink, I'm all shaky.'

Maja made a pistol with two fingers and shot her in the forehead. 'Don't even think about it! Stimulants on the job are forbidden. That's when things start to go wrong, Eva. But afterwards we'll go to Hannah's and eat. I promise you one thing: when you start earning money you really begin to get a taste for it. Whenever I want something, I just put my hand into a bowl and lift out a wad of notes. I've got money all over the place, in drawers and cupboards, in the bathroom, in the kitchen, crammed into boots and shoes, I hardly know where it all is any more.'

Eva had turned pale. 'Surely you haven't got two million floating around the flat, have you?'

'No, no. Only what I need for pocket money. The bulk of it is hidden away in the holiday cabin.'

'The holiday cabin?'

'Dad's cabin. He died some time ago, so it's my cabin now. You went there once, don't you remember, a gang of us girls went on a trip? Up on the Hardanger Plateau?'

'Your father's dead?'

'Yes, four years ago. I dare say you can guess what got him in the end.'

Eva politely refrained from replying. 'Just imagine if someone broke in.'

'It's well hidden. No one would think of looking there. And paper money is fairly flat, it doesn't take up much room. I can't exactly put it in the bank.'

'Money isn't everything,' Eva said knowingly. 'Perhaps you'll die before you can enjoy it.'

'Perhaps you'll die before you've even lived,' Maja countered. 'But if I do happen to die all of a sudden, you are hereby nominated as my sole heir. I'd like you to have the money.'

'Well, thanks. I think I need a shower,' Eva said. 'I'm sweating with fear.'

'Go straight ahead. I'll get out your dress. Has anyone told you that you look lovely in black?'

'Thanks.'

'It wasn't a compliment. I just meant that you always seem to be wearing black!'

'Oh,' Eva said bashfully. 'No, not that I can remember. Jostein couldn't bear it.'

'I can't quite see what you've got against colours.'

'They're – distracting in a way.'

'Distracting from what?'

'From what's really important.'

'And that is . . .?'

'All the other things.'

Maja sighed and cleared away the glasses and plates. 'Artists certainly aren't easy people.'

'No,' Eva giggled, 'but somebody's got to take the trouble to emphasise the depths of existence. So that the rest of you have a surface to skate over.'

She went into the room that was to be hers and undressed. She heard Maja humming next door and the sound of clothes-hangers clicking. Maja's room was green, with plenty of gold, and it made Eva think about her own black and white home; there was a world of difference between them.

The shower cabinet was tiny and had a large mirror as its back wall. It reflected her tall body, and she thought it looked strange, as if she'd already relinquished her proprietorial rights. Steam clouded the mirror. For an instant she looked young and sleek, with a pink tinge from the flowery curtain, then she vanished entirely.

'I mustn't think,' she said to herself. 'Just do what Maja tells me.'

She finished, dried herself and walked out into the room again, which seemed cool by comparison. Maja entered with something red over her arm, a dressing gown. Eva put it on.

'Great. It's just what you needed. Get yourself some red clothes, you look like a woman when you dress in red, rather than a beanpole. Can you do anything about your hair?'

'No.'

'OK. Then there's just one little thing I need to show you. Lie down on the bed, Eva.'

'What?'

'Just do as I say, lie down on the bed.'

Eva hesitated, but then went to the bed and lay down in the middle of it.

'No, out to the side, the right side, otherwise you're lying on the join.'

Eva pulled herself over to the edge.

'Move your right hand towards the floor.'

'What?'

'Drop your arm over the edge. And then on the side of the bed, can you feel something hard underneath the bedspread?'

'Yes.'

'Slip your hand under and pull it loose, it's taped into position.'

Eva fumbled under the fringe of the counterpane, she felt something long and smooth fastened to the bedside. She gripped it and pulled. It was a knife.

'You see that knife, Eva? It's a Hunter, from Brusletto. If you think it looks nasty, that's the whole point. It's to engender fear and respect. If anyone should try any funny business. If you slide your hand down and bring it up again holding that knife, while he's sitting there with a bare bum and all his equipment out, I think he'll calm down pretty quickly.'

'But – you said nothing like that ever happens.' Eva was stammering. She was beginning to feel unwell.

'No,' she said evasively, 'just a few pathetic try-ons.' She bent down by the side of the bed and replaced the knife. Eva couldn't see her face. 'But occasionally someone gets above themselves. I don't know everyone equally well. And then, men are so much stronger than us.' She fiddled with the tape. 'In fact I forget it's there. But I'd remember quickly enough if anything should happen, I can promise you that.' She raised herself again. The old smile was back in place. 'I may be frivolous, but I'm not unprepared. Come here, you need a bit of lipstick.'

Eva hesitated for a moment, then crossed the thick carpet in her bare feet. This is a different world, she thought, with its own rules. Afterwards, when I get home again, everything will be as it was before. Two worlds, with a wall between them.

Chapter 20

She sat stock-still on a footstool behind the door. The room lay in darkness and no one could spot her from outside. Through the crack in the door she could see Maja's bed, she could make out the bedside table and the lamp with its big shade, decorated with a pink flamingo. Otherwise the room was dim. She was waiting for the two short rings of the doorbell, it was the agreed signal. It was five to eight. The building was situated in a quiet street, there wasn't a sound outside, only the subdued music from the stereo system. She was playing Joe Cocker. Hoarser every year, thought Eva. There was the sound of a car, it stopped in the street right under their windows. She looked at the clock again, it was showing three minutes to and her heart began to thump harder. A car door slammed. Then there was the dull thud of the door downstairs shutting. A sudden impulse made her get up and go to the window. She found herself looking down at a white car. It was parked by the pavement. A sporty model, she thought, peering through the opening in the curtains. She had a sharp eye for detail. This was an Opel, quite nice, but not a new model. It seemed familiar. Jostein had driven one like it when they'd met all those years ago. She crept back, seated herself on the stool and placed her hands in her lap. The doorbell sounded the signal of two rings. Maja rose and walked across the room, suddenly she turned and gave a thumbs-up. Then she went out and opened the door. Eva tried to breathe calmly. There was so much material in the room, she felt everything constricting. A man entered. She couldn't see him clearly, but he seemed to be in his thirties, a stocky man with thin, fair hair. It was long at the neck, he'd gathered it into a sad little ponytail with a rubber band. His denim trousers were a bad fit because of his beer belly. It was her greatest aversion, men who couldn't wear trousers properly because of their stomachs. Jostein was the same, but he was Jostein and that was different. The man yanked off his jacket and threw it nonchalantly on the bed, as if he were in his own home. Eva didn't like it, it seemed brazen. Then he reached into his back pocket and fished out a note which he also threw on the bed. She heard Maja's voice, but she was speaking so softly that Eva had to listen hard to make out what she said. Carefully, she bent forward so that her ear was as close to the opening as possible.

'I've been waiting for you,' she heard. 'Come!'

Her voice was as soft as silk. I couldn't speak like that, Eva thought despairingly. The man suddenly moved in close and Maja seemed tiny even though he wasn't especially tall. There wasn't much light in the room, but she saw him open Maja's green dressing gown and pull it off her shoulders. It fell and lay in a heap on the floor. Eva stared hard at Maja's round, white body, and at the man, but she couldn't make out his expression. The music murmured pleasantly in the background and Maja went to the bed now; she lay down slowly on her back with her arms out to the side. The man followed. He wore a checked shirt which he suddenly wrenched out of the waist of his trousers. He'd done his paying, now he could lay claim to the goods he'd bought, and he did. He knelt next to her and began to fumble with his belt. Eva could see Maja's black panties and her chubby thighs. They weren't speaking at all now, both moved with accustomed slowness, they'd done this many times, they had a fixed routine. Then he went straight to it, opened his belt completely and Eva heard his zip as he pulled it down. The bed creaked slightly as he got into position. Maja remained motionless, as did Eva, she saw through the gap that he was pulling his trousers down his thighs, then he took hold of Maja's panties and pulled them off. She helped by lifting her bottom languidly. Then she opened her legs. Just then something changed in him. He began to pant hard, he straddled Maja and pushed her legs even further apart. Then he dived in. Maja had turned her face to the side. She could only make out the man's stringy hair and his white bottom working rapidly up and down at an ever increasing tempo. Shortly after, he raised himself, straightening his arms and tilting his head back. He gave a long, drawn-out, throaty groan, then he subsided. It had taken maybe a minute. Just as he collapsed with his chin on the mattress, his hand slid over the edge. He fumbled along the side of the bed for a handhold, and there was a small thud. It made him lean over and look down, Eva saw that he was scrabbling for something on the carpet. Maja had turned her head, her dark eyebrows lifted as he suddenly raised himself once more. In his hand he held the knife. It flashed in the light of the flamingo lamp. He stared at it in amazement, and then at Maja who was trying to sit up. Eva put a hand to her mouth and stifled a gasp. There was total silence in the room for several seconds. Joe Cocker had just finished 'Up Where We Belong' and was now pausing before his next number. The scene she beheld through the crack in the door made her blood freeze in her veins, and she found it hard to breathe. Maja, still naked and lying on the bed, her eyes watchful, the man on top of her, with his trousers about his knees and the sharp knife in his hand.

'What the fuck is this?' His voice was suspicious. He

was staring at Maja, but she was as soft and mild as she had been when he arrived. She was a professional.

'Just a little protection for a lone woman. Lots of strange people come here.'

'Oh, really?' thought Eva.

'Oh, really?' he said. 'So that's what you think of us? You weren't planning to stick this in me by any chance?'

'It's more you that's stuck something into me,' she laughed huskily.

He was kneeling as before, still with the knife in his hand, and didn't budge. 'I've heard of prostitutes who fleece people like this.' He looked at the knife, turned it in his hand, looked down at the naked body and chalk-white skin, as if he were enjoying it.

'Thank you,' she said, 'I've already been paid. Now I think you ought to put it down. I don't like you pointing that knife at me.'

'And I don't like finding knives in the bed when I come here on honest business. You women are as treacherous as hell!'

He was beginning to work himself up. Eva bit her lip and had almost stopped breathing. Maja tried to rise, but he pushed her down.

'Calm down now!' she said loudly. 'Stop being oversensitive.'

'I'm not oversensitive,' he snapped back. 'You're the ones who're oversensitive, you think we're after you the whole time. Fuck! Knives and stuff. Have you got a firearm as well?'

'Naturally.'

'You're one of those paranoid types, I thought as much.'

'It's you who's paranoid. I had no cause to stick that in you. At least not then. But enough's enough. Get moving now, otherwise you'll have to pay extra.'

'Hah! I'll go when I'm good and ready,' he answered, as he tugged at his trousers and struggled with the zip.

'You were ready a long time ago, and there are others waiting.'

'They'll have to wait, then. You tarts are fucking greedy. I've laid out a thousand for a five-minute job, d'you know how long it takes me to earn that much at the brewery?'

'No,' said Maja wearily. She was staring at the ceiling now. Eva waited with three fingers stuffed into her mouth.

'Fucking bloody hell,' he muttered as he struggled with his belt buckle. 'Cunts!'

'Right! That's quite enough! You needn't bloody well come again. You're not welcome here from now on. And I should have said that a long time ago.'

'Oh, I see!' He stopped and nodded, as if the scales had suddenly fallen from his eyes. 'So that's how it is! You lot welcome us with open arms, get us to empty our wallets, when really none of you can stand the sight of us! That's it, isn't it? Christ, you tarts are the most cynical bunch I've ever met!'

With a huge effort Maja rose and got herself on to her elbows. She tried to pull up her legs, but the man was furious and stopped her, she jabbed him with an elbow and twisted out from between his legs as she clutched for the knife, got a hold and pulled as hard as she could. Suddenly she was holding it in her hand. She rose on to her knees with the knife raised. The point quivered. She was staring at the man now, he was still kneeling on the bed as if he were about to spring, the little ponytail stuck out, like a young boy's erection, Eva thought. She'd got her entire hand in her mouth and bit as hard as she could to suppress a scream. If he'd turned to the left, he would have seen Eva's eye, a small gleaming point in the blackness of the slightly open door. But he didn't, he grabbed a pillow and held it in front of him for protection. He glowered at Maja who was kneeling and shaking with the knife in front of her. A pillow and a knife. Everything went deathly quiet.

Eva buried her face in her hands. She had to make the appalling scene vanish, she was terrified the man would catch sight of her, come bolting across the floor and wrench open the door, she wondered what he would make of that, and what sort of rage would fill him then, if he knew she'd been sitting there in the dark staring at them. She crouched, still as a statue on her

stool, struggled to breathe calmly, noticed that Joe
Cocker had begun another song, 'When a Woman
Cries'. In the midst of her despair she felt a tremendous
sense of relief. Never, ever would she allow some strange
man into this room and let him pull her clothes off.
Not only would she put an end to her own career before
it started, but she would persuade Maja to give up as
well. Maja's a decent person really, she thought, considerate of others, and with almost two million, that was
quite enough. She'd just have to make do with a little
hotel. Eva looked up again and through the gap: the
man had finally got off the bed, and was now pulling
on his jacket. She saw the back of his head and his
gaze flitting round the room, as if to assure himself
that he hadn't left anything behind. She held her breath
when his eyes discovered that her door stood ajar. He
stared hard for a few seconds, then turned and crossed
the floor. Something was wrong. Not a word was
spoken, it was suddenly so quiet. She could see Maja's
feet, they lay motionless on the golden counterpane,
pointing out to the sides. And the man wasn't dawdling
any more, he opened the door quickly, and slipped out.

Eva didn't move.

She was waiting for Maja to call. Inside she felt her
anger rising. It was directed at Maja, who had dragged
her into this dubious flat and who'd maintained that
it was safe. But she heard no sound from the bed. At

last she got up, pushed open the door, and now she could see everything, Maja's white body lying diagonally across the bed. She lay quite still with a pillow over her face.

Eva didn't scream. This was a normal Maja jape, and quite typical of her. She would stop at nothing if she wanted a good laugh. She folded her arms and shook her head. 'If you let that one in again, you'll lose all my respect,' she said dryly.

A car started outside, she turned quickly and ran to the window, peered down at the pavement as it moved into the street. It's an Opel Manta, she thought, just like the one Jostein had owned. She caught a glimpse of the number. BL 74 . . .

The tyres screeched angrily. He did a U-turn and almost hit a sign on the edge of the pavement. Then he roared off in the direction of the pub. Eva followed him with her eyes, then turned and walked back. She reached across the bed and carefully gripped the corner of the large pillow. And then she screamed.

It was a piercing sound from deep in her throat. Maja was staring at the ceiling with wide-open eyes, her fingers splayed on the counterpane. Eva backed away in horror and bumped into the bedside table, the large flamingo lamp wobbled precariously, and automatically she put out both hands to save it. She turned and ran to the window again, peered down into the empty street which now was completely deserted, not a car, not a pedestrian was visible, but she heard a soft hum from the traffic a little further off. She ran back again, bent down and grabbed her shoulders, shook her hard and watched as her mouth fell slightly open. Now she was lying there gaping. In despair, she looked around for a phone, but she couldn't see one anywhere, rushed into the other room, searched on the bedside table, on the window ledge, came back, never thought about turning more lights on and still couldn't see a phone, just a shiny red model sports car on a shelf. That was the phone. She grabbed it, lifted the body and was about to ring for help, but she couldn't remember the number of the emergency services, the number had just changed, she'd heard it on the news, so she had to find a phone book and look there. Then she couldn't find a phone book. She put back the receiver and dropped into a chair. She stared down at her red dressing gown and suddenly imagined the room crowded with uniformed police, photographers flashing away and her, sitting in a chair, naked beneath the red dressing gown, like any old whore.

LIKE A WHORE.

What would she say? That she'd been sitting watching from behind the door? Why didn't I do anything? she wondered in amazement. Because it had all happened so fast. She'd been frightened of being discovered, frightened that his anger would turn against her instead. She'd been sure that Maja could handle the situation on her own. Maja, the professional. She got up suddenly and bolted into the other room. She found her own clothes and changed as rapidly as she could. She was listening for sounds the whole time, what if the doorbell suddenly rang and there was a new customer standing there – the thought made her run out and check that the door was locked. She couldn't control her fingers, and doing up buttons was difficult. Out of the corner of her eye she could see Maja's white feet the whole time. Nobody knows I've been here, she told herself, nobody except Maja. If anyone finds out, Jostein, or the police, or Child Welfare, they'll take Emma away from me. I'll run home and pretend it never happened. This has nothing to do with me or my life, I don't belong here, in this velvet and plush flat. She stumbled through the rooms and found her handbag, her long coat, then suddenly realised that her fingerprints must be everywhere. The idea brought her to a complete full stop. But as she wasn't on any files, they couldn't incriminate her. Or so she thought. She halted by the bed once more. She went right up to the headboard and bent down. There was a fly in the corner of Maja's mouth. It walked across her cheek and settled in the corner of her eye, began to rub its long legs. Eva watched it despondently, tried to brush it away. But it kept on walking up her cheek and into the lower lashes, and finally, a little hesitantly, out on to her eyeball. There it stayed. It looked as if it sank slightly on to the eye.

Eva clapped her hand to her mouth and rushed out to the bathroom. She was violently sick, bending down far into the toilet bowl in an attempt not to make a mess. For a long while she remained there dribbling and panting. It left a rank, sour taste; she flushed the loo, was about to get up to have a drink, when she suddenly slipped in her own vomit, fell forward and knocked her chin on the porcelain rim of the bowl. Her lower lip split. Her teeth dug into her tongue and the blood seeped out. Tears came. She mustn't look at Maja any more, or she'd never get out. She pulled out several handfuls of loo paper and began to wipe the floor. Some of it had splashed up the wall and down the pedestal of the toilet. She went on wiping and threw the tissue into the bowl, flushing occasionally so that it wouldn't get blocked. But it did anyway, the blockage of wet tissue with her own vomit on it lodged in the bend of the toilet. She gave up, went to the washbasin and drank some water, tried to hold it in her mouth to stop the bleeding. Finally, she went back to the room again, stood with her back turned wondering how long Maja would lie like that before someone found her. Then she sat down again. The block was quiet, it was evening, she mustn't be in too much of a hurry now. If anyone rang the bell, she must just keep still. She wondered if she could be convicted as an accessory to murder, because she'd just sat there and watched. If she phoned right away and told the whole story, right from their chance meeting in Glassmagasinet, would they believe her? She looked around at all the things Maja had collected. She'd had lavish taste and liked plenty of colour. A great, strawberry-shaped tureen with the green leaves as the lid. It stood on a small table near the window. Eva got up slowly, she wasn't quite sure where the thought came from, but she went to the window and carefully lifted the lid. It was full of notes. Quickly, she turned and looked at Maja. But, of course, she hadn't seen anything. The roll of paper money was fat, it must have contained several thousand kroner. She looked about for other hiding places, caught sight of a blue and white vase with artificial roses in it, lifted the flowers and found another cache of money. A sewing box turned out to be crammed with money, then all at once she remembered the boots in the hall cupboard, went out into the little hall and opened it. She turned the three pairs of boots upside down and the money came tumbling out. Eva began to sweat heavily, she stuffed the money into her bag and continued searching. She found money in both bedside tables and in the medicine cabinet in the bathroom. Gradually, as she put money into her bag, her anger rose. She now avoided glancing at Maja's corpse. Her friend had destroyed something in her life. She had revealed a side to her nature she didn't know she had, a side she'd rather be without. It was Maja's fault, and Maja didn't need the money any more. Her bag was now completely full of fifty-, hundred- and thousand-kroner notes. She put her hand to her forehead and wiped away the sweat. The doorbell rang. She cowered in a corner, terrified at the thought that someone outside might be able to see her through the keyhole. Two short rings. That man out there would have been my first client, she thought, and held her breath, forcing herself against the wall. The bell rang again. Now she'd have to wait a while before leaving the flat, she mustn't be seen. She'd never been part of this, it had been an accident. At last she heard steps retreating down the stairs. She heard the front door bang and glanced at the time. It was a quarter to nine. Then she looked at Maja for the last time. She wasn't so pretty now, something about her gaping mouth and staring eyes. 'It's your fault,' Eva sobbed. Then she waited, stiff as a board for exactly five minutes, standing with her back to the corpse and counting the seconds. Finally, cautiously, she opened the door and crept out.

She met no one in the stairwell. The air was dark and dank when she slipped out of the front door and turned to the left. Not to the right past the King's Arms. She turned left again by the Methodist church, passed the Esso service station, turned left at the Gjensidige Forsiking insurance company building and walked along the river until she came to the roundabout. Her tongue felt numb and painful, but the bleeding had stopped. She clutched her bag tightly to her. She continued up the hill at a steady pace, she kept her head down and was careful not to look at anyone, she mustn't walk too quickly, no one must witness a woman hurrying away along these streets, on this evening, at just this hour, and so she sauntered. There's nothing suspicious about a woman ambling through town, she thought. It was only when she'd reached the bridge that she broke into a run.

An hour later she was back in her own living room, still holding her handbag tightly to her. She was exhausted after coming all that way, but she hadn't dared hail a taxi. She was breathing hard and had a stitch; she wanted to sit down, but had to hide her bag first. She felt it couldn't sit on the table as usual, it was full of money, it had to be put away. Somebody might come. She looked about for a cupboard or a drawer, rejected the idea and went into the utility room. She peered into the drum of the washing machine, it was empty. She shoved the bag inside and closed the door. Then she went back to the living room, was about to sit down, but turned and went to the kitchen for some wine. The bottle was open, she filled a tumbler and returned, stared out through the windows at the darkness and silence. She took two large gulps and suddenly decided to close the curtains, so that no one could look in. Although there wasn't anybody outside. She drew all the curtains and was just about to sit down with her glass when she remembered that her cigarettes were in her bag in the washing machine. She went to the utility room and retrieved them. She walked back again, forgot that she needed a light and retraced her steps. Her pulse was rising all the time, but she found her lighter and thought that now she could sit down – but then she remembered the ashtray. She got up yet again feeling her fingers beginning to twitch. A car turned slowly into the street, she ran to the window and peeped out through a chink in the curtains. It was a taxi. It's only looking for a house, she thought, went out again, found the ashtray on the kitchen work surface and lit a cigarette. The phone's been cut off, was her next thought, it was a relief, no one could get hold of her now. The door was locked. She took another drag on her cigarette and left it in the ashtray. If she turned off most of the lights, it would look as if she wasn't at home. She went round the house switching the lights off one by one. It got darker, the corners were completely black.

Then at last she sat down on the edge of the chair, ready to get up again quickly. She had an unpleasant feeling that there was something she'd forgotten, so she drank the wine and smoked, breathing fast and unevenly, and after a while she felt dizzy. She attempted to shape thoughts into sentences inside her mind, but she never finished them before more thoughts came crowding in. This confused her. She had more wine and smoked more cigarettes. It was almost eleven o'clock. Perhaps they'd already found Maja, perhaps one of her clients had tried the door and found it unlocked. But if it was a man with a wife and children he might have fled just as she had done. A prostitute can die without anyone bothering to lift a finger, she thought with horror. Maybe she'd be there for a long time before anyone took responsibility, maybe days or weeks. Until the smell in the stairwell was such that they began to wonder what was wrong. She went into the kitchen and poured more wine. Soon Emma would be home, she thought, and then everything would be back to normal. She drained the glass standing by the work surface and went to the bathroom. It was better to go to bed and let the time pass. The quicker the time passed the better. She cleaned her teeth and got under the duvet. Perhaps the police would trace her anyway, it would be best to work out what to say.

She closed her eyes and tried to sleep, but was constantly troubled by new thoughts. Had anybody seen her when she'd entered the flats? She didn't think so. But at Hannah's and in the café in Glassmagasinet? She couldn't hide the fact that they'd met each other, it was too risky. She would have to describe that day just as it had been, that they'd been for a meal, that they'd been back to Maja's flat afterwards. The painting, she thought suddenly. Leaning against the wall in the living room. But she could have gone home to collect that the same day. And ought she to admit that she knew Maja was a prostitute? Wasn't it best to tell the truth wherever possible? Yes, she knew that, because Maja had told her. Quite voluntarily. They had never had secrets from one another. She forced her eyes closed again, wanting to escape her thoughts. The taxi, she thought suddenly – the one they'd ordered. The one that had driven her to Tordenskioldsgate with the painting wrapped in a blanket, could they track it down? But she might only have gone to deliver it, stayed with her for a short while, and then had to leave because Maja was expecting a client. That was how it had been, of course. They'd met on Wednesday morning and had coffee. They hadn't seen each other for twenty-five years. Later they had dinner together. Maja paid. She wanted to buy a picture and the following day she'd sent a taxi to pick her up. Had she seen this client? Heard a name mentioned? Had she met anyone on the stairs or out in the street? No, no, she'd left in plenty of time before he was due. She knew nothing about this man, didn't want to know anything about him, she thought it was ghastly. It was gruesome. I don't know how she died, she reasoned, only what's been in the newspapers. I must read the papers. I must listen to what they say on the radio. I mustn't make any mistakes. She kept staring on and on at the ceiling as she wrung her hands beneath the duvet. When did they broadcast the first news bulletin? Six o'clock? She looked at the alarm clock which told her it was almost midnight. The light-green hands were splayed just as Maja's legs had been splayed on the golden counterpane. She blinked and opened her eyes. Nightmares were queuing up in her head. She got out of bed and went to the bathroom, put on her dressing gown and sat down in the living room. She got up again and turned on the radio, which was playing music. She thought: I'd better stay awake. As long as I'm awake I know what's happening.

Chapter 21

Killed in her own bed.

Eva saw the headline on the stand outside Omar's before she'd even got out of the car. In just a few night-time hours the case had begun spreading across the town, across the country. She ran in and put the money on the counter, opened the paper in the car and rested it against the steering wheel. Her hands shook.

Late yesterday evening a thirty-nine-year-old woman was found dead in her own bed. The woman appears to have been suffocated, but because of their investigation the police are giving no more details at present. There were no signs of a struggle in the flat, and nothing to indicate that anything was taken. The woman, who was previously known to the police in connection with prostitution, was found by a male acquaintance at ten o'clock last night. He told the paper that he had gone there to buy sex and had accidentally found the door open. He discovered the woman dead in bed and immediately rang the police. One provisional theory is that the woman was killed by a client, but the motive is unknown. More on pages 6 and 7.

Eva turned the pages of the newspaper. There wasn't much more, except some large photos. A picture of the block with Maja's window marked with a cross. It must have been an old picture as there was a lot of foliage on the trees in front of the building. A picture of the man who found her, fuzzy and taken from behind so that nobody could recognise him. And the picture of a policeman. The one who was in charge of the case. A serious man with greying hair in a light-blue shirt. Inspector Konrad Sejer, some name, she thought. Anyone who was in the area on Thursday evening was asked to get in touch with the police.

She folded the newspaper. If the police did discover that she'd been with Maja, they'd turn up quite soon, maybe even during the course of the day. If a week passed she could begin to feel safe. But their first move would certainly be to review the past few days to see what Maja had been doing and whom she'd been with. Eva started the car and drove slowly back to her house. She went in and decided to do a bit of work, wash and tidy up and think about what she'd say. There were great piles of dirty clothes in the utility room, she began to feed them into the washing machine, then suddenly remembered that her bag and the money was in there, and pulled it out. Then she filled the machine with clothes. Maja and I were childhood friends, she said to herself, but we lost contact with each other in '69. Because my family had to move. We were both fifteen at the time.

She poured powder into the washing machine and pressed the button.

So we hadn't seen one another for nearly twenty-five years. I met her at Glassmagasinet, I'd been to the paint shop and exchanged a canister of fixative. We went to the café on the first floor and had coffee.

She went into the kitchen and filled the sink with water.

And we talked about the old days, the way girls do. Did I know she was a prostitute? Well, she did tell me that, as a matter of fact. She wasn't ashamed of it either. She treated me to dinner, we went to Hannah's Kitchen.

Eva squirted washing-up liquid in the sink and put glasses and cutlery into the hot water. The washing machine was slowly filling in the utility room.

After the meal I went back to her home. Yes, that's right, we took a taxi. But I wasn't there all that long. Oh yes, she talked about her clients, but she didn't mention any names or anything. The painting?

Eva picked up a glass with a stem, held it up to the light and began to wash it.

Yes, it's my painting. Or rather, Maja bought it from me. For ten thousand kroner. But only because she felt sorry for me, I don't think she really liked it. But then she hadn't got much idea about art anyway. So the following evening I went round to deliver it, I took a taxi. I had a cup of coffee and left quite soon. She was expecting a client. Did I see him? No, no, I didn't see anyone, I went before he arrived. I didn't want to be there then.

She rinsed the glass under the tap and took another. It was frightening how many wine glasses had accumulated. The washing machine began to slosh. It was really fairly simple, she thought, as she'd obviously never be suspected of the murder itself. A woman doesn't murder a friend, another woman. So they had no reason to suspect her at all. *No one could prove what she'd seen*.

But the money, which she'd taken . . .

She inhaled and tried to calm herself. Suddenly the full force of it shook her: she'd taken Maja's money. Why on earth had she done that? Simply because she needed it? She was just picking up another glass when the doorbell rang. The ring was firm and authoritative.

No! It couldn't be! Eva started so violently that she crushed the glass. Her hand began to bleed, the water turned red. She bent towards the window to peer out, but she couldn't see who it was, only that someone was standing there. For goodness' sake, who could possibly . . .

She raised her hand and wrapped a dishcloth around it so that blood wouldn't drip on the floor. She went out into the hall, regretting that she'd chosen frosted glass for the narrow window next to the door, as it was impossible to see through it. Then she opened the door. A man was standing outside, very tall, slim and grey-haired, he seemed rather familiar. He resembled the man in the paper, the one who was leading the investigation, but surely it was too soon for that, it was only Friday morning after all, and there were limits to what they could discover in a single night, even though they'd certainly . . .

'Konrad Sejer,' he said. 'Police.'

Her heart sank and landed in the region of her stomach. Her throat tightened with a little cluck, not a sound emerged. He stood motionless, staring enquiringly at her, and when she didn't say anything, nodded at the dishcloth: 'Has something happened?'

'No, I was just washing up.' She found it impossible to move her legs.

'Eva Marie Magnus?'

'Yes, that's me.'

He gazed at her intensely. 'May I come in?'

How has he managed to find me? In only a few hours, how the hell . . .

'Yes, of course, I was just a bit preoccupied with my

hand, I'll get a plaster. It was only a cheap glass, so it doesn't matter, but I'm bleeding like a stuck pig and it's so annoying when you get blood on the furniture and carpets. Impossible to get it off . . . police?'

She backed away, trying to remember what to say, it had all gone right out of her head now, but obviously he had to ask something before she could answer, the best thing was to say as little as possible, just answer the questions, not go cackling on like a hen about this and that, or he'd simply think she was nervous, which she was, but he mustn't find that out.

They were in the living room.

'You deal with that hand first,' he said briskly. 'I'll wait here till you're ready.' He studied her carefully, noted the split lip, which had swollen up.

She went to the bathroom, didn't dare look at herself in the mirror in case she got a shock. She took a roll of plaster out of the medicine cabinet and cut off a bit, slapped it over the cut and inhaled deeply three times. Maja and I were childhood friends, she whispered. Then she returned.

He was still standing, so she nodded for him to sit. In the second he opened his mouth it struck her like a bolt of lightning that there was something she'd forgotten to work out, something critically important. She wanted to hurry and solve the problem, but it was too late, he'd already begun to speak now and she could no longer think.

'Do you know Maja Durban?'

She steadied herself on the chair back. 'Yes. Yes, I do.'

'Has it been long since you saw her last?'

'No. It was – yesterday. Yesterday evening.'

He nodded slowly. 'At what time yesterday?'

'Er, between six and seven I should think.'

'Did you know that she was found dead at her flat at 10 p.m. last night?'

Eva sat down, moistened her lips and gulped. Did I know? she thought, have I heard already, this early in the morning . . . Suddenly she was staring right at the newspaper, front page up. 'Yes. I saw it in the paper.'

He picked it up, turned it and looked at the back. 'Ah? You're not on the mailing list, I see. No address label. So you go out and buy the paper early in the morning?'

There was something tenacious about him, he was the type who could get a stone to talk. She had no chance. 'Well, not every single day. But quite often.'

'How did you know it was Ms Durban who was killed?'

'What do you mean?'

'Her name,' he said quietly, 'isn't mentioned in the article.'

Eva felt she was about to faint. 'Well, I recognised the building in the picture. And her window was marked. I mean I knew from the content of the article that it was Maja. She was a bit unusual. It says' – she leant forward and pointed with her finger – '"known to the police" and "prostitution". And she was thirty-nine. So I knew it was her, I knew at once.'

'Uh huh? And what did you think then? Once you realised she'd been murdered?'

Eva struggled manically to find the right words. 'That she should have listened to me. I tried to warn her.'

He was silent. She thought he was going to continue, but he didn't, he looked round the living room, studied her large paintings, not without a certain interest, and gazed at her again for a while, still without speaking. Eva felt herself sweating and her hand began to ache.

'You'd have got in touch with us, I assume, if I hadn't come along here first?'

'How d'you mean?'

'You visit a friend, and next day you read in the paper that she's been murdered. I assume you'd have made contact, to make a statement, to help us?'

'Oh, yes, of course. I just hadn't got round to it.'

'The washing-up was more important?'

Eva was slowly disintegrating in front of his eyes. 'Maja and I were childhood friends,' she said lamely.

'Go on.'

Despair was almost getting the better of her, she tried to pull herself together, but could no longer remember the story as she'd rehearsed it.

'We bumped into each other at Glassmagasinet, we

hadn't seen each other for twenty-five years, so we went and had a coffee together. She told me about her occupation.'

'Yes. She'd been going for a while.'

He was silent once more, but she couldn't stick to her intention of only answering questions.

'We had dinner together, on Wednesday evening. And had coffee at her home afterwards.'

'So you've been to her flat?'

'Yes, only a quick visit. I took a taxi home that night, and Maja wanted me to bring her a painting. Which she wanted to buy. Because I'm a painter, and she thought that was pretty hopeless, particularly as I hardly sell any paintings, and when I said they'd cut off the phone, she wanted to help me by buying a painting. She had a lot of money.' She thought of the money at the cabin, but didn't mention it.

'What did she pay for the picture?'

'Ten thousand. Just what I owed in unpaid bills.'

'That was a good buy,' he said suddenly.

She was so amazed that her eyes widened.

'So she wanted you to go back, and you did?'

'Yes. But only to deliver the painting,' she said quickly. 'I took a taxi. I'd wrapped it up in a blanket. . .'

'We know that. You were picked up by cab number F16. I'd imagine that was a bit of a ride,' he said smiling. 'How long were you there?'

Eva battled not to let the mask slip. 'An hour maybe.

I had a sandwich and then we chatted a bit.' She got up to find a cigarette, opened her bag which she'd placed on the dining table and found herself staring down at wads of notes. She closed it again with a snap.

'D'you smoke?' he asked, proffering a packet of Prince.

'Thanks.'

She pulled a cigarette from the packet and reached for the Zippo lighter he'd slid across the table.

'The taxi picked you up at six, so you'd have been at Ms Durban's by about six-twenty I should imagine?'

'Yes, that's probably about right. But I wasn't actually checking the time.'

She took a deep drag on the cigarette and exhaled, trying to ease the tension that was building up inside her. It didn't help.

'And you were there for an hour, so you would have left about seven-twenty?'

'As I said I wasn't watching the clock. But she was expecting a client and I didn't want to be there then, so I left a good while before he was due.'

'When was he due?'

'At eight. She told me that straight away, that she had a client coming at eight. They rang twice. It was an arranged signal.'

Sejer nodded. 'And do you know who he was?'

'No. I didn't want to know, I thought what she was doing was awful, disgusting, I can't understand how she, or anyone, can do that.'

'You may have been the last person to see her alive. The man who came at eight may well have been her murderer.'

'Oh?' She gasped as if shuddering at the thought.

'Did you meet anyone in the street?'

'No.'

'Which way did you go?'

Tell the truth, she thought, for as long as you can. 'To the left. Past the Esso station and Gjensidige. Along the river and over the bridge.'

'That's a bit of a detour.'

'I didn't want to walk past the pub.'

'Why not?'

'There are so many drunks outside it in the evenings.'

This was certainly true. She hated walking past large groups of inebriated men.

'I see.' He looked at her bandaged hand. 'Did she see you out?'

'No.'

'Did she lock the door after you?'

'I don't think so. But I didn't pay much attention to that.'

'And you didn't meet anyone on the stairs or on the pavement?'

'No. No one.'

'Did you notice if there were any cars parked in the street?'

'I can't remember any.'

'I see. Then you walked across the bridge – then what?'

'What d'you mean?'

'Where did you go then?'

'I walked home.'

'You *walked* home? From Tordenskioldsgate to Engelstad?'

'Yes.'

'That's quite a long way, isn't it?'

'I suppose so, but I wanted to walk. I had such a lot to think about.'

'And what did you have to think about that required such a long walk?'

'Well, Maja and all that,' she mumbled. 'That she'd turned out like that. We'd known each other so well in the past, I couldn't understand it. I thought I knew her,' she said pensively and almost to herself. She crushed out her cigarette and pushed her hair back over her shoulder.

'So you met Maja Durban on Wednesday morning, and that was the first time in twenty-five years?'

'Yes.'

'And popped in for a short while yesterday evening between six and seven?'

'Yes.'

'And that's all?'

'Yes. That's it, that's all.'

'You haven't forgotten anything?'

'No, I don't think so.'

He rose from the sofa and nodded again, picked up his Zippo lighter which now had Eva's fingerprints all over it, and slipped it into his breast pocket.

'Did she strike you as anxious about anything?'

'No, definitely not. Maja was just as upbeat as always. She was in complete control.'

'And during the conversation there was no hint that someone was after her? Or that she was in dispute with anyone?'

'No, there wasn't, not in any way.'

'Did she receive any phone calls while you were there?'

'No.'

'Well, I shan't detain you any longer. Please give us a ring if something turns up that you think might be important. Anything at all.'

'Yes!'

'I'll get your phone reconnected immediately.'

'What?'

'I tried to phone you. The phone people told me you hadn't paid.'

'Oh, yes. Thanks a lot.'

'In case we need to talk to you again.'

Eva bit her lip, bemused. 'Er,' she asked tentatively, 'how did you know I was there?'

He reached into his inside pocket and drew out a little red leather book. 'Ms Durban's pocket diary. Entry for the thirtieth of September reads: "Met Eva at Glassmagasinet. Dinner at Hannah's." At the back she'd entered your name and address.'

So simple, she thought.

'Don't get up,' he went on, 'I'll find my own way out.' She plumped down again. She felt totally drained, twined her fingers in her lap until the cut began to bleed again. Sejer walked across the room and stopped suddenly by one of her pictures. He cocked his head and turned to her again. 'What does it represent?'

Eva squirmed. 'I don't usually try to explain my pictures.'

'No, I can understand that well enough. But this' – he pointed to a spire rising up from the blackness – 'reminds me of a church. And this small grey thing in the background, could be something like a headstone. Slightly arched at the top. A long way from the church, but you can still see they're linked. A churchyard,' he said simply. 'With just one headstone. Who's buried there?'

Eva stared at him in amazement. 'Me, I suppose.'

He walked on into the hall. 'It's the most powerful image I've ever seen,' he said.

Just as the front door slammed, it occurred to her that maybe she should have shed a few tears, but it was too late now. She sat with her hand in her lap listening to the washing machine, it had begun its spinning cycle, turning faster and faster until it became an ominous whine.

Chapter 22

She shook off her fear and began to work up a slowly rising anger. It was an alien feeling; she was never angry, only despondent. She'd fetched her handbag from the dining table, opened it and turned it upside down so that the money fluttered out. Most of it was in hundred-kroner notes, a few fifties and a clutch of thousands. She counted on and on, unable to believe her own eyes. More than sixty thousand kroner! Pocket money, Maja had said. She arranged it in tidy piles and shook her head. She could live for an eternity on sixty thousand, six months at least. And no one would miss it. Nobody even knew it existed. Where would it have gone otherwise, she thought, to the state? Eva had the strange feeling that she deserved it. That it was hers. She gathered up the piles, found a rubber band and bound them up neatly. It no longer troubled her that she'd taken the money. It ought to have troubled her, she couldn't quite understand why it didn't, she'd never stolen anything in her life before, apart from Mrs Skollenborg's plums. But why should it just lie there, in bowls and vases, when she needed it so badly?

After a short pause for reflection she went down to the cellar. She rummaged around for a while on the workbench and found an empty paint tin that was dry inside. Lime green, satin finish. She put the wad of notes in the tin, replaced the lid and pushed it back under the bench. Whenever I need something I can simply put my hand in the tin and fish out a few notes, she thought in amazement, just as Maja had done. She went back up again. It's because no one will find me out, she thought. Maybe we're all thieves at heart provided the opportunity is good enough. This was a good opportunity. Money that belongs to no one any more has been redistributed to people who really need it. Like me and Emma. And Maja had almost two million more hidden at her cabin. She shook her head. There was no point in even thinking about such large sums. But what if it was so well hidden that it would never be found? Was it just to lie there and rot? I'd like you to have the money, Maja had said. Perhaps it was meant as a joke, but the thought made her give a little gasp. Perhaps she really had meant it. A possibility tried to insinuate itself, but she pushed it away. Money that no one knew about. It was quite impossible to imagine what she could do with so much. Of course it would never work. You could never hide a fortune like that, even Emma would start asking questions if she suddenly had all that money in her hands, she might babble about it to Jostein, who in turn would start asking questions, or perhaps to her grandfather, or to friends or parents of friends. That's why it's so difficult to be a thief, she mused, there's always someone to be suspicious, someone who knew how badly off you'd been, and gossip spread so quickly. If only Maja knew what she was sitting here thinking. Perhaps she was in a cold-storage drawer now, with a label tied to her toe. Durban, Maja, DOB 04.08.1954.

She shuddered. But the man with the ponytail wouldn't be free for long, they were always caught. It was just a matter of waiting while they closed in on him; he hadn't got a chance, not now with all the modern DNA testing, and he had actually had intercourse with Maja. He'd left quite a visiting card, as well as fingerprints and hairs and fibres from his clothing and all sorts of other things, she'd read about such methods in crime novels. Suddenly, it struck her with horror that she'd left a lot of traces there herself. The man from the police would return, she was sure of that. Then she must tell her story just as she'd done before, perhaps it got easier after a while. She stepped purposefully into her studio. She put on her smock and set about staring fiercely at the black canvas that stood on the easel. Sixty by ninety, it was a good format, not too large, not too restricting. She had sandpaper and blocks in a drawer. She tore off a piece and folded it round a block, clenched her hand and made a few tentative movements in the air. Then she attacked the canvas. She landed on the right and did four or five powerful strokes. The colour turned mid-grey, something like lead, a little lighter where the canvas weave had thicker fibres. She stood back. What if they didn't find him? What if he simply went free? Opel Manta, BL 74, wasn't that it? Not everybody gets caught, she thought now, if he wasn't already on the file, how could they find him? It had all happened so fast and so completely silently. He slid out and disappeared in a matter of seconds. If she were the only one who'd seen the car they would never find out he was driving an Opel Manta, just the sort of uncommon car that would have made him so easy to trace.

She advanced again and worked intensively at a point a bit further to the left, smaller movements now, but harder. What had he said? Something about his job – how long it took him to earn a thousand kroner. In her mind's eye she could see the back of his fair hair and the little ponytail at his neck. Hadn't he said the brewery?

She stopped. She'd got to the white canvas and a piercing brightness. The block fell to the floor. She glanced at the time, thought for a second and shook her head hard. Continued scraping. Glanced again.

Pulled the smock over her head, got dressed and went out.

The car needed full choke to start. It made a terrific roar and the exhaust was black as she changed up and nosed into the road. Maybe he was already over the border in Sweden for all she knew. Perhaps he had a cabin where he could hide, perhaps he'd committed suicide. Or perhaps he was at work just like everyone else, as if nothing had happened. At the brewery, with his white Manta parked outside.

She sat hunched over the steering wheel and drove fast. She wanted to see if she was right, if the car really was standing there. If it really existed and wasn't a figment of her imagination. She shot past the power station on the right and suddenly remembered the unpaid bills, she mustn't forget about them. She had the money now, even enough to frame some of her pictures. People didn't buy pictures with unpainted canvas round the edges. She couldn't understand them. Now she had the Spice Garden on her left and was approaching the hill with its nine sleeping policemen. She changed down into second. He never saw me, she thought. I run no risk strolling around outside the brewery; he has no idea who I am or what I've seen. But he is scared, and on his guard. I'll have to be careful. She lurched over the first bump. If he's clever, he'll carry on with his life as if nothing's happened. Go to work.

Tell dirty jokes in the canteen. Maybe, she thought suddenly, he's got a wife and children. She drove on carefully over the bumps trying to spare the old car. Secretly, she christened him Elmer. It was a suitable name she thought, slightly pale and watery. Anyway, she couldn't imagine him being called anything ordinary, like other people, Trygve, or Kåre, or perhaps Jens. Not when she saw him with her inner eye, kneeling on the bed with his trousers round his knees and the sharp knife glinting in his hand. There was nothing ordinary about him. Did he feel different now? Was he shaken and scared, or was he simply angry that he'd over-stepped a mark that might possibly cost him dear? What did it really feel like?

Eva accelerated and turned tightly into the round-about. She bowled past the light-bulb factory, and noticed the newspaper stand outside the bakery door, 'Found suffocated' it said, and the same at the Esso service station. Maja was all over town and Elmer would certainly have read it too, if he read newspapers, and surely everyone did. She slackened speed, she was in Oscarsgate now, glided past the brewery, went on to the swimming baths and parked round the back. She remained seated in the car for a few moments. The brewery car park was large and there were lots of white cars. She locked up and walked slowly past the swimming baths, smelling the chlorine that wafted out, and continued to the bosses' car park, right by the brewery's main entrance. Elmer definitely wasn't one of the bosses, he wasn't dressed like a boss, and he'd also moaned about his wages. She ambled slowly on, now she had the car park on her left. It was protected by a barrier. A card machine blinked red and a large sign on the right declared that the car park was kept under surveillance, but not what form it took. She couldn't see cameras anywhere. She squeezed past the barrier and turned to the left, it was a case of searching systematically, there were a great many cars. Her heart thumped harder, she pushed her hands into her coat pockets and attempted to stroll unhurriedly, occasionally raising her face to the sun. She formed her mouth into a small smile and hoped it looked trustworthy. Here was a Honda Civic, white, and almost unnaturally shiny, as if it had come straight from the showroom. She went on down the line, needing to look at all of them, including the number plates, but at the same time appearing not to be checking if someone was watching her. Could a man kill in the evening and then go to work the next day? Was it possible? A BMW, rather worn and dirty with a lot of rubbish on the dashboard. A Beetle, which was not actually white, but more a dirty yellow. She went on to the second row, felt a tiny bit of warmth from the sun even though it was October now, a wistful little caress on her cheek. Suddenly, Maja was irretrievably dead. It was unbelievable. She wasn't really sure if it had sunk in. She'd popped up from nowhere, and just as suddenly she'd gone. She'd seemed to flit by like some strange dream. A white Mercedes, an old Audi, she sauntered on her long legs with her coat open, until all at once a man was blocking her way. A navy blue boiler suit with lots of luminous strips on it. Securitas.

'You got an entry card?'

Eva frowned. He was only a spotty boy, but large. 'What?'

'This is a private car park. Looking for something?'

'Yes, a car. I'm not touching anything.'

'You'll have to leave, this is for employees only.' He had spiky yellow hair and loads of self-confidence.

'It's only to check something. Just going round to take a look. It's important to me,' she added.

'No way! Come on, I'll see you out.' He came towards her, his arm authoritative.

'You can follow me if you like, I only want to look at the cars. I'm looking for a guy I need to talk to, it's important. Please. I've got a car and a stereo of my own.'

He hesitated. 'OK then, but be quick. My job is getting unauthorised persons off the car park, so that's why.'

She continued along the lines of cars hearing his steps behind her.

'What kind of car is it?' he fretted.

She didn't answer. Elmer mustn't know someone was

looking for him. This puppy in his blue romper suit would certainly tell.

'I know lots of the blokes who work here,' he added.

A Toyota Tercel, an old Volvo, a Nissan Sunny. The security man coughed.

'Is he on production? On the taps?'

'I don't know him,' she said curtly. 'Only the car.'

'This is some big secret, eh?'

'Correct.'

He stopped and nodded. He stood with his arms folded feeling foolish. A lone woman was trespassing in a private area and he was following her about like a poodle. What kind of security man was he? Some of his self-assurance seeped away.

'And what d'you want with a bloke you don't know?' He overtook her and propped himself against the bonnet of a car. His legs were long, they were blocking her way.

'I'm thinking of throttling him,' she said smiling sweetly.

'Oh yeah, right.' He chuckled, as if he suddenly understood. His beaver nylon boiler suit sat snugly on his toned body. Eva stared at the number plate between his open legs. BL 744. She turned to the car opposite, which was a silver Golf, walked right up to it and peered in through the window. He followed her. 'That one's in the canteen, can't remember his name. A little squirt with wavy hair. Is that him?'

She smiled patiently, straightened up and threw a quick glance at the white Opel behind him, now she could make out the full number. BL 74470. It was a Manta. She'd been right, it was just like Jostein's old one, but this one was nicer-looking, newer and better looked after. The trim of the seats was red. She walked back, heading for the barrier, she'd seen enough. She'd found him just like that. A perfectly normal brewery worker with a murder on his conscience. And she, Eva, knew enough to put him inside for fifteen or twenty years. Inside a tiny cell. It's unbelievable, she thought. Yesterday he killed Maja. Today he's at work as if nothing had happened. So he's clever. A cold fish. Perhaps he was talking about the murder over a sandwich in the canteen. She could imagine him smacking his lips and chewing with bits of mayonnaise on his upper lip. Terrible wasn't it, boys, about that woman – must have been an excitable customer. Then he'd wash it down with some Coke, pick out the lemon and bits of parsley before taking another bite. I'll bet he's away over the Swedish border already.

Maybe several of them had visited Maja, she thought suddenly. And perhaps he felt the way she did, that he could hardly believe it had happened and pushed it away like a nasty dream.

'I remember his name now!' the security man yelled after her. 'The one with the Golf. His name's Bendiksen. From Finnmark!'

Eva waved without turning and walked on. Then she halted again. 'Do they work shifts?'

'Seven to three to eleven to seven.'

She nodded again, glanced at her watch and walked out of the car park, back past the swimming baths and got into her own car. Her heart was beating fast now, she had a huge secret and wasn't quite sure what to do with it. But she started the car and drove homewards. Three o'clock was a long way off. Then she could wait and follow him. Find out where he lived. If he had a wife and children. A terrific urge surfaced within her, he had to know that someone was on to him! No more than that. She couldn't bear the thought that he felt safe, that he'd got up and gone to work as usual, after killing Maja for no reason at all. She couldn't understand why he'd done it, where all the fury had come from. As if the knife on the side of the bed was the greatest insult he'd ever suffered. But murderers aren't like other people, she mused, and swung out to pass a cyclist who was weaving about on her right. They must lack something. Or perhaps he'd quite simply been terrified by the sight of the knife. Had he really believed that Maja would stab him? She wondered for a moment if some crafty lawyer could save him by asserting that he'd acted in self-defence. In that case I'd have to come forward, Eva thought, but then dismissed the idea. To give evidence as a friend of the prostitute, no, she couldn't do it. I'm not a coward, she thought, not really.

But I have to think of Emma. She repeated it to herself again and again. But a great restlessness had taken charge of her body, a thousand little ants crawling through her veins. At the thought that nobody knew anything. That such a thing could happen to her friend, Maja – the very best of friends – and end up as just a tiny paragraph in the newspaper.

Chapter 23

The phone rang as she was closing the front door.

She jumped. The line had been restored. For a moment she hesitated, made a rapid decision and lifted the receiver.

'Eva my dear! Where on earth have you been? I've been ringing for days!'

'My phone's been cut off. But I've got it back now, I was just a bit late with a payment.'

'I've told you you're to let me know if you need anything,' her father growled.

'Not having a phone for a couple of days won't kill me,' she said easily, 'and you're not exactly flush with money yourself.'

'It's better for me to starve than you. Fetch Emma to the phone, I want to hear her unsullied little voice.'

'She's with Jostein for a few days, it's the autumn break. So tell me, do I sound sullied, is that it?'

'Your voice has a tainted undertone now and then. I always have the feeling you only tell me a fraction of what's going on.'

'Yes, that's right. It's called being considerate. You're not a spring chicken any more, you know.'

'I think you should come over soon so that we can tease each other properly, over a glass of wine. I can't do good ripostes on the phone.' He was snuffling a bit as if he had a cold.

'I'll be along one of these days. You could always ring Jostein and get Emma there. Besides, she isn't entirely unsullied, I think she takes after you basically.'

'I'll take that as a compliment. Will he be embarrassed if I phone?'

'No, don't be silly. He's really fond of you. He's always frightened you're angry that he walked out, so if you phone he'll be pleased.'

'I'm extremely angry! You didn't think otherwise, surely?'

'Don't say that to him.'

'I'll never understand why you're so loyal to a man who ran off like that.'

'I'll tell you sometime, over a glass of wine.'

'A father should know everything about his only child,' he scolded crossly. 'The life you lead is just one almighty secret.'

'Yes,' she said quietly. 'It certainly is, Dad. But you know, important truths will out. When the time is ripe.'

'The time's almost up,' he answered. 'I'm old.'

'That's what you always say when you're feeling sorry for yourself. Get some wine, and I'll come over. I'll ring and tell you when. You are wearing your slippers, aren't you?'

'That's for me to know, and you to wonder. When you start dressing like a woman, I'll start dressing like an old man.'

'That's a deal, Dad.'

They said nothing for a while, but she could hear his breathing. Eva felt he was so close that she could almost sense his warm breath coming down the phone line and caressing her cheek. Her father was a sturdy root from which Eva derived all her strength. Somewhere at the back of her mind she would occasionally register that he would die soon and that all the intimacy she knew in life would be torn from her, stripped away, as if someone were tearing the hide and hair from her body.

Her thoughts made her feel icy.

'You're not thinking pleasant thoughts, Eva.'

'I'll come soon. I don't think life's much fun really.'

'Then we can console one another.'

She put down the phone. It was so quiet after that, she went to the window and her thoughts ran wild even though she tried to control them. What way did we go, she thought, to get to the cabin that time, didn't we go through Kongsberg first? It was so long ago. More than twenty-five years. Maja's father had driven them in the van. And they'd got drunk, the heather round the hut had been dappled with little blotches of stew and fruit cocktail, and some of their clothes had to be left outside at night. Through Kongsberg, she thought, and across the bridge. Up towards Sigdal, wasn't that the way? A red cabin with green window frames. Tiny, standing almost totally by itself. But it was a long way. Two hundred, maybe three hundred kilometres. Nearly two million. How much room did a sum like that take up, she thought, if it was in various denominations it would hardly fit into a shoebox. And where in a small cabin could one hide such a sum? In the cellar? Up the chimney? Or maybe down that outside toilet. They'd had to throw in handfuls of earth and bark, each time they'd used it. Or was it hidden in empty food tins in the fridge? Maja was ingenious. It wouldn't be easy if anyone decided to search for it, she thought. But who would search for it? Nobody knew about it, and so it would lie there for ever and crumble to dust, or had she told anyone else? If that were the case, perhaps others were thinking along the same lines as she was now, thinking about the two million and dreaming.

She went back to the studio and began scraping at the black canvas again. October wasn't exactly high season for mountain cabins at that sort of altitude, perhaps there wasn't a soul up there, nobody to see her. If she parked a little way off and walked the final bit

– if she could even remember the way. Turn left at a yellow shop, she recalled, then on, up and up, almost to the treeline. Millions of sheep. The tourist hostel and the large lake, she could park there, down by the water. She kept scraping at the canvas. Two million. Her own gallery. Just paint and paint and never worry about money, not for years. Take good care of her father and of Emma. Just reach into a bowl and pull the money out whenever she needed it. Or a safe-deposit box. Why on earth hadn't Maja put the money in a safe-deposit box? Perhaps because a safe-deposit box had to be registered and could be traced. The money wasn't legitimate. Eva scratched harder. If she wanted to get hold of the money she'd have to break into the cabin, and she couldn't imagine herself daring to do that. Breaking open the door with a crowbar or smashing a pane of glass would certainly be audible a long way off. But if there wasn't anyone up there . . . She could go in the evening and arrive during the night. Although it would be hard to search in the dark. A torch maybe. She threw away the piece of sandpaper and walked slowly down the stairs to the cellar. A drawer in the workbench contained a torch that Jostein had left. It gave a miserably poor light. She put her hand into the paint pot where she'd hidden Maja's pocket money and pulled out a bundle of notes, mounted the stairs and put on her coat. She pushed away the small stabbings of her conscience, and the slight, almost inaudible note of caution sounding from her common sense. First, she'd pay all her bills and then there were a couple of things she needed as well. It was now midday. In three hours Elmer would have finished his shift, and would walk to his car. Eva put on her sunglasses. She stared at herself in the mirror: dark hair, dark glasses and coat. She was unrecognisable.

There was an ironmonger's in the square. She didn't dare ask for a crowbar, but instead wandered along the shelves looking for something she could push into the crack round a door. She found a sturdy chisel, extra large and with a sharp edge, and a solid hammer. It had a grooved rubber handle. She had to enquire about the torch.

'What are you going to use it for?' asked the ironmonger.

'For lighting,' Eva said nonplussed. She stared at his stomach bulging beneath the nylon coat. Its buttons strained dangerously.

'Aha, yes, I realise that. But they make torches for different purposes. I mean, are you going to use it for *working*, or for walking at night, or for signalling . . .?'

'Working,' she said quickly.

He produced a water- and shock-resistant Maglite torch, it was long and neat with a narrow body and a beam that could be focused as required. 'This is about the best you can get. Lifetime guarantee. The American cops use them. Four hundred and fifty kroner.'

'Oh God! Yes, I'll take it,' she said quickly.

'It's also good for bashing people on the head with,' he said earnestly. 'Burglars and the like.'

Eva frowned. She wasn't sure if he was being serious.

The tools cost a fortune, more than seven hundred kroner. She paid and carried them out in a grey paper bag. She felt like the archetypal housebreaker herself, all she needed were some sneakers and a balaclava. Then she realised she hadn't eaten. She went to the first-floor café at Jensen Manufaktur where she bought two sandwiches, one smoked salmon and egg and one cheese, a glass of milk and a coffee. She saw no one she knew. She didn't really know anyone anyway, was merely surrounded by nameless faces which demanded nothing of her, and she liked that. She had such a lot to think about now. When she'd finished she went to the bookshop and bought a road atlas. She sat on some steps in the pedestrian precinct, partly hidden by an ice-cream sign, and began to search. She rediscovered the way fairly quickly, did a provisional measurement with her fingers and came to the conclusion that it was at least two hundred kilometres. At all events it would take two and a half hours to drive there. If she left at nine she'd be up there before midnight. Alone, in a cabin on the Hardanger Plateau with a hammer and chisel, did she dare?

She glanced at the time again. She was waiting for Elmer who'd now been at work for six hours and who'd soon have got through his first working day as a murderer. From now on he would count the days, watch the calendar as time passed. Sigh with relief each evening he went to his bed as a free man. One day, somehow or other, she'd send him a little reminder. So that he'd lose his feeling of security and lie awake at night, waiting and waiting. Slowly, he'd go to pieces, perhaps start drinking, and finally skip work. And then he'd go straight to the dogs. Eva smiled an acid smile. She got up from her seat and went to G-Sport. There she bought a well waterproofed windcheater with a hood, dark green, a pair of Nike trainers and a small daysack. She'd never possessed such things in her life before. But if she were to trudge along mountain tracks in the middle of the night she should at least resemble a hut owner. In case anyone saw her. She paid almost fourteen hundred kroner for the stuff and rolled her eyes, but it didn't make much of a dent in her wallet. How simple everything was when you didn't have to count the kroner. Just pull them out and slap them down on the counter. She felt so light-headed and strange, almost like some other person, but it was she, Eva, who stood here strewing notes about her. It wasn't that she yearned for luxury of any kind, she cared nothing for that at all. Simply an existence that was untroubled, so that she could paint in peace. She wanted no more. Lastly, she went to the bank and paid her bills. Electricity, phone, road tax, insurance and council tax. She stuffed

all the receipts into her bag and walked out again with
head held high. She crossed the square and down to the
benches by the river, where she watched the dark water
rushing past. The current was strong. A paper carton
which once, perhaps, had contained fast food flew past
like a miniature speed boat. Maybe Elmer was looking
at the clock now, more often than he usually did. But
no one had asked after him, no one had come through
the production hall to lead him away to a waiting car.
Nobody had seen anything. He thought he could get
away with it. Perhaps, perhaps he could get away with
it. Eva rose again and went back to her car. She drove
to the swimming baths and parked at the front so that
she could see the barrier. The Securitas guard was still
patrolling the lines of cars. She lowered her head and
began studying her road atlas. It was a quarter to three.

At last they appeared, a group of three men together.
He halted by the white car and ran a hand through his
hair. It hung loose now, but she recognised his profile,
and his beer belly. He chatted and gesticulated, and
thumped the other two good-naturedly with his fist.

As if nothing had happened!
They were talking about the car. She saw that from
their gestures, they examined the tyres, one of them bent
down and pointed under the radiator, Elmer shook his
head as if in disagreement. He placed a hand on the
roof of the car, as if to demonstrate that it was his. A

strutting type with macho body language. Eva put the car in gear and slid slowly out of the lot. Maybe he was a real hot-rodder and would pull away from her immediately. His car looked lively, hers was falling to bits. But the traffic was dense at this time of day, it should be all right. His engine roared angrily as he started up, as if there was something quite special beneath the bonnet. The other two leapt clear. He waved, and came slowly towards the barrier which was open. She was in luck. He was indicating right and would drive past her, if she were quick she could get in right behind him. He'd put on a pair of sunglasses. Just as she nipped out, he looked in his mirror. She had an unpleasant feeling, tried to keep a courteous distance and rolled slowly along behind him down the congested main street, and out of town. He drove past the hospital and the undertaker, and soon afterwards moved into the right-hand lane, he was driving well but fairly fast, past the video shop and the Data superstore. They were approaching Rosenkrantzgate now, he glanced in the mirror once and suddenly indicated right. She had to drive straight on, but in her mirror she managed to see that he'd drawn up at the first entrance of a green house. A small boy had just run out. Perhaps it was his son. Then they were gone.

So he lived in that green house in Rosenkrantzgate. Possibly he had a son, of about five or six. Same age as Emma, she thought.

Could he continue to be a father after all that had happened? Take the boy on his lap in the evenings and sing songs? Help him brush his teeth? With the same hands that had made him a murderer? She couldn't turn until she got to the trotting course, but then she made a cheeky U-turn and drove back the way she'd come. Now she had the green house on her left. A woman stood outside with a wash basket in her hands. Bleached hair piled high. A typical bimbo, just the sort he *would* like, she thought. She had him now. And soon, quite soon, she'd have two million.

Chapter 24

It was nine in the evening when she set off in the car. Two and a half hours later she'd smoked ten cigarettes and the yellow shop was nowhere to be seen. Her legs had begun to feel stiff and her back ached. All at once, the project seemed more like some idiotic stunt. Outside it was as black as pitch, she'd passed Veggli, and the café with the big troll, she'd left the small towns behind and gradually the names began to awaken memories. This must be right. The shop should be on the left and it should be lit up, the way shops were, fully illuminated all night. But everything was dark, not a house to be seen, no traffic. The forest lined the road on each side like black walls, as if she were driving along the bottom of a ravine. There was music on the radio, but now she found it annoying. Bloody shop!

She pulled into the side of the road and stopped. Lit another cigarette and pondered a bit. It was almost midnight and she was tired. Perhaps she wouldn't find it, perhaps her memory was playing tricks on her. It had been so long ago, over twenty-five years, they were just kids then. Maja had led the gang and the others had trotted along behind like sheep, Eva, Hanne, Ina and Else Gro. Old, green sleeping bags and tinned food. Cigarettes and lager. Maybe the old shop had been pulled down and they'd put up some huge shopping centre instead, she thought, or maybe they didn't build shopping centres deep in the forest. She'd just have to drive on, she gave herself twenty minutes more and if she didn't find it she'd have to turn back. Or she could spend the night in the car and carry on looking when it got light. But the notion of sleeping on the back seat wasn't very appealing, this was pure wilderness, she didn't know if she dared. She put the car in gear and moved out on to the road again, extinguishing her cigarette in the ashtray which was now full to overflowing. She took another look at the time and accelerated. She seemed to recall that the road had crossed a bridge, there'd been sheep and goats there, then they'd zigzagged upwards driving round hairpin bends. In the winter they cleared the road only as far as the tourist hostel, and Maja had to do the final bit on skis. But luckily there was no snow yet, or perhaps there was higher up, perhaps she'd have to wade through it on the final stretch, she hadn't considered that. Eva wasn't exactly the outdoors type, but now she felt ridiculous. She lit yet another cigarette, they were making her feel thoroughly queasy by this time, and peered into the gloomy forest searching for light. She turned up the heater. The air was different up here, sharper. It was so damned far! Elmer was probably in bed now, nightmares lurking, or perhaps he sat alone in his living room with his third whisky, his wife long since gone to bed, sleeping the sleep of the innocent under the duvet. It couldn't be easy lying there with the image of Maja in his head, the feeling of those legs kicking under him as he pushed her into the mattress with the pillow, she must have put up a fight. Maja was strong, but men were so much stronger, it never ceased to amaze her. They didn't even need to be particularly big, it was as if they were made of totally different stuff. Suddenly she braked. There was a light in the distance, on the left. Soon she saw the familiar orange sign of the Co-op.

The Co-op. And there was the road and the bridge. She flipped the indicator arm, lurched across the bridge and drove carefully up the mountainside in second gear. Her pulse began to race again, and she saw the cabin in her mind's eye, a small dark wedge, simple and modest, with its totally improbable treasure, a pure fairy tale, the key to an untroubled life. Maja should have seen her now, she would have approved, the way she liked people who helped themselves to the good things in life. At any rate she wouldn't have wanted the money to go to the state. Two million – how much interest would that be at six or seven per cent? No, she couldn't use a bank. She bit her lip, she'd have to keep it in the cellar. Nobody must know about it, not Emma, not anyone. And she mustn't throw money around or talk in her sleep or get drunk. In fact, she reflected, life would become rather complicated. The Ascona crept on upwards, Eva didn't meet a single car, it was as if she were on a different planet, completely uninhabited, even the sheep were absent. It was probably too cold, Eva didn't know much about such things. Fifteen minutes later she passed the tourist hostel on the right. She drove on, with the lake on her right now, and searched for a turning that would take her down to the shore. There was no snow, but up here it was lighter, the sky was so big. On her left was a large cabin, with a light in one window. It gave her a bit of a start. If there were people up here she'd have to watch out. The people with mountain cabins – Oslo types who'd had cabins up here for generations – would probably keep in touch with one another. Yes, we saw a car pass by here yesterday evening, well it would be about midnight. We didn't recognise the sound of the engine, Amundsen drives a Volvo and Bertrandsen has a diesel Merc. It must have been a stranger, we're sure of that.

Eva drove on round the bend, following the lake all the time. It was so calm it was like glass and glowed with an almost metallic glint, as if it were covered with ice. She caught sight of a small shed by the waterside and assumed there'd be a track leading to it. It was awfully bumpy. She crept down it, staring about her all the time, but she couldn't see lights anywhere else. She didn't stop until she was right by the water's edge. It was possible to drive round the shed and park behind it. So she did. She switched off the ignition and head-lights, and for a few seconds she sat still in the pitch blackness.

She was just about to slam the door, when she changed her mind. The sound of a car door would reverberate like a gunshot in this silence. Instead, she pushed it gently to, didn't bother to lock up, and put the keys in her pocket. Then she lifted the daysack on to her back, the sack that contained the hammer and chisel and torch, did up her zip and tightened the hood round her face. She couldn't remember just how long it took to walk from here, but thought it was about fifteen to twenty minutes. It was freezing now, the cold stung her cheeks as she walked with head bent, up the potholed track, and then strode out along the road. She hoped she would recognise the cabin when she saw it. There was a stream behind it where they'd brushed their teeth and got water for coffee. The mountains reared up in every direction. They'd climbed the biggest, Johovda; she'd looked out across the Hardanger Plateau and felt so very small, but it was a good feeling, the feeling that most things in the world were bigger than herself. She liked it. Funny, she thought suddenly, as she walked on alone in the dark, we all know we're going to die, and yet we live as hard as we can. She found the thought strangely moving.

She rounded a bend and saw some cabins in the distance. There were several, four or five, but no lights in any of them. This caused her to increase her pace a bit. Could it be there? Hadn't it stood alone by its stream, or was her memory playing tricks? No, the others had probably been built since then, but it made no difference provided they were unlit, and she couldn't see any parked cars. They were so oddly arranged, almost like emergency rations dropped from a plane, spread out as if at random. From here they all looked black, but she approached the first and thought it was brown, the windows were white. A set of antlers splayed under the gable. She stared at the one on the left, it lay closer to the stream, but it wasn't red. This meant nothing, it could have been painted. She walked more slowly, there was a wooden sign hanging on one of the walls, it looked new, and even though she couldn't remember what the cabin had been called before, she was certain now. This was Maja's cabin. It proclaimed itself to be 'Hilton'.

She went round the back. The stream cut into the heather, more deeply than she recalled, but she recognised the boulders they'd sat on and the small path like a pale snake up to the entrance. She'd arrived. She was alone. Nobody knew a thing and the night was long. I'll find that money, she thought, even if I have to claw my way through the floorboards to get it!

She didn't dare use the torch. She examined the windows with the little night vision she had, they looked pretty rotten. Especially the kitchen window. But it was rather high up, she needed something to stand on. She walked round the cabin again, found a small wood store and a chopping block. The block was heavy, almost impossible to move, but it would make a good platform, sturdy and smooth. She got a firm grip of it and tried to roll it. It worked. She took off the daysack and pushed and up-ended the great slab round the corner and over to the kitchen window. Then she fetched the sack, took out the chisel and got up on the block. Just as she was standing there in the autumn darkness with the chisel in her hand and her heart thumping at the sheer notion of the money, almost all her breath was sucked out of her. She hardly recognised herself. This wasn't her cabin, her money. She jumped down, pressed her hands to her chest for a few moments and drew the ice-cold air into her lungs. Johovda was suddenly pointing heavenwards so threateningly, as if to warn her. She could scuttle back home again, with her morality largely intact, apart from the sixty thousand she'd already taken, but then she hadn't been herself, she'd been almost out of control, so that could be forgiven. This was quite different. This was pure theft, exploitation of Maja's death. The thumping gradually subsided. She stepped up again. A little hesitantly she pushed the chisel into a gap between the window and the frame. The wood was as soft as putty, the chisel dug in deeply. When she let go, it remained there. She jumped down, found the hammer and carefully tapped the big chisel even further in. Then she let the hammer fall and levered the chisel to the side. The whole lot gave. She heard splintering wood, and the catch on the inside snap with a small bang. The window jumped out ten or fifteen centimetres and hung loosely on its top hinges. Eva looked about, picked up the daysack and opened the window fully. It was blacked out with a thick curtain. She shoved the sack through and dropped the tools in after it. She pushed her head in, stretched her arms across and tried to haul herself after. The chopping block could have done with being a bit higher, she'd have to do a little hop. The window was very narrow. She bent her knees slightly and gave a jump, lay across the opening with her head and arms inside and her legs outside. The window scraped at her back. The kitchen was in total darkness, but she could feel the work surface beneath her hands, so she wriggled carefully across the edge, hooked her foot round the window frame and slid to the floor. She brought pots and pans clattering and crashing down from every direction, and her chin banged on the floor. For an instant she lay there floundering, partially tangled up in a rug. Then she sat up and gasped for breath. She was inside.

All the windows were thoroughly blacked out. There was no chance that light could seep out. She switched on her torch.

It sent a bright white beam straight into the fireplace. She moved to the middle of the floor and tried to get her bearings. The sofa was covered with a checked travelling rug, Maja had once sat there relating all her adventures, and there'd been many of them. Even though they were no more than thirteen at the time. And they'd gawped at her, with a mixture of trepidation and awe. Some had lowered their eyes. Ina pursed her lips and didn't want to hear more, she was a committed Christian.

A troll with a warty nose and a spruce tree in its hand stood in the fireplace. A witch doll was hanging from the ceiling; it glowered down at her with shiny button eyes. She saw the dining table, a small corner cabinet high up on the wall, a dresser displaying cups and plates. A chest of drawers, probably containing mittens and woolly hats. Two diminutive bedrooms, with their doors open. The little kitchen with drawers and cupboards. The iron ring in the floor and the trapdoor she'd have to open to get into the cellar. An excellent hiding place, dark and cold. Or the shed with all its tools, and the outside loo which had been incorporated into the cabin. They just had to pass through the lobby first, they'd gone in twos, petrified and hysterical because Maja had been reading them some blood-curdling real-life murders. They went with shoulders hunched and the paraffin lamp quivering. And there was the gas stove. 'Now, don't go blowing the hut to bits!' were her father's parting words as he went back to his van. There were two large bookshelves above the sofa, lots of paperbacks and some cartoon series. Maja had brought several issues of *Cocktail* with her, she remembered, they read aloud to each other, but only after Ina had gone to bed.

Eva felt cold. There was no point just sitting there in a daze, she had to make a plan. Try to put herself in Maja's place, work out what had gone through her mind as she'd stood there with her money in her hands and wanted to make sure no one would find it. She had lots of imagination and could have come up with something quite improbable. Eva immediately thought of the earth closet. That the cache was submerged in the night soil. Or, good God . . . could it be buried outside amongst the heather? She got up, trying to hold the panic at bay. Time was limited, she had to get away before it was light. Elimination, she thought, forget about the places where the money certainly *wasn't*. The obvious places. Like the desk, the corner cupboard and the chest of drawers. Search systematically and calmly, she imagined it might be in plastic bags or envelopes secured by rubber bands, protected from the damp. The first bedroom contained a chest of drawers. She rejected that too, and concentrated on the more unusual possibilities. First the cellar, it was the least pleasant place, after all. She got hold of the iron ring and raised the trapdoor. A black hole yawned at her, and an icy draught arose from the darkness. Perhaps there were rats down there. The trapdoor could be hooked open and she climbed down with the torch in her hand. It was impossible to stand upright, so she crouched on her haunches and directed her light at the shelves, at jam jars and pickled cucumbers, red and white wine, port, sherry and more jam jars. A cake tin with pictures of Snow White and Cinderella. She shook it and heard the small cakes inside leap and dance with fear. Frozen potatoes with long chits, cans, which she lifted – they were heavy and intact. Some bottles of beer and more of wine. Maja never managed to empty her cabin for the winter. The beam of light played over the uneven stone floor; there was the smell of rot and decay, but otherwise it was completely bare. Finally, she seated herself on the bottom step and shone her torch right over the tiny room once more, slowly and carefully. No cartons or crates by the stone walls and no cavities in them. Was it possible to roll notes up and push them into empty wine bottles? No, for goodness' sake, she rose and climbed back up again, replaced the trapdoor carefully and began opening the kitchen cabinets. The ones that contained crockery and glass she closed again immediately, but cupboards with saucepans were examined more thoroughly, she lifted them off one another, looked into them, shone her torch into the back of the compartment. Nothing. She peered into the oven, moved into the living room and looked under the sofa. Inside the books on the shelves perhaps, it would be a bit of a job if she had to open each one individually, but obviously she hadn't put the money there either, but it might be in the fireplace, perhaps a little way up the chimney. She put one foot into the grate and pointed the torch upwards. Nothing. Then she thought of the settle bed by the dining table. They usually contained storage space, and this turned out to be the case here, too. Inside were slippers and old ski boots, thick sweaters, an aged anorak and a couple of rugs. And then she caught sight of an old radio, and had the idea that maybe Maja had opened it, taken the insides out and hidden the money there, but she doubted that Maja had the technical ability for such an operation.

The bread bin, she thought suddenly, on the kitchen work surface. Or the tureen on top of the corner cupboard. Inside the wall clock perhaps? What about the old rucksack hanging on a nail – that's where it is, she thought, and pulled it down. Empty. Eva illuminated her watch, which showed almost one o'clock. Then she went into the bedrooms, removed the bedclothes and mattresses, took a quick look through the chests of drawers anyway and two narrow wardrobes which contained windcheaters and down jackets. An old salt tub was full of scarves and thick woollen socks. Back to the kitchen again where she opened all the small china jars, which were filled with exactly what their labels proclaimed: salt, flour, pearl barley and coffee. Out to the lobby where she fumbled behind a small curtain beneath a bench, but found nothing other than a washing basket, a brush and a sticky bottle of disinfectant.

There remained the extension. The workshop, the tool shed, the earth closet. The door creaked ominously as she opened it, and the room was windowless. The floor sagged slightly. Eva could hear her starchy windcheater crackling in the silence. A large workbench stretched along the room. There was a tool-board on the wall, and someone had drawn round each individual item with a pencil, so that it was easy to replace after use. Another chopping block. Old garden furniture, an old mouse-nibbled foam rubber mattress, skis and ski poles. Snow shovel. She didn't know where to begin. Unless to try the earth closet first and shine the torch down there. She crossed to it and opened the door. The toilet was tiny, but it had two seats, and it was a long way to the soil beneath. Both holes were covered with squares of polystyrene and there wasn't much of a smell inside, it probably hadn't been used for a long time, and it was cold. A picture of Crown Prince Haakon wearing a blue v-necked jumper graced the wall. His teeth shone chalky white in the darkness. Did he realise, she wondered, that people hung his picture in their loos? There was a piece of rug on the floor. Eva pushed off one polystyrene square and bent over. She tried to hold her breath as she looked round the underside in case it was taped in position. She could see nothing. She removed the other square and shone her torch there too, the dark mass down below was indistinct, but she could make out individual bits of white paper. She imagined how millions might lie at the bottom of that heap, in a metal box, for example. That would have been a job.

She stood up again and breathed out. Perhaps she should prod the mass with a ski pole or something, there were several pairs by the workbench. Some really old ones with tattered rings, others of fibreglass with little white plastic discs on the bottom. Then all at once she felt silly, realised that of course the money wasn't buried in the ordure, there were limits. For a moment she stood indecisively looking about. An old, flecked plastic bucket stood beneath the workbench with a couple of bottles of turpentine – and a tin of paint. It was a large tin, maybe ten litres. She stole over to it, crouched down and read: Protective Wood Stain,

Mahogany. Shook it and heard something flop about inside the tin. She put her nails under the lid and tried to prise it off, but it wouldn't budge. She found a screwdriver on the board above the workbench, forced it under the rim and eased it up. The tin was full of flat packets. Packets covered with aluminium foil, they resembled ordinary packets of sandwiches. She gasped and stuck the torch under her chin, picked up one of the packets and began to tear off the foil. A wad of notes. She'd found it!

Eva sat down on her backside with a thump. She clutched the packet tightly. Maja's idea had been exactly the same as hers, to hide the money in an empty paint tin! She buried her head in her hands for a moment, overwhelmed by it all, money that no one knew about, that no one owned, a staggering sum was now lying in her lap. An enormous life insurance. She pulled out the remainder of the packets, there were eleven in all. They were fat, roughly the thickness of four or five slices of bread, she imagined, and she laid them one on top of the other on the floor, it was a real pile by the time she'd finished. She no longer felt cold. Her blood was singing in her veins, she was panting as if she'd been on a long run, she could almost fancy her brow was beaded in sweat. She fumbled with the zips in her jacket so that she could stuff her treasure in the pockets, with which it was well supplied. Two packets in each jacket pocket and the rest in her trouser pockets, that might do. But she had to do the zips up properly afterwards, she couldn't risk them falling out on the way back. She'd made up her mind to run back to the car, somehow she just had to get rid of all this unaccustomed energy that was coursing through her body. A run, a wild run through the heather, that was what she needed now. She stood up. She'd risen to gain better access to her pockets, but just at that moment she heard a sound. It was a familiar sound, a sound she heard every single day and so recognised instantly, but now her heart stopped with a nasty jolt and stood still for a long moment. It was a car.

It came purring towards the cabin, she heard it change down and the sound of brittle, frozen heather beating against the bumper. Its bright headlights penetrated the split timber of the walls in places, she stood as if turned to stone with the packets of money in her hands, not a thought in her head. Her mind was absolutely empty, all she felt was blind panic, and then her body took over, it acted, and her thoughts followed it, she watched almost in amazement as she shoved the packets back into the paint tin, pressed down the lid, tiptoed across the floor, which creaked a little, but the car's engine was still running. She opened the loo door, pushed away one polystyrene square and dropped the tin down the hole. Then she switched off the torch.

A car door slammed. She heard rapid steps and shortly after the jangling of keys in the lock. It was the middle of the night and someone was letting themselves into Maja's cabin! It couldn't be anyone with honest intentions, she thought, and heard the screeching of rusty hinges, now someone was tramping into the little covered entrance. In a few moments the person out there would discover the open window. The entire cabin would be searched. Eva wasn't thinking any more, she stood as if on a burning ship, and now she chose the foaming ice-cold sea. Resolutely, she put one leg into the toilet. She steadied herself on the frame, realised that she couldn't get her other leg in because the hole wasn't big enough, lifted her leg out again, and instead stuck both her legs in at the same time, allowing herself to sink into the dark space. Her feet kicked wildly as she waited to touch bottom, and at last she felt it, a sort of soft mass into which she sank. The footsteps up above were entering the cabin as she grabbed the torch and threw it down at her feet. Then she hunkered down, strained a little to get her shoulders through and scrabbled in the dark for the square to cover the hole with, balanced it on her fingertips and manoeuvred it carefully into place above her head. Then she was left in total blackness, not a gleam of light anywhere, and she sank down a bit further, gave up trying to crouch and seated herself properly. She sank a bit more. She rested her forehead on her knees. There hadn't been much smell when she'd first gone into the toilet and looked down, now the stink began to worsen as her body heat warmed up the contents. She sat there breathing as carefully as she could with her nose stuck between her knees, the torch had rolled to the side and was out of reach. The tin with the two million in it was between her legs. A door slammed in the cabin, and now she heard violent curses. It was a man and he was livid.

Chapter 25

She had to breathe through her mouth. She didn't open her nasal passages even for an instant. Eva was afraid she might faint. She tried to listen to what he was doing, he was certainly searching for something. He didn't bother to keep quiet, maybe he'd even switched the light on, she thought, and suddenly remembered her daysack which she'd left on the living room floor. The thought of it almost made her sick. Could he have seen the light of her torch? She didn't think so. But the daysack on the floor – would he realise that she was still here? Would he search the cabin from top to bottom? Perhaps that was what he was doing right now, and at any moment he might come tramping into the extension and tear open the door of the earth closet. But would he remove the lid and look down? She forced her nose into her kneecaps and breathed carefully through her mouth. There would be silence in the cabin for a while, and then the racket would break out afresh. After some minutes she heard his footsteps approaching, they were in the lobby again, she heard something topple and crash, and more swearing. Then he came into the workshop. Silence fell again.

She imagined him standing staring at the door of the loo now, and thinking as everyone else would have done, that perhaps someone was hiding inside. There were more footsteps, Eva ducked and waited, heard a great creak as he opened the door. The world stood still for several seconds, she was just one quivering mass of terror, hot blood pumping through her body, but then everything stopped completely, breathing, heart and blood which had become viscous as oil. Perhaps he was only a metre away, perhaps he could hear her breathing, so she stopped, until her lungs began to feel as if they were bursting. Each second was an eternity. Then she heard footsteps again, he'd retreated and was clattering about with something near the workbench. Suddenly it struck Eva that he might need to use the toilet, if he went on searching for long enough he might need to relieve himself, and then he'd come in again, remove one of the pieces of polystyrene and pee into the hole. He'd either get her feet, if he chose the hole next to the outer wall, but if he used the other one, he'd pee on her head. And if he switched on the light he'd see that there was someone sitting down there with a paint tin between her legs. She had no idea who he was. Maja hadn't told the truth, there was something she'd left out, and it was Maja who'd got her into this crazy situation, just as she'd done a thousand times before, and Maja who'd provided the opportunity for her to get hold of some money, tons of money, even though she'd never wanted it, only enough for food and bills. She didn't need any more. She'd willingly have given him the lot, or perhaps they could go halves, she thought, why did he have any more right to it than she did, it was the money of a child-hood friend and they had shared everything. She'd been named by Maja as her beneficiary.

The man was now tearing through drawers of tools and rubbish, he sounded violent, agitated; judging by the noise the cabin would look like a battlefield before he'd finished. She wondered if he'd decide to spend the night there, perhaps bed down in one of the bunks beneath a thick winter duvet, while she sat here on this pile of faeces with numb feet. She might get frostbite; if she had to sit here till the morning she'd die of cold and despair and the stink, but perhaps he was a common thief like herself and had to get away before daylight. That was what she hoped. She hoped and prayed, while he stamped about the cabin searching continuously. She felt herself becoming drowsy, realised that she mustn't sleep, but she kept slipping away, the smell wasn't so obvious then, or perhaps she was completely anaesthetised. It would have been lovely to sleep a while, it struck her that it might be difficult to get out again, it would be impossible to get a firm footing in the boggy morass she was sitting in, perhaps she'd be left down here on her own to die with two million in her lap. Maybe she ought to call for help, get out and take her clothes off and simply share the money with the bastard who was in there rummaging about not knowing where to look. She thought about this as she became vaguely conscious that it had gone quiet at last, as if he really had turned in, possibly on the sofa under the checked rug. Possibly he'd been down to the cellar and found a bottle of red wine which he'd warmed on the gas stove and added sugar; hot, sweet red wine, the fringed woollen rug and a little fire in the grate. She flexed her fingers and discovered they were stiff. Slowly she seemed to shut down, against the cold and the smell, closed her eyes and her mind, leaving only one small corner of consciousness open in case he came in again to pee, or to search more thoroughly, but the corner became smaller, she receded inwards and downwards in the dark, and a last thought flew quickly through her mind: how on earth had she ended up here?

There was a loud bang.

Eva started. She flung out her arms in a pure reflex action and thumped her elbow on the semi-rotten woodwork. Perhaps he'd heard it. The walls were thin and everything was quiet. She realised it had been the door slamming, he was outside the cabin now, just by the wall of the earth closet. He took three or four paces then halted. Eva waited and listened, trying to guess what he was doing, she was as stiff as a post and couldn't move her arms or legs. Then he coughed and immediately afterwards came the well-known sound of a strong stream of urine hitting the frozen ground. Typical bloke, she thought, they were lazy, couldn't even be bothered to go to the loo, but just poked the manservant out of the door, and it was presumably this that had saved her from being discovered. She almost laughed aloud with relief. The peeing went on and on, he must have been holding himself in a long time, and perhaps he'd had a beer, perhaps he was finished now and would be leaving. Strange that he hadn't checked down the toilet but he probably hadn't the imagination for that, she thought. She, who would have prodded the night soil with a ski stick if she hadn't found the paint tin. Hope began to dawn that everything might soon be over now, and with hope returned the cold and stiffness, as well as the stench, which was unbearable by this time.

He went inside again. What's the time, how long have I been in this torpor? she thought, and struggled to breathe calmly. Again there was a variety of sounds, doors, drawers and pacing to and fro. Perhaps it was fully day and quite light, he might have pulled down the blackout curtains and now wished to search again.

Then he'd revisit the extension, and look down into the night soil too, the thought would suddenly strike him like lightning, just as it had her. She tried to imagine what he'd feel when he saw her head and realised she'd been sitting there all the time, disbelief and fury, or if he were an innocent man on a lawful mission simply fear and alarm. But she didn't give that any credence. She heard the door again and the key in the lock. She could hardly believe that he might be leaving. She didn't move a muscle, but the footsteps through the heather really were receding, and at last the sound she'd been longing for most of all, it was almost too good to be true. The sound of a car door slamming. Eva began to tremble violently. The engine started with a roar and she sobbed with relief, it revved for a good while, and still she didn't budge, just waited while the car manoeuvred, perhaps he was turning around. She heard twigs scratching against metal and the engine slowing for a moment. Then he gathered speed. He was safely out on the road now, he changed up and drove off, and the engine faded slowly away, until at last, at long last, it could be heard no more.

A great peace filled her body.

She placed her hands on the tin and exhaled, sniffed a bit and tried to extend her legs. They were as crooked as ancient tree roots and she had no feeling in her feet at all. She pushed the polystyrene cover off with one hand. It was as dark as before, as if it were still the middle of the night. The torch, she thought suddenly, what's happened to the torch? She clenched her fists and steeled herself, then began unwillingly to scrabble about in the muck searching for it, between her legs, out in the corners, it wasn't a large area, she must find it. She fumbled behind her back and felt the ice-cold metal against her hand. Perhaps it was broken. She found the switch. It was working. With a sigh of relief she looked at her watch. It was half past three. It would be dark for a long time yet, she had plenty of time. She stuck the torch through the hole and laid it on the top of the toilet, then she took hold of the seat and tried to lift herself up. Her back ached and her legs would hardly support her, but she got her head through, squeezed her shoulders out, and suddenly it was as if she was being suffocated and couldn't get out fast enough. She floundered and gasped and wriggled her way up, kicking as hard as she could at the soft heap beneath her, twisting herself through the hole, lay across the toilet, wrenched her legs after her and knocked the torch which fell on the floor. She stared down at the striped rug which was now illuminated, and pulled her feet through. She placed a foot to the floor. It was like being paralysed. But she was standing on her own feet, she bent once again, aimed the torch down for the very last time and reached for the handle of the tin. She had fought for this. Now the money was hers. She left the extension and entered the cabin. It was completely wrecked. Everything had been emptied and strewn about. She shone her torch round, he hadn't removed the blackout curtains. Everything was dark, but the air was strangely fresh and soothing, she'd almost forgotten what ordinary air was, it was like inhaling cool mineral water through her nose. Unsteadily she tottered over to an armchair and threw herself into it. Her clothes had stiffened on her body. Everything would have to be thrown away, every stitch she had on. Perhaps she ought to cut her hair, too, maybe she'd never get the smell out of it. It was a long way to drive home covered in filth from top to toe, but possibly there were clothes in the cabin she could change into. She struggled up again and went into one of the bedrooms. Holding the torch she pulled out garment after garment from the chest of drawers, she found underwear, socks, an old undershirt and a knitted jumper, but trousers were more difficult. She came out again, remembered the small entry where the outdoor clothes were kept, and was in luck. She found an old down snowsuit hanging there, it was lovely and soft, but possibly a bit on the small side. It would be like trying to get into a sausage skin. But it was clean. In comparison with what she had on now, it was clean. The scent of ski wax and firewood clung to it. She put the clothes on the floor and began to undress. Her hands were the worst, she tried to keep them away from her face, she couldn't bear to smell them. Maybe she could slosh some disinfectant over them and dry them with a towel. She began to shiver with cold again, but at the same time she was in high spirits. She kept looking across at the tin, a flecked paint tin, it looked so innocent, who would have thought it contained a fortune, apart from her. But she, of course, was a person of imagination. An artist.

Finally, she found a pair of ski boots inside the settle bed and struggled with the laces. Her hands had begun to thaw, but they worked slowly. She pushed her filthy clothes into the daysack, which he'd chucked into a corner. She put the sack on her back, held the torch in one hand, the paint tin in the other. No need to struggle with the little kitchen window, after everything that had happened. The front door was locked from the outside. She went into the bedroom again, tore down the blackout curtain and opened the window wide. She took a deep breath of mountain air and stepped up on to the sill. Then she jumped out.

Chapter 26

The man drove a dark blue Saab. His face had an evil expression just then, fury and frustration gleamed in his eyes. The money had gone. Someone had got there before him, but he couldn't understand who. The car bounced and shook on the gravel road and he cursed again. He had the lake on his left, it was dead calm, most of the cabins were dark now. He felt cheated. Something had happened that he couldn't fathom, and he searched his memory for anything that might explain this catastrophe, the barely credible fact that someone had broken into the cabin and stolen the money. His money. Obviously, that was what had happened. Nothing else was missing, the binoculars, the camera, the television and the radio were all there. Even the wine in the cellar was untouched. He banged his fist on the steering wheel and braked a little on the bend. He turned to the left on a sudden whim. He'd caught sight of a narrow, potholed track that ran down to the lake, down to a small shed-like cabin. The cabin was clearly unoccupied and didn't look as if it had been inhabited for a long time. He drove his car right down to the shore and left the engine running. He had to calm down. He took his cigarettes out of his inner pocket and lit one, as he stared pensively out across the great shining expanse of water. His face was narrow, his eyes close together, his hair and brows dark. He was quite a good-looking man, but his demeanour ruined it, he had a forbidding, injured expression, and when occasionally he did smile, it wasn't convincing. He wasn't smiling now. He smoked eagerly, became irritated by the purring of the engine in the silence and turned it off. He opened the door and took a few steps towards the water the better to observe the impressive landscape. It was very dark when the headlights went out, but gradually the mountains loomed up in the blackness, like huge primeval beasts lying sleeping round a waterhole. He felt an irrepressible urge to growl loudly in the gloom, perhaps they'd wake up and growl back. Just at that moment he caught sight of the car. An old Ascona. It was parked at the back of the cabin, a somewhat run-down car, all on its own. That was strange. Could there be people in the cabin after all? He crept over to it, suddenly unsure if he were alone, and tried to see in through the side window of the car. The door was unlocked, that was even stranger. The car was empty, there was nothing on the seats or dashboard. He straightened up again and looked around. An odd thought struck him, it made him return to his own car and get in. He sat there pondering as he smoked his cigarette. When he'd smoked it to the filter, he crushed it out in the ashtray and lit a new one.

Suddenly Eva realised how tired she was. She could hardly lift her legs and kept tripping over heather and tussocks. The tin weighed a ton in her weary hand, but there were no pockets in the down snowsuit, and she didn't want to put the money in with her dirty clothes in the daysack. It might get tainted with the smell, you could never tell. Now she was out on the road the walking was easier. She went as fast as she could, but her legs didn't seem to be able to keep up with her. She felt her heels come down, but not the push from the flat of her foot, that part was numb. The plateau lay before her completely deserted; she looked for the cabin that had had the light in it, but it was dark now. The thought of the long car journey ahead almost demoralised her, but if she'd got this far, she'd manage to get home again as well, and maybe she'd find an open service station along the way. Somewhere they sold sausages and hamburgers, Coke and chocolate, or perhaps those Danish pastries in packets of two. And hot coffee. She was terribly hungry. Now that she'd begun to think about food she couldn't stop. Even if she did find somewhere, it was hard to know what people might think if she was to enter the place stinking to high heaven. Presumably the smell was stronger than she realised herself, she'd simply become accustomed to it. And now she could make out the little road down to the lake, she moved the tin over to her left hand and held the torch in her right. Everything seemed empty and deserted, but she wouldn't switch it on until she was down by the car and ready to go. The less visible she was the better. Never before had she longed for her own car and a cigarette so much. She'd refrained from smoking, didn't want to leave butts around. She sniffed a little out of pure emotion at all the things that had happened and increased her speed.

She had only a few metres to go when something brought her up short. A tremendous roar split the silence and suddenly she found herself bathed in a flood of halogen light. She stood paralysed with her tin and torch and for a moment she couldn't move her feet. Then she recognised the light and sound as a car starting up right in front of her, and she ran out of the beam, out into the heather and tussocks of grass. She ran for her life, clutching the paint tin tightly. She could still hear the engine, and as long as she heard it she would continue running, if it stopped she'd have to get down. But she didn't get that far. All at once she tripped and fell forward, full length on to her stomach, she twisted one foot and felt twigs and straws scratching at her face. She lay quite still. The engine died too, and a car door opened. She understood now. He'd found her car, he'd sat there waiting for her. It's all over, she thought. Perhaps he had a gun. Perhaps a bullet in the back of the head would be the last episode in her life. Money didn't mean that much, she marvelled suddenly at all the exertions she'd undergone just for money. It was really quite amazing. The only things that really mattered were Emma, and her father. That you had a bit of bread, and a bit of light and warmth. She thought all this as she heard his movements through the heather, but she couldn't tell if he was getting closer, or going in the wrong direction.

She rested her head on one arm and just wanted to sleep, the money wasn't to be hers after all, that was why it had all gone wrong, and she didn't give a damn about money. But then she pulled herself together again, she thought of Emma, how she had to get away from this man who was tearing through the heather. She began to crawl on her stomach, sliding cautiously away in the smooth down suit. She could still hear his footsteps and, as long as he was moving, he couldn't hear her. She crawled a little way then stopped, crawled and stopped, and kept on like this. He was still some distance away, the plateau was large and he had no torch with him. Talk about being ill-prepared, she thought, as she struggled to drag the tin along without making too much noise. Then she heard his car start up again, and saw the headlights sweeping across the landscape. She ducked and flattened herself as much as she could. It was lucky that her hair was dark and the suit was navy blue, but the tin was almost white. She had to cover it with her body or it would be visible as a bright spot. It was ridiculous of her to have lugged this big tin along, he'd certainly have seen it. Soon he'd come crashing through the heather in his car and catch her in his headlights. Perhaps he'd just run her down, run over her with all four wheels, and nobody would be able to work out what had happened. Why she was lying there; killed by a car high up in the mountains, in an undersized down snowsuit. Smelling of sewage. No one would ever know. And maybe, she thought, maybe Maja's killer would go free.

The man shook his head and accelerated. He was certain he'd seen something in the darkness, something white which seemed to fly through the air. He scanned the sides of the road as he drove slowly up it, but the headlights left the mountain landscape around him in complete darkness. It must have been something he'd imagined. A sheep perhaps. They probably weren't grazing up here any more, but perhaps there were birds up here, and foxes and hares. There were lots of explanations. It had taken him a little by surprise as he'd just bent forward to stub out his cigarette. But it was odd about the car. Unless there'd been someone staying in that small cabin after all. He hadn't got time to think about it any more. There were many things that had to be cleared up. He was going to get the money. It was his now, and no one should think otherwise. He accelerated and turned on to the road. There he changed up into third and shortly afterwards passed the tourist hostel on the left. Then his lights vanished round a bend.

Chapter 27

The blobs of foam were like the mountains of Hardanger and the water was boiling hot. Eva dipped one foot in cautiously, it was almost scalded, but the bath couldn't be hot enough. She would have liked the water inside her body too, inside her veins. On the edge of the tub was a large glass of red wine. She'd thrown the daysack into the rubbish bin and unplugged the phone. Now, she sank into the water which had turned a pale turquoise colour from the bath salts. Heaven couldn't be better than this. As they thawed, she stretched her fingers and toes. She took a sip of wine and felt the pain in her foot recede a little. Driving had been a nightmare, as her ankle had swollen considerably. She pinched her nose and submerged completely for a moment. When she surfaced again she had a large dot of foam on the top of her head. That's the picture of a millionaire, she thought with surprise, as she looked at her reflection in the mirror above the bath. The soft blob began to teeter sideways, then slide down to hang beneath her ear. She settled in the water again and did some mental arithmetic. She tried to work out how long the money would last if she used two hundred thousand per year. Well, it would be around ten years. If there really *was* two million there, she hadn't counted it yet, but she would once she'd bathed and cleaned up and had some food. The only thing she'd found on the way home was a sweet dispenser that contained nothing but raspberry drops and throat lozenges. She closed her eyes and heard how the foam rustled in her ear as it disintegrated. Her skin was beginning to accustom itself to the temperature; afterwards she'd be wrinkled and pink from the hot soapy water, like a baby. It had been a long time since she'd taken a bath. She usually made do with a quick shower, and she'd forgotten just how good it was. Emma was the one who always liked a bath.

She reached out for her wine glass and took several large sips. Afterwards, when she'd bathed and counted the money, she would sleep, perhaps right through until it was evening again. The tiredness lay across her eyes like a lump of lead. Now it pulled her head forward until her chin rested on her chest. The last thing she knew was the taste of soap in her mouth.

It was nine o'clock on the morning of 3 October. Eva slept on in the cold bath water. She was in the middle of a disturbing dream. As she squirmed in the water to escape it, she slipped forward a little in the bath. Her face submerged. She gasped and inhaled soapy water, coughed and spluttered, attempted to sit up, but the sides of the ceramic tub were slippery; she slid down again, spat and dribbled until the tears flowed, before she finally managed to get herself into a sitting position. She was cold again. Then she heard the doorbell.

Alarmed, she got up and stepped out of the bath. She'd forgotten her injured foot and yelped, staggered a bit because she'd risen so quickly and reached for her dressing gown. Her watch was on the shelf under the mirror, she looked at it quickly and wondered who it could possibly be at this time of day. It was too early for salesmen and beggars, her father didn't go out and Emma hadn't given notice of her arrival. The police! she thought, and tied the belt of the dressing gown. She hadn't prepared herself, hadn't had time to think about what she'd say if he actually came again, and now he was here, she was quite certain it was him. That inspector with the searching glance. Of course, she didn't have to open the door. She was the mistress of her own house, she was in the middle of a bath and it was an ungodly hour to come asking questions. She only had to remain in the bathroom until he went. He would think she hadn't got up yet, or perhaps that she'd gone away. Except that the car was outside, but she might have taken the bus, as she sometimes did when she had no money for petrol. What did he want now? At least he knew nothing about Maja's money, unless she'd left a will which he'd found, perhaps that was precisely what she had done, left all her money to the Women's Refuge! The thought made her reel. Of course she could. She hadn't put her money in a safe-deposit box, she had put her will in there instead, a small red book containing the truth about her life. The doorbell rang again. Eva came to a swift decision. There was little point in hiding in the bathroom, he wasn't going to give up. She made a turban out of her towel, went out into the hall in her bare feet, limping and gasping at each step.

'Mrs Magnus,' he said smiling, 'I'm disturbing you in the middle of your bath, it's unforgivable of me. I should have come later.'

'I've finished anyway,' she answered tersely, standing on the doorstep. He was wearing a leather jacket and jeans and looked like a normal man, not like the enemy at all, she thought. The man by the lake was the enemy, whoever he might be. Perhaps he'd taken the number of her car. She almost had a fit at the thought of it. If so, it wouldn't be long before he turned up at her door. She hadn't considered that. A deep furrow appeared in her brow.

'May I come in for a moment?'

She said nothing, just backed against the wall and

nodded. In the living room she nodded again at the sofa; she just stood there, stood there like a wall of resistance, he thought, as he seated himself with a studied calm on her black sofa. His trained eye made an almost imperceptible sweep of the black and white room, he noted the bag of raspberry drops on the table, the car keys, her handbag, open, a packet of cigarettes.

'Hurt your foot?' he asked abruptly.

'Only twisted it a bit. Was there anything in particular?' Reluctantly she sat down in the chair facing him.

'Just a few things. I'd like to go through the statement you made last time, from start to finish. There are some details I need more information about.'

Eva was nervous. She fumbled for a cigarette straight away and wondered suddenly if she could refuse to answer. She wasn't suspected of anything after all. Or was she? 'Tell me,' she said in a cocky tone, 'am I actually obliged to make a statement about this?'

Sejer stared open-mouthed. 'No,' he said in surprise, 'certainly not!' His eyes, grey in reality, took on an innocent blue tint. 'But does that mean you've got something against making one? I thought, as she was your friend, that you'd be only too willing. So that we can find the perpetrator. But if you've got objections . . .'

'No, no, I didn't mean it like that.' She recoiled quickly, regretting her question.

'The first of October,' he went on, 'Thursday. Let's begin at the beginning. You took a taxi to Tordenskioldsgate. The taxi got here at 6 p.m.?'

'Yes, as I said.'

'From what you told me, you spent roughly an hour at Ms Durban's flat.'

'Yes, I must have done. Not much longer anyway.' How long had it really been, she thought – two hours?

He'd opened a notebook and was reading from it. It was horrible. Everything she'd said was written down, now he could use it against her. 'Can you tell me what you did during that hour? In as much detail as you can?'

'What?' She stared uneasily at him.

'From the time you entered the flat until she closed the door behind you. Absolutely everything that happened. Just begin at the beginning.'

'Well, er, I had a cup of coffee.'

'Did you wash it up afterwards?'

'Uh?' She felt her head begin to spin.

'I ask because there was no used coffee cup found. But there was a glass which had obviously contained Coke.'

'Oh yes! Of course! Coke. I'm getting mixed up. Does that *really* matter?'

He gave her a sharp look. And she fell silent again just like the last time. Eva sat staring and waiting, she knew she was sinking in deeper and deeper, there were so many things she hadn't thought of, far too many.

'Yes, I had a sandwich and a Coke. Maja made me a sandwich.'

'Yes. A tuna sandwich?'

Eva shook her head in wonder. She couldn't keep up any more, maybe he'd been there when it happened, she thought, maybe he'd been hiding in a cupboard and seen everything.

'Can you tell me,' he asked all at once, as he changed position on the sofa, he was looking thoughtful and inquisitive, 'can you tell me why you vomited that sandwich up again?'

Eva felt like passing out. 'Well, I felt ill,' she stammered. 'I'd had a couple of beers, and fish doesn't really agree with me all that much. We'd had such a late night the evening before. And I hadn't eaten much, I'm not that bothered about food, so I hadn't eaten anything, and she absolutely insisted I had it, she thought I was thin.' She stopped and drew breath. What was that about saying as little as possible, why couldn't she remember!

'Was that why you took a shower while you were there? Because you felt ill?'

'Yes!' she replied quickly. Now she was the one who was silent. He saw the beginnings of rebellion in her eyes. Quite soon she would clam up completely.

'You managed to do quite a lot while you were there.

In only one hour. Did you also take a little nap, too, in the guest room?'

'A nap?' she asked wanly.

'Someone had lain on the bed in there. Or is the simple truth, Mrs Magnus, that you were really Durban's partner, and that you shared the flat? Just like her, you had a little sideline in prostitution to ease the finances?'

'NO!' Eva screamed and stood up. Her chair shot back. 'No, I did not! I didn't want anything to do with it. Maja was the one who tried to persuade me, but I wouldn't!' She was shaking like a leaf and her face was chalky white. 'Maja was always trying to persuade me, she had the oddest ideas. Once, when we were thirteen . . .' Then she began to sob.

Somewhat taken aback, he stared at the tabletop and waited. Outbursts like these made him embarrassed. Suddenly she looked so pathetic. Her turban had come undone and had fallen to her shoulders, her hair was wringing wet.

'I'm beginning to wonder,' Eva whispered, 'if you don't think I'm the one who did it.'

'Obviously that's a possibility we've considered,' he said quietly, 'and here I'm not thinking so much about any motive you may have had, or whether you're capable of killing someone and all that. We go into that later on. In the first instance we look at who was in the vicinity, who, in purely physical terms, had the opportunity to commit this murder. Then we look at alibi. And lastly,' he said nodding, 'we consider motive. And in this case the fact is that you were there just a short time before she died. But let me make it quite clear at once – we're certain that Ms Durban's murderer was a man.'

'Yes,' she said.

'Yes?'

'I mean, wasn't it one of her clients?'

'Is that what you believe?'

'Well, I – wasn't it though? That was what the papers said!'

He nodded and leant forward. He smells nice, she thought, like Dad when he was younger.

'Tell me what happened.'

She sat down again, made a terrific effort and approached the truth in tiny increments. She ought to tell him now, what had happened, that evening on the footstool. And he'd ask why on earth she hadn't confessed all this at once. It was because, she thought, she was a fickle person, someone lacking discipline and character, undependable, cowardly, with questionable morals, who didn't stand up for an old friend who'd meant so much, but who'd then taken her money instead, she could hardly believe it was true, it was unbearable.

'We haven't got much money, me and Emma,' she mumbled. 'It's always been like that, ever since Jostein went away. I told Maja about it. She wanted me to solve the problem her way. I was to borrow the spare room. We were at Hannah's and we were drunk. I began to consider her proposition, I was so tired and I couldn't take any more sleepless nights, threats in the mail and disconnected phones. So we arranged that I'd return – and try it. She would help. Show me the ropes.'

'Yes?'

'I was slightly pissed when I arrived, I couldn't face being sober, because then the decision would sort of become concrete, I came as arranged, and I'd decided . . .'

She stopped, because just then it had actually dawned on her, in all its horror. She was a potential prostitute. And now *he* knew it too.

'But then I couldn't go through with it. Maja gave me a Coke and I sobered up as I was sitting there, and my courage evaporated. I thought they might take Emma away if it got out. It made me ill, I ran away from the whole thing. But before that she explained certain things to me.'

'Explained what?'

'Well, how things worked.'

'Did she show you the knife?'

Eva held back for a moment. 'She did show me the knife. She said it was to engender fear and respect. I was lying on the bed. That was when I got frightened,' Eva said quickly. 'That was when I decided to pull out.

I don't know how you managed to find all this out, I don't understand anything.'

'The knife obviously wasn't much help?' he said doubtfully.

'No, she . . .' Eva stopped dead.

'What were you about to say?'

'She probably wasn't tough enough.'

'Your fingerprints were all over the flat,' he went on. 'Even,' he said slowly, 'on the phone. Who did you phone?'

'Fingerprints?' Her fingers curled at the thought of it. Perhaps they'd been in her house while she was up in the mountains, perhaps they'd picked the lock and tiptoed about with those small brushes they used.

'Who did you phone, Eva?'

'No one! But I did consider – phoning Jostein,' she lied.

'Jostein Magnus?'

'Yes, my ex. Emma's father.'

'And why didn't you?'

'Well, I simply changed my mind. He walked out on me, I didn't want to ask him for anything. I got dressed and left. I told Maja that what she was doing could be dangerous, but she only smiled. Maja never listened to anyone.'

'Why didn't you tell me all this the first time I came?'

'I was embarrassed. I really did consider becoming a prostitute, and I couldn't bear the thought of anyone knowing it.'

'I've never, ever, in all my life looked down on women who are prostitutes,' he said simply.

He rose from the sofa as if he were satisfied. She couldn't believe her eyes.

He stood for a short while out on the steps, gazing at the drive, looking at the car and at Emma's bike which was propped against the house. Then his stare moved further out, down the street to the other houses, as if trying to form an opinion about the area she lived in, what sort of person she was to live just here, in this neighbourhood, in this house.

'Did you get the impression that Ms Durban had a lot of money?'

The question came suddenly.

'Oh yes. All her things were expensive. She ate in restaurants and that sort of thing.'

'We're wondering if she might have had a tidy sum stashed away somewhere,' he said, 'and that someone might have known about it.' His gaze struck her like a laser beam right between the eyes and she blinked in terror. 'Her husband arrived by plane from France yesterday, we're hoping he can tell us something when we get him in for questioning.'

'What?' She steadied herself on the door frame.

'Ms Durban's husband,' Sejer repeated. 'You look frightened.'

'I didn't know she had one,' she said lamely.

'No? Didn't she say?' He frowned. 'That's a bit

strange, her not saying anything, if you were old friends?'

If, she thought. If we really were old friends. If I'm telling the truth. She could go on talking till the cows came home, he obviously wouldn't believe her.

'Nothing more to add, Mrs Magnus?'

Eva shook her head. She was petrified. The man who'd arrived at the cabin could have been Maja's husband. Searching for his inheritance. Perhaps, perhaps one day he'd turn up on her doorstep. Maybe during the night when she was asleep. Maja could have told him that they'd met. If she'd had time. She might have phoned. International call to France. Sejer went down the four wrought-iron steps and halted on the gravel.

'You should put an ankle like that in hot water. Make sure you wrap a bandage round it.'

Then he left.

Chapter 28

The money had to be moved out of the house. As the big Peugeot slowly disappeared, she pushed the door shut with a bang and rushed down to the cellar. Her foot was feeling numb again. She prised the lid off the tin with a knife and emptied the packets on to the concrete floor; then she sat and began tearing the foil off them. They were bound with rubber bands. She realised quite quickly that there was a system to the bundles. All the thousand-kroner notes were together, and the hundreds, it was easy to count them. The floor was very cold and she lost sensation in her bottom. On and on she counted, keeping a mental tally of each, laying it aside, and counting the next. Her heart thumped ever louder. Where could she hide such a huge sum? A safe-deposit box was too risky, she had the feeling that they'd be watching her now, watching her every move, Sejer and his people. And Maja's husband.

Maja was married. Why hadn't she said so? Had she felt that a husband, a companion for life, was an impediment? Or was he more a kind of business partner to share the running of the hotel? Or just a bloke she didn't want to acknowledge? The last seemed the most likely.

The paint tin was a wonderful hiding place really, but she had to keep it somewhere else, somewhere no one would think of looking and where she could easily help herself to more when she needed it. At her father's, of course, in his cellar, along with all the old junk he'd accumulated over the years. Eva's childhood bed. The apples which lay rotting in the old potato bin. The defective washing machine. She lost count and had to begin again. Her hands were sweating and this made it easy to separate the crisp notes from one another, soon she had half a million in one big heap and there was masses more. Maja's husband. Maybe he was a really shady character – if Maja had been a prostitute, what might he be? A drug dealer or something similar. Perhaps neither of them had any moral sense. Have *I* got any? she thought suddenly, she was getting close to a million now and she was making inroads into the money. This, she thought, probably represents a good deal of the housekeeping money of hundreds of housewives in this town, money that should have been used for nappies and tins of food. It was an odd thought.

She was on the hundred-kroner notes now, and it took

longer. She thought the five hundreds were the nicest-looking, the colour and the pattern, beautiful blue bills. One point six, her fingers were icy, she was counting fifties. If he'd got her registration number, it would only take minutes for him to find her address, if he phoned the Vehicle Registration Office, if he'd even noticed the car; if he'd had some imagination he'd probably have looked at it and considered the possibility, been surprised that it was standing there unlocked. Up in the mountains, not far from the cabin. But he hadn't had the imagination to search in the earth closet. One point seven million. And a few fifties. Maja had been close to her goal. One point seven million kroner. Pieces of foil lay glinting in the light from the bare bulb in the ceiling. She put the money in the tin again and went up the stairs, the swelling in her foot seemed to have eased, perhaps because of the cellar's coldness. Her dark hair hung like frozen twigs down her neck. She put the tin in the utility room and went back to the bathroom, took a quick hot shower and got dressed.

The millionaire in the mirror was tenser now. She had to get hold of a tarpaulin for the car in case he was sniffing around. Or she could buy a new car. An Audi perhaps? Not one of the biggest ones, perhaps even second-hand. Suddenly she realised it was impossible. She could only buy bread and milk as before. Even Omar would begin to speculate if her shopping basket grew larger. She limped out and fetched the tin.

This would have to do. And anyway, they could move. She got some aluminium foil from a kitchen drawer, wrapped the bundles up neatly and laid them in the tin, all except one. On this she stuck a piece of masking tape, pondered a second and wrote 'Bacon' on it. Then she put it in the freezer. No point in running out straight away. The sixty thousand in the little tin had been considerably depleted. She put on her coat and went out. But first she examined her mailbox, which had entirely escaped her mind. A green envelope lay in it, from the Arts Council. She gave a smile of surprise. Her grant had come.

'You've started going out at night,' smiled her father, 'that's a good sign.'

'How so?'

'I kept ringing you yesterday, right through till eleven o'clock.'

'Oh yes, I was out.'

'Have you found someone to keep you warm at last?' he asked expectantly.

I was just about freezing to death, she thought, I was sitting waist-high in excrement half the night.

'Well, yes, sort of. I'm not saying any more.'

She played secretive, hugged him and went inside. The paint tin was in the car boot, she'd fetch it later and smuggle it down to the cellar.

'Was there something in particular?'

'My fire alarm was wailing and I couldn't switch it off.'

'Ah,' she said quickly, 'so what did you do?'

'I rang the fire station and they came at once. Nice people. Sit down now, how long can you stay, can you stay a while? By the way, how long's Emma going to be at Jostein's, you're not thinking of giving her up?'

'Don't be so silly, I'd never even entertain the idea. I can certainly stay for a bit, I could make us dinner.'

'I don't think I've got anything in.'

'Then I'll go out and buy something.'

'No, you haven't got the money to feed me, I'll have a bowl of porridge.'

'What about fillet steak?' she asked with a smile.

'I don't like you saying silly things,' he said crossly.

'My grant came today, and I've got nobody else to celebrate with.'

At that he gave way. Eva began to potter about the house, and his mind gradually became tranquil. It was the sounds he missed most of all, the sounds of another human being who breathed and padded about, radio and television weren't the same.

'Have you seen the papers?' he growled a little later. 'Some poor girl's been suffocated in her own bed. People who do that sort of thing should be knocked on the head with a club. Poor young thing. Treating a girl like that, when she's offering a service and a bed and everything, never heard the like. I thought her name sounded rather familiar, but I can't place it, did you read about it, Eva? Is it anyone we know?'

'No,' she called from the kitchen.

He frowned. 'Well, that's a mercy anyway. If it had been someone I knew, I'd have tracked the bloke down and knocked him on the head with a club. Only punishment he'll get is a cell with TV and three meals a day. I mean, does anybody even ask if they're sorry?'

'Someone certainly will.' Eva knotted the neck of the rubbish sack and went to the door. She had to be careful now. 'They take that into consideration during sentencing, whether they show signs of remorse or not.'

'Ha! So they simply say sorry for all they're worth and get off lightly.'

'It won't be that easy. They have experts who can tell if you're lying for that sort of thing.' She shuddered at the sound of her own words.

Then she vanished outside, and he heard her banging the lid of the refuse bin. He waited a bit, but she didn't return. There's something up with the girl, he thought, as if she's doing something I'm not supposed to know about, I know her too well to be fooled when she's hiding things, just like that time when Mrs Skollenborg died, she went quite hysterical about it, it wasn't normal, the old woman was almost ninety and none of the children liked her, but then she was a horrible old bag. There was something fishy about it. And now she's doing something in the cellar, what in the name of all that's holy is she doing down there?

He thought as he struggled with a disposable lighter which wouldn't light; he rubbed it hard between his rough hands until the gas pressure had built up sufficiently, and finally he got a light. He'd managed to get a flame out of a supposedly empty lighter up to ten times. You really do learn to economise when you're a pensioner, he reflected.

'What d'you want with your steak?' asked Eva, who'd finally emerged from the cellar holding an ovenproof dish in her hands.

'What are you going to do with that?'

'I found it in the cellar,' she replied rapidly, 'I'll roast vegetables in it.'

'Don't you boil vegetables?'

'Yes, sometimes. Do you like broccoli? Just tender with salt and butter?'

'See if I've got enough wine.'

'You've got plenty. I didn't know you'd got an extra supply in the cellar?'

'That's in case I lose my home help. You never know. The council's trying to save money, this year alone they want to save twenty million.' He took a long drag at his cigarette to indicate that he didn't want any comments.

'When did you start getting interested in food?' he said all at once. 'You normally only eat bread.'

'Well, maybe I'm starting to grow up. No, I don't know, I just felt like it. Porridge and red wine just don't go together.'

'That's pure nonsense. A good, well-salted rye porridge made with pork fat washed down with red wine is a really fine meal.'

'I'm going to Lorentzen's, to their fresh-produce counter. Is there anything else you want?'

'Eternal youth,' he grunted.

Eva frowned. She hated him talking like that.

Without batting an eyelid she asked for half a kilo of fillet steak. The woman behind the counter was sturdy and wore disposable gloves, she reached resolutely for a large piece of meat that was almost the colour of liver. Was that *really* what fillet steak looked like?

'Whole or in slices?' She raised her knife to cut.

'Well, what would be best?'

'Thin slices. Wait till the butter turns brown and then skim them quickly across the pan. Just as if you were running barefoot across newly laid asphalt. Whatever you do, don't fry them.'

'I don't think my father would take to raw meat.'

'Don't ask what he wants, just do as I say.'

She smiled suddenly, and Eva was captivated by this chubby woman in her white nylon coat and becoming little net cap. A symbol of hygiene perhaps, but it looked more like a little crown, she thought, and all the dead meat on the counter was the realm over which she reigned.

She weighed the meat and put the price sticker on, gently, as if bandaging a wound. A hundred and thirty kroner, it was an unbelievable price. She wandered for a while amongst the shelves picking out the odd small item which she dropped in her basket, it was best to put them straight into the fridge without saying a word to her father, otherwise he wouldn't accept them. Cheese, liver pâté, two bags of the best coffee, butter, cream. Biscuits with fillings. And on an impulse she grabbed three pairs of pants from the clothes rack. It was just a case of smuggling them into his chest of drawers and hoping he'd use them. By the checkout she added a box of marzipan and nougat chocolates, two magazines and a carton of cigarettes. The final bill was overwhelming. But it struck her that all old people ought to be able to buy such a basket of groceries, at least once a week, so that they could enjoy themselves a little at the end of their lives. Young people can eat porridge, she thought. She paid, carried the bags out to the car and drove back.

'Why did he do it, d'you think?' said her father, as he chewed the tender meat.

'Do what?'

'Kill her. In her bed and everything.'

'Why are you curious about it?'

'Aren't you?'

Eva waited a moment and chewed slowly, mostly for show, she could have swallowed the meat whole. 'Yes, a bit. But why do you ask?'

'I'm interested in the dark side of human nature. You're an artist, aren't you interested? In the drama of humanity?'

'It was a bit unusual, the world she lived in. I don't know anything about it.'

'She was about your age.'

'Yes, and rather silly. Laying yourself open to that kind of trade isn't particularly clever. She was probably only thinking of one thing: the most money in the shortest possible time. Tax free. They must have started arguing or something.' She filled her father's glass and ladled a spoonful of gravy over his meat.

'It's a sort of threshold they cross,' he said pensively. 'I wonder what it is, what it means. Why some people overstep it, and others could never dream of doing so.'

'Everyone can,' Eva said. 'It's circumstances which dictate. And they don't step over either – they stray over. They don't see it until they're on the other side, and then it's too late.' It is too late, she thought in astonishment. I've stolen a fortune. I really have.

'I socked someone at work once,' her father said all at once, 'because he was malicious. A really rotten character. Afterwards he showed me real respect, as if he acknowledged the fact. I've never forgotten it. It's the only time in my life I've ever hit someone, but just then it was totally necessary. Nothing else in the world could have soothed my fury, I felt that I'd have gone mad if I hadn't given him one, it was as if my brain was seething.' He took a few sips of wine and smacked his lips thoughtfully.

'Aggression is fear,' Eva blurted out suddenly. 'Aggression is always really just self-defence, in one way or another. A method of defending oneself, one's own body, one's own intelligence, one's own honour.'

'There are people who kill merely for gain.'

'Yes, of course, but that's something different again. The woman in the paper certainly wasn't killed for money.'

'In any case, they'll get him soon. One of the residents in the block saw the car. I think it's so funny, the way their cars always give them away. They haven't even got the sense to use their bloody feet when they go off to commit their awful crimes.'

'What did you say?'

'Didn't you see that bit? He hadn't realised it was important. He'd been away until this morning. But he'd seen a car go round the corner at high speed, early in the evening. A white car, not entirely new. Probably a Renault.'

'A what?' Eva dropped her knife on her plate so the gravy splashed.

'A Renault. A special model that's not very common, so they thought it would be easy to find him. These car-registration places are good, it's just a matter of searching for everyone with that type of car and visiting them one by one. And then they have to produce an alibi, and God help the ones who can't. Clever stuff.'

'A Renault?' Eva ceased chewing.

'Yes. Elderly taxi driver, knew about cars. Lucky it wasn't some old woman, they can't tell the difference between a Porsche and a Volkswagen.'

Eva prodded her broccoli and felt her hands shaking. What a nuisance, she thought, talk about a blind alley! 'He could have made a mistake. Think of all the time they'll waste!'

'But they haven't got anything else to go on, have they?' her father said in a surprised voice. 'Why should he make a mistake? He knows about cars, that's what they said on the radio.'

She gulped at her wine and tried to conceal her despair. Could a Renault really resemble an Opel? French cars looked so completely different. Perhaps he was some fool who wanted to seem important. She thought of Elmer and how happy such a ridiculous observation must be making him, he must have heard it, he was probably glued to the radio during the news bulletins and was even now rubbing his hands with relief, it was enough to make you weep.

'D'you want mousse for pudding?' she said abruptly.

'Yes, if I can have coffee as well.'

'You always do!'

'Yes, yes,' he said disconcerted, 'it was only a joke!'

She got up and cleared the table, there was a clatter and clash of plates and cutlery, she'd have to do something about this. It was her fault that he was still free, they could have got him already if she'd told the truth. Now perhaps they'd arrest someone else. She placed a cigar next to her father's glass and rinsed the plates. Afterwards they ate their mousse in silence, it stuck to her father's upper lip like white foam and he licked it off with great relish. He glanced at her now and again, he'd adopted a slightly lower profile. Perhaps, he thought, it was a bad time of the month. When she'd settled him on the sofa, she went to wash up. First she stuffed four hundred-kroner notes into his jam jar and hoped that he didn't know exactly what his financial resources were. Afterwards, they sat next to each other on the sofa, sleepy from the food and wine. Eva had calmed down.

'They'll get him all right,' she said slowly. 'There's always someone who's seen something, who's just a little slow off the mark, but they come forward eventually. Nobody gets away with that sort of thing. The world isn't that unjust. It's difficult to keep quiet as well, perhaps he'll confide in someone when he's drunk or something like that. A man who's capable of killing like that, in anger for example, who's that unstable, he won't be able to control himself for the remainder of his life without giving himself away. And then he'll have to confide in somebody. Who'll go to the police. Or perhaps they'll offer a reward, and then someone or other will rush out and report him, some greedy type.' Her own words stuck in her throat. 'What I mean is, somewhere there's a person who feels responsible for seeing that right prevails. People are just a little slow, that's all. Or they're scared.'

'No, they're cowardly,' mumbled her father sleepily. 'That's the point. People are cowardly, they only think about their own hide, don't want to get mixed up in anything. It's nice you've got such faith in justice, my dear, but it's not much help. To her, I mean. No one can help her any more.'

Eva made no reply, her voice would have broken. She drew on her cigarette.

'Why did you thump that man?' she asked suddenly.

'Who?'

'The man at work, the one you were talking about.'

'I said. Because he was malicious.'

'That's no answer.'

'Why did you go into such hysterics when Mrs Skollenborg died?' he asked.

'I'll tell you about it some other time.'

'On my deathbed?'

'You can ask on your deathbed, and then we'll see.'

Night was coming on. Eva thought about Elmer and wondered what he was doing. Perhaps he was sitting staring at the wall, at the pattern of the wallpaper, at his own hands, as he marvelled at the way they could live their own life like that and act beyond his control. While Maja lay in a refrigerated drawer, without consciousness, without a single thought in her cold head. Eva had no thoughts left either, she poured more wine, and felt them fade away into a mist she could no longer penetrate.

Chapter 29

The morning arrived, misty and breezy, but the mist cleared as they were having breakfast. The radio murmured in the background. Eva listened with half an ear which suddenly pricked up. It was the news. A man had been detained in connection with the killing. A fifty-seven-year-old bus driver with a white Renault. They both listened, ignoring their food.

'Ha!' said her father. 'He's got no alibi.'

Eva felt her heart sinking. The suspect admitted to having bought sex from the victim on several occasions. Not surprising, there were lots of them, they had virtually besieged Maja for two years. She could see his future falling apart now, this innocent bloke, perhaps he had a family. She thought: it's my fault.

'Wasn't it just what I said,' said her father triumphantly, 'they've got him already.'

'It all sounds a bit too simple to me. Just because

he's got that make of car and no alibi. And anyway, there's no law against buying sex. In the old days,' she said raising her voice, 'men weren't men unless they visited a brothel.'

'My goodness,' said her father glancing up.

Eva was sweating.

'Why are you being so negative? Don't they always catch them straight away? This is a small town.'

'They sometimes get it wrong,' Eva retorted. She was struggling with the tough crust of her father's whole-meal loaf as she felt a decision force itself on her. She had to do something.

'There must be loads of men who've paid visits to . . . that woman, and have got white cars, and no alibis.'

She finished eating and got up. Cleared the table. Washed up, pushed her wallet in between two newspapers in the living room and got her coat. She gave her father a quick hug.

'See you again,' she said waving, 'soon.'

'I certainly hope so.'

He pushed back his false teeth, which had a tendency to drop down if he smiled too broadly, and waved after her. As he watched the Ascona lurching up the road, he felt the trembling start as it always did when he'd had company for some time and suddenly was alone again. Soon she was moving at a good speed down towards Hov tunnel. I'll head for Rosenkrantzgate, she thought, to the green house. And find out who he is. She had a shoulder bag in the car, and with her long skirt she could pass for a saleswoman, or the representative of some sect or other. Perhaps she might catch a glimpse or two of his wife or get a word with the boy, if that was his son, she thought. Jehovah's Witnesses, didn't they always wear skirts? And long hair, at least they'd done so when she was a girl. Or was that the Mormons, or were they the same?

She was inside the tunnel now. She glanced quickly at her own unmade-up face in the mirror, but saw it only in short, orange-tinged glimpses, as the lights of the tunnel roof were reflected in her eyes. She hardly knew herself, as she gripped the steering wheel and felt a smouldering beneath her black overcoat. It was something she hadn't felt since those childhood days with Maja, that passion had died along the way, in her difficult marriage, in the piles of unpaid bills and the worries over Emma's weight, in the frustration of not breaking through as an artist. It began somewhere in her chest, but gradually worked its way down to end up in her genitals. The feeling made her come alive, she had the feeling she could stroll into her studio and create a picture of primeval force, stronger than anything she'd ever done before, driven by righteous anger. It excited her. Her pulse rose, and the flaming orange light from the roof of the tunnel kept the fire alight until she was back in the centre of town. There she moved into the right-hand lane and drove to Rosenkrantzgate.

The area round the colourful houses was deserted, it was early in the day. She drove a little past the green house and parked behind a cycle shed on the outskirts of the estate. She walked briskly between the houses, trying to look purposeful and satisfied, as if she carried a joyful message in the large bag slung over her shoulder; she noted the details, like the cycle racks, the small area with its swing and sandbox, the washing lines and the hedge littered with the remnants of yellow flowers. The odd faded plastic toy lay discarded on the tiny patches of garden. She turned towards the green house and went up to the first entrance. She'd recognise the blonde woman again if she saw her, that slender creature with her frivolous body language. Eva looked at the doorbell, she chose the upper button which was labelled Helland, but stood there a moment gathering her courage. She peered at the door with its wired safety glass which she couldn't see through. She couldn't hear anything either, so it gave her quite a start when the door suddenly opened and a man was looking directly at her. It wasn't Elmer. Only two families shared each entrance, so she nodded quickly and stepped aside to let him past. He was looking suspicious. Quickly, she looked at the bells.

'Helland?' she enquired rapidly.

'Yes, that's me.'

'Oh, then it's Einarsson I need!'

He turned to look at her before disappearing in the direction of the garage, and she sneaked in through the door like a thief.

It was a porcelain nameplate, crudely painted to depict a mother, a father and a child, with names under each, Jorun, Egil and Jan Henry. She nodded slowly to herself and stole out again. Egil Einarsson, Rosenkrantzgate 16, she thought – I know who you are and what you've done. And soon you'll know that I know.

She was back at home again, and in deep concentration. All other tasks had been laid aside, all scruples burst like tiny bubbles as they reached the surface of her consciousness, all fear had turned in her and become energy. In her mind she could see the unfortunate bus driver, a bit overweight perhaps, rather bald, that was how she imagined him, sitting now in some interview room drinking instant coffee and smoking all the cigarettes he wanted, and that would be quite a lot. The enjoyment had probably gone out of them, but at least it was something for his hands to do, what else could he do with them when he was surrounded on all sides by uniformed officers studying those very hands, and wondering whether he could have killed Maja with them. Naturally they'd do a DNA test, but that would take time, perhaps weeks, and in the meantime he'd have to wait, and even if he hadn't had sex with Maja that evening, he could have killed her all the same, they'd think. Of course they'd be humane, even though it was a case of murder, the worst and most brutal of all crimes. Nevertheless she had no difficulty imagining some nasty man with ferrety eyes hacking away any security and sense of worth he might possess. Perhaps even Sejer, with all his quiet patience, could be transformed into such a nightmare. It wasn't impossible. And perhaps somewhere in the background there was a wife fretting, mad with fear. When you get down to it, she thought, none of us can be sure of one another.

She searched through her wardrobe for clothes she didn't normally wear. An old pair of army surplus trousers, with pockets on the thighs. They were thick and stiff and uncomfortable and weren't at all like her, so they were just right now. She had to get outside herself, then it would be easier. A black polo-necked jumper and short white rubber boots also fitted the bill. Then she sat down at the dining table with a notepad and pencil. She chewed and chewed, enjoying the taste of porous wood and soft graphite, just as she enjoyed gently licking her brushes after she'd rinsed them in turpentine. She'd never told anyone about this, it was a secret vice. After three attempts, the text was ready. It was short and simple, without any refinements, it could easily have been written by a man, she thought, as she wallowed in her own vigour. It was something new, a new force that drove her on. She hadn't experienced such a thing for a long time but had dragged herself forward, her feet following unwilling after her, nothing pushing, nothing motivating her. Now she had some real momentum. Maja would have approved of it.

'WILL OFFER GOOD PRICE IF YOU'RE THINKING OF SELLING THE CAR.'

Nothing more. And a signature. She hesitated a little over this, she mustn't use her own name, but she couldn't make anything up. Whatever she chose looked silly. In the end it sorted itself out. A real name that he didn't know and a real phone number which wasn't hers. 'After 7 p.m.' There, it was done. She discarded her handbag and coat and instead found an old down jacket. She put the note in one of its pockets. On a whim she found a band and caught up her hair at the nape of her neck. When she stopped in front of the hall mirror to check her appearance, she saw a stranger with protruding ears. She looked like an overgrown child. It didn't matter, the effect wasn't too silly. The most important thing was that she shouldn't resemble Eva. Finally, she went down to the cellar, rooted around under the workbench and found one of Jostein's old fishing bags. In the bottom lay a knife. Long and narrow, it fitted neatly into the thigh pocket of her trousers. Just a little security for a lone woman. To engender fear and respect, should Egil Einarsson do something stupid.

She parked a good way off by the corner of the swimming baths. The Securitas guard was nowhere to be seen; for goodness' sake, he had other areas to patrol as well, she thought. Perhaps he was lurking near the staff lockers or the toilets, perhaps he was keeping an eye on the stocks of beer and mineral water. Presumably there were thieves here as in all other workplaces. She crossed the road and squeezed past the barrier. Again she was amazed by the number of white cars, but she automatically looked for his in the same place as last time, and it wasn't there. A disturbing thought, that perhaps he wasn't at work that day, that he'd finally broken down and run away, crept into her mind and threatened her equilibrium. Or perhaps he was on the evening shift, but she continued along the rows of cars. Maybe he already knew about the bus driver and was feeling safer than ever. A Renault, how stupid could you get! Now and again she glanced quickly over her shoulder, but there was no one in view. Quick as a spider she scurried round the car park and at length found the Opel right on the perimeter. Today he'd parked askew in the marked parking place, as if he'd been in a hurry. Things will get worse for you, she mumbled to herself. She fished out the note from her pocket, unfolded it and placed it beneath a wiper blade. She stood for a moment or two admiring the car, in case anyone was looking at her from a window. Then she went back again and drove up the town's main street. It was like beginning a marathon without having trained for it, the task overwhelmed her, but she felt rested and ready, determined to finish. She would always remember that day. It was lightly overcast with a strong breeze, Sunday 4 October.

She looked at the clock practically every quarter of an hour.

When it was approaching 6 p.m. she got into her car and drove the twenty-five kilometres out to her father's. He'd seen the car a long way off and was standing on the steps as she arrived, wearing a frown. What odd clothes the girl had on, as if she was going on a forest hike, or worse. He shook his head.

'Are you going to rob a bank?'

'That's the idea. Perhaps you could drive the getaway car?'

'You forgot your wallet,' he said.

'I know, that's why I've come.'

She patted his cheek and went inside, throwing a quick glance at the door of his workroom, where he kept the phone. It stood ajar. The phone almost never rang. She darted a glance at the time again, thought that he might not phone at all, or perhaps not until late in the evening. But men and their cars was a subject she understood. Boasting about them, discussing road-holding and construction, horsepower, braking effect and German thoroughness, as they drooled like small boys and nodded knowingly, this was a man's greatest weakness. The vague impression she had should prove to be correct. This car was important to him. His wife and child took second place. It wasn't certain he would sell, but then she didn't intend to buy. When he realised she was a woman, he'd be even more intrigued. He, a man who went to prostitutes, a deceiver who used his wages to buy pleasure from other women when he was married and had a child. A heel. A shady customer. Perhaps a bit of a drinker and obviously psychologically unstable. A real turd, a . . .

'Why are you so red in the face?'

She started and pulled herself together. 'I've got things to think about.'

'Well, you don't say. Have you heard anything from Emma?'

'She'll be coming soon. D'you think I'm a bad mother?'

He spluttered a bit. 'You're not so bad. You do the best you can. No one is good enough really, not for Emma at least.' He hobbled after her, heading towards the kitchen.

'My God, you're more concerned about that girl than you ever were about me.'

'Naturally. Just wait till you're a grandmother. It's a

sort of second chance, you see, to make a better job than you did the first time round.'

'You were good enough for me.'

'Even though we moved?'

She turned with the bag of coffee in her hand. 'Oh yes.'

'I thought you hadn't forgiven me.'

'Well, perhaps not. But everyone's allowed a certain quota of mistakes, even you.'

'Wasn't it because of your best friend, you lost your best friend – that must have been hard. What was her name again?' His voice was perfectly innocent.

'Er . . . May Britt.'

'May Britt? Was that her name?'

She shook coffee into the paper filter and held her breath. Fortunately he was an old man now, his memory wasn't what it had been. But she felt a louse. Lies flew from lips like flies.

'You're missing Emma too, that's why you've started coming over here all the time. If she stays at Jostein's for too long you'll have to make a contribution to her keep, did you know that?'

'He'd never even dream of it. Don't be unfair.'

'I'm only saying you should be careful. This woman of his, how well do you really know her?'

'Not at all. I'm not interested. But she's blonde with big tits.'

'Be careful, she might get up to something.'

'Dad!' Eva turned and groaned. 'Don't add to the worries I've already got!'

He stared ruefully at the floor. 'Sorry. I'm only trying to find out what's up with you.'

'Thanks, but I'm in complete control, I really am. Sit down. You ought to keep your legs raised, you're being careless. Are you using the electric blanket I gave you?'

'I forget to plug it in. I'm an old man, I can't remember every little thing. Anyway, I'm always frightened it's going to short-circuit.'

'We'll have to organise a time switch or something.'

'Have you come into money?'

It went deathly quiet. The first drops of boiling water dripped into the filter and the smell of coffee spread through the kitchen.

'No,' she said quietly. 'But I'm not letting lack of money take all the pleasure out of my life any more.'

'Ah, you've got yourself a printing press! I thought as much.' He sat down contented. 'I'd like a Tia Maria as well.'

'I know.'

'So you remembered? That today's the fourth of October?'

'Yes. I wouldn't forget this date, I won't ever forget it. You'll have a Tia Maria for Mum just as she asked you to.'

'You don't need to make it too small, either.'

'I never do, I know you.'

He got his liqueur, they had their coffee and sat looking out of the window. It wasn't hard for the two of them to sit in silence, they'd done it so often. Now they gazed at his neighbour's barn, at the maple tree, which was blood-red and yellow, and they noticed that the bark was loosening from one side of its trunk.

'He'll be taking that tree down soon,' her father said softly. 'Look. Hardly any branches left on one side.'

'But it's beautiful for all that. It'll be very bare without that tree.'

'It's diseased, you know. The tree will die anyway.'

'Should we cut down big trees just because they're not perfect any more?'

'No. But because they're ill. He's already planted a replacement, on the left there.'

'That tiny sprig?'

'That's how they begin. They get bigger gradually, but it takes forty to fifty years.'

Eva slurped her coffee and glanced clandestinely at the time. He'd certainly be at home by now, he'd have read her note, perhaps he was talking to his wife about whether they ought to think about selling. No he wasn't, he'd decide without asking her. But maybe he was phoning a mate for advice about what he could ask for a well-maintained Manta. She hoped he wouldn't ask her to make an offer. She hadn't a clue.

She could say that she'd need to make some enquiries herself. Perhaps he was washing it at this very moment, and going over it with the vacuum cleaner. Or perhaps he'd read the note, snorted with contempt and thrown it away; possibly the wind had torn it from under the windscreen wiper and he'd never even read it at all. Maybe he was just sitting watching television, a beer at his side and his feet on the table, while his wife minced around telling the boy to be quiet, at least while Dad was watching the news. Or perhaps he'd gone into town with the lads for a bowling session. She thought about all of this and went on sipping her coffee, there were thousands of possible reasons why he might not phone. But there was also a reason why he might: money. She'd find out if he was as greedy as her, and she believed he was. It would be an opportunity to rid himself of something that could link him to the murder as well. Her cup was just on its way to her lips and her gaze was fixed on the dying tree outside, when suddenly the phone rang. Coffee sloshed down her chin as she jumped up.

'What's the matter?' Her father stared at her in astonishment.

'Your phone's ringing, I'll get it.'

She ran to his workroom. She closed the door carefully behind her and had to calm herself down a little before lifting the receiver with a trembling hand. It might not be him. Perhaps it was the home help saying she was ill. Or perhaps it was Emma, or someone with the wrong number.

'Liland,' she said quietly.

There was a moment's silence. His voice sounded uncertain, as if he was scared of being made to look foolish. Or perhaps he sensed danger.

'Yes, it's about an Opel Manta. I want to speak to Liland.'

'Speaking.' For an instant she was totally overwhelmed by the sound of his voice. 'So you're interested?'

'It's more you that's interested. But I thought it was a man.'

'Does it make any difference?'

'No, course not. So long as you know what we're talking about.'

'Oh, God!' She gave a small laugh. 'Why, we're talking about money, aren't we? Most things are for sale, if the price is good enough.' She'd adopted a hearty tone. It was easy.

'Yeah, yeah, but the price'll have to be really good.'

'It will be, provided the car's as good as it looks.' Her heart was thumping wildly under her sweater. He sounded sulky; she realised that she couldn't stand him.

'The car's tip-top. Just a tiny oil leak.'

'OK, that can be fixed. Can I have a look at it?'

'Course. You can see her tonight if you want. I've

been over her with the vac and tidied inside. But you must give her a test drive.'

'I wasn't exactly going to buy without giving it a test.'

'It's not definite I'm going to sell.'

Both were silent, and she listened to the hostility that quivered on the line between them without quite knowing where it came from. As if they'd both hated each other for a long time.

'It's ten past seven now. I've got a couple of things to take care of first, but could you be in town for half past nine, for example? D'you live in town?'

'Yes,' she said curtly.

'What about – at the bus station?'

'Fine by me. At half past nine. I'll see you when you arrive, I'll be by the kiosk.'

He hung up, she stood for a time listening to the dialling tone. Her father was shouting from the kitchen. She stared at the handset and marvelled at how unaffected he was. As if nothing had happened. That was it. For him it really was over. He'd put it behind him. Now he was interested in money. But she had been, too. She shuddered and went out again, slid behind the kitchen table. Things were happening almost too fast now, she must gather her wits, but her heart was thumping away and she knew she had more colour in her cheeks than usual.

'Well?' said her father expectantly. 'Don't they want to speak to me?'

'He had the wrong number.'

'Oh? That took a long time to find out.'

'No, he was just talkative. A pleasant sort. Asked if I wanted to buy his car.'

'Nah. You'd better leave that to others. When you want a new car, you ask Jostein for help.'

'I'll remember that.'

She filled her cup and stared out at the maple again. The tear in the bark really was ugly. It resembled nothing so much as a large, suppurating wound.

Chapter 30

She waited in the dark. There wasn't a breeze any more, the wind came in capricious squalls over the roof of the bus station, and her ponytail slapped about her ears, which were freezing now, because her hair wasn't hanging over them and warming them as it usually did. Her thoughts wandered, here and there, back to the time when they'd been girls. Suddenly she saw her so clearly in her mind's eye, an image from a summer, perhaps they'd been eleven at the time. Maja was wearing that American bathing costume she'd been so proud of. Her uncle had bought it for her, the uncle who was on a whaler and always came home bearing exciting gifts. Sometimes a little of his bounty even showered down on Eva as well. Boxes of chocolates and American chewing gum. The bathing costume was bright red and amusingly crinkly. It had elastic criss-crossing it and this made the material crinkle into tiny bubbles. No one else had a swimming costume like it. When Maja came out of the sea, the bubbles were full of water and even bigger, and made her look like a huge raspberry. This was the image she gazed at now, Maja coming out of the water, the water running off and splashing round her feet, her hair even darker because it was wet, wearing the best swimming costume on the entire beach. Again and again Maja comes up from the water. She grins and displays her white teeth, for she knows nothing about the future and how it will all end.

The money was now safely stashed in her father's cellar. She'd practically slung the tin in a corner, where it looked almost as valueless as it had done in the workroom at the cabin. Her father never went down there, he couldn't manage the difficult cellar stairs. Nobody else went there either, unless his home help went down for something, but she didn't think so. Home helps didn't do either attics or cellars, it said so in their terms and conditions.

The bus station was the ugliest building Eva knew, a long grey concrete box with empty windows. She'd parked round the back, down by the railway lines, now she leant against the kiosk and looked up at the bridge from where she knew he'd come. He would turn right, disappear behind the bank for a moment and then glide up to the front of the kiosk. He wouldn't come out and introduce himself, he wasn't that sort, just remain sitting in the car, push his nose under the windscreen and peer up at her, maybe give a quick nod, a sort of signal that she could come. She'd have to sit next to him with only the gear stick between them. You sat quite close together in a car, she thought, so close that she'd catch his smell, and his voice would be directly in her left ear. That terse, unfriendly voice. She cleared her throat nervously as she formulated her opening line. Maybe one to make the blood freeze in his veins? She rejected the idea and stared at the cars passing regularly with a brief swish over the bridge above. They couldn't wait to get out of the windswept town. Everyone had an objective, no one strolled about at random, not on an evening like this.

The buses rumbled good-naturedly over by their stops, and people dived into their brightness and warmth. There was something nice about the red buses. The trusty driver bent over his steering wheel, giving a lazy nod each time a few coins jingled into his hand, and the faces behind the windows, autumn-pale with eyes that stared, unseeing. On a bus you were in no-man's-land, left to your own thoughts, all you did was sit and vibrate in the warmth. All at once she felt the urge to sit at one of those windows, take the bus round the town and see how everyone found their own secure bolt-holes. Instead she stood here getting cold, rubbing herself with icy hands in the gloves that were far too thin, waiting for a murderer. When he suddenly turned the corner, Eva let out all the air she had in her lungs. From then on they filled and emptied in a special rhythm, one that nothing could influence, it was like being inside an iron lung. It was vital to keep concentrating, she mustn't let it slip, mustn't say too much, just feel her way cautiously. He was slowing down, she saw him put the car in neutral and lean against the window. His expression was doltish and vaguely sceptical. She opened the door and sat down. He was grasping the gear stick, as if this was a toy he wasn't going to share with anyone, as if sending out a warning. Then he nodded quickly.

She did up her seat belt. 'Drive round for a bit, then I'll have a go afterwards.'

He made no reply, but put the car in gear and drove away across the marked bus lanes. She knew he was waiting for something, as if she should speak first, because she was the one who'd taken the initiative, who wanted a new car.

I'm no bloody coward, Eva thought.

'So you're not frightened of picking up strangers on the road?' she said sweetly.

It was 9.40 on 4 October and Eva's record was as clean as new-fallen snow.

His left hand rested languidly on the steering wheel, and he never let go of the gear change, that stubby, sporty gear stick, with his right. She sat staring at them.

Short, square hands with thick fingers. They were smooth, hairless, the one on the steering wheel was relaxed, the one grasping the gear stick was a pale claw. They were like something she'd seen in Emma's books, blind, colourless submarine creatures. His thighs were short and fat, and threatened to burst the seams of his jeans, his stomach protruded from his skimpy, ribbed leather jacket. He could have been five months pregnant.

'So now you want to get yourself a Manta?' he said jiggling backwards and forwards in his seat.

'I'm a little sentimental,' she said tersely. 'I had one once, but had to sell it. I never got over it.'

I'm sitting right next to him, she thought with astonishment, and I'm talking as if nothing's happened.

'So what do you drive now?'

'An old Ascona,' she said and smiled. 'It's not quite the same.'

'Too right.'

They were halfway across the bridge now, he indicated left as they came to the main street.

'Drive out towards Fossen,' she said, 'there's a bit of flat country there where we can speed up a bit.'

'Oh yes? You want some speed?'

He chuckled and rocked backwards and forwards again; it was a juvenile habit which made him seem unintelligent, primitive, exactly the way she remembered him. She felt old next to him, but presumably they were the same age, possibly he was a couple of years younger. His pot belly didn't budge when he moved, it appeared to be as hard as stone. His pale face flared up with each street light. A wan face without character, almost expressionless.

'I'll drive out to the aerodrome, and you can drive back. Far enough, isn't it?'

'Yes, sure.'

He flexed his right hand to get some air across his sweaty palm and drove even faster. The porky figure in his tight-fitting clothes was reminiscent of a well-filled sausage. He was certainly much stronger than she was, in any case he'd been stronger than Maja. But he'd been sitting on top. She tried to imagine how it would have been if Maja had been quicker and had stabbed him instead, then the two of them would have had a corpse on their hands. It could easily have happened like that, it was strange. Life was so fortuitous.

'This is the GSi model, in case you're wondering.'

'D'you think I'm a complete beginner?'

'No, no, I was just mentioning it,' he mumbled. 'There's nothing wrong with the engine, let me tell you. Nought to a hundred in ten seconds. She can get close to two hundred, if you're up for it. But women have a funny way of driving,' he said jiggling, 'they let the car decide. Just sort of sit there and get taken along for the ride.'

'That's fast enough for me. The seats are good,' she added.

'Recaro seats.'

'Is the sunroof electric?'

'No, manual. Much better, the electric ones pack up quicker. Cost an arm and a leg to repair. The boot is 490 litres, and has a light. If you're fannying about with a kid's buggy, and that.'

'Well, thank you! Does it drink petrol?'

'No, no, this here's just average. It does nought point six. A litre maybe in cities. You've got to reckon on that.'

'I've looked at it several times,' she let drop.

'Oh? What for?' Now he sounded suspicious.

'I had to get some money together first.'

'Have you got enough, that's the question.'

'I have.'

'You haven't asked the price.'

'I haven't thought about that yet. I'll make you an offer you won't be able to refuse.'

'Wow, you talk like a Mafia boss.'

'Yup.'

'I don't really want to sell it.'

'No, but you're greedy like everyone else, so that'll be all right.' She wriggled a bit. She could feel the knife, it was pressing into her thigh. I'm no bloody coward, she thought.

'And this offer of yours,' he said clearing his throat, 'how big is it?'

'Wouldn't you like to know. I'll drive it first, check under the bonnet and the body, and in daylight too. And I'll need an AA test, of course.'

'D'you want a Manta or don't you?'

'I thought you said you weren't going to sell.'

There was silence in the car, which had become hot and humid, the windows were misting up. He turned on the fan to clear them. Eva turned one last time and stared back at the town. The occasional welder's flame could be seen from the new railway bridge that was under construction. The traffic became sparser and they were approaching the point where the street lighting ended. He went left at the roundabout and continued along the south side of the river. It was less of a torrent up here, but the current was powerful enough. After a few minutes' silence he suddenly turned to the right. The aerodrome was on their left, while he rolled down a bumpy track and through a small clump of trees, halting on an open piece of ground right down by the river's edge. Eva felt uncomfortable. There were no people nearby. The engine was still running, it purred softly and dependably, there was no doubting the car was in good condition.

'Ace fishing spot,' he said pulling on the handbrake.

'Ninety-two thousand,' she put in quickly, 'is that right? You haven't wound the clock back?'

'Christ, is there no limit to your bloody suspicions!'

'I just think it seems very low. This is a typical bloke's car, and blokes tend to drive a lot. My Ascona is an '82 model and it's done a hundred and sixty.'

'Well, it's about time you had a new car, then. Want to take a look at the works?'

'It's pitch black outside.'

'I've got a torch.' He turned off the engine and climbed out of the car.

Eva gathered herself for a moment and opened the door, a terrific gust of wind almost tore it out of her hand. 'Bloody weather!'

'It's called autumn.' He raised the bonnet and secured it. 'I admit that the engine's been cleaned today. You wouldn't have been able to see anything otherwise.'

Eva moved to his side and stared down at the shiny engine. 'God, just like the family silver.'

'Yeah, isn't it just?' He turned and grinned. One eye tooth was missing. 'Nice stuff they make at Opel. Really great to work on.'

'Possibly so, but I won't be doing it myself.'

'Didn't think so. I've got some spare parts, they're included in the sale, if we go ahead, that is.'

'And what'll you get instead?'

'Not quite sure, I'm very tempted by a BMW. We'll have to see. About this famous offer of yours.' He bent down again, and Eva saw his large bottom in the tight jeans. There was a wide strip of naked skin between his belt and his leather jacket. White and moist as bread dough. 'I think I've found that oil leak here. It's only a gasket. It'll cost – maybe thirty or forty kroner. I'm sure to have one at home.'

Eva didn't answer. She kept on staring at his backside, his white skin. He had a bald patch at the back of his head. She forgot to reply. In the silence she heard the rush of the river, an even roar. That poor bus driver, she thought, he's probably still sitting in the interview room. He's sick of the instant coffee by now and is struggling with his missing alibi. People haven't always got an alibi, or perhaps he had one he didn't want to use. Perhaps he had a girlfriend, and if he said anything about her his marriage would fall apart, if it hadn't already done so. And his neighbours would be thinking things, and his grandchildren would have to find something to say to all those snotty little faces in the playground, when the rumour began to circulate that their grandfather was suspected of killing that tart in Tordenskioldsgate. Maybe he'd got a weak heart, maybe he'd have a heart attack and die while he was being interviewed. He was the right age, fifty-seven. Or maybe he didn't have a girlfriend at all, but only dreamt of one, and had simply been driving around to be on his own, to get away for a bit. Stopped at a roadside kiosk and had something to eat, perhaps, or wandered along the river and got a bit of fresh air. And no one believed it, because grown men who're old enough to be grandads don't drive round aimlessly, unless they're perverts, or have a lover. That one about the hot-dog stand won't wash with us, you'll have to do better than that. So, for the last time: when did you last visit Maja Durban?

'Here, the torch.' He'd straightened up again. He pushed it into her hand. She stood shining the light down at the grass. 'Or I can hold it and you can look.'

'No,' she stammered, 'it's not necessary. I'm sure it's fine. I mean, I'll take your word. Buying a car is a matter of trust.'

'I think you ought to give it the once over. You've got to see just how great this is, there aren't many blokes who keep engines the way I do. And it's only had one previous owner. No one else is allowed to drive it either, the wife hasn't got a licence. I'm telling you, your offer better be good. And when we've signed the contract, I want you to have seen all over it, I don't want any of this coming back afterwards, complaining about this and that.'

'I'm not a fool,' she riposted. 'As far as this car's concerned, I think I can trust you.'

'You bet you can. But women sometimes get funny ideas, that's why I'm mentioning it. Sometimes they've got unpleasant things up their sleeve, in a manner of speaking.'

The knife, she thought.

He snorted mucus up his nose, and went on: 'I've just got to make certain you can do a proper deal.'

She trembled. Raised the torch and shone it in his

face. 'Yes I can. I'll pay, and I'll get the goods I've asked for. Don't you think it's wonderful, the way everything can be bought for money?'

'I haven't been offered any money yet.'

'That'll come after the AA test.'

'I thought you said you trusted me.'

'Only as regards the car.'

He snorted. 'What the fuck does that mean?'

'You just think about it for a bit.'

The river sent up a surge of writhing water, gave a great swish and settled again.

He shook his head in disbelief and ducked down over the engine again. 'Bloody women,' he mumbled. 'Coming here dragging some innocent bugger out of his warm garage and into this sodding storm, just to talk a load of piss!'

'Innocent?'

Eva felt the ground sinking beneath her. It made her fade a bit, feel relaxed and strange, she had to support herself on the car, she was standing on the left, just by the rod that was propping up the bonnet.

'What I mean is,' he boomed from the depths of the engine, 'that you were the one who wanted the car. And I turn up just like we'd agreed. Don't see why you're so bloody touchy.'

'Touchy?' she snapped. 'D'you call this being touchy? I've seen a hell of a lot worse, I've seen people go completely berserk for nothing at all!'

He twisted round and looked at her suspiciously. 'Christ's sake, are you schizophrenic or something?' He bent down once more.

Eva gasped and felt her fury gaining the upper hand. It felt like a release, it rose at terrible speed, white hot like a stream of lava, poured up through the regions of her stomach, on into her breast and out along her arms, and she gesticulated wildly in the darkness, suddenly felt that she'd struck something and heard a scraping sound. The prop holding the bonnet up had been knocked away. The heavy metal lid came down with a clang. His bottom and legs protruded from the lip, the rest of him was hidden.

She backed away and screamed. From deep within there came some gurgling noises and a few choice oaths. Terrified, she stared at the bonnet, it must have been heavy, but it lifted a fraction, fell down again and lifted once more. Eva's heart was pounding so hard that he must have been able to hear it. She'd ignited his rage, just as Maja had done, and now that blind fury would be directed at her, in just a second or two he'd extricate himself and attack her with all his strength, so she took a few paces forwards, fumbled down her thigh for the pocket, pushed her hand in and found the knife. She pulled it out of its sheath.

'For fuck's sake!'

He wanted to get up, turn round, but Eva sprang to the side of the car and lay across the bonnet with all her weight. He gave a hollow-sounding scream, as if he were inside a tin. 'What the hell are you doing?'

'Losing control!' she screamed. Her voice broke.

'You're a total fucking nutcase!'

'You're the one who's the nutcase!'

'What d'you want, for God's sake!'

Eva caught her breath and shouted. 'I want to know why Maja had to die!'

It went deathly quiet. He attempted to move, but couldn't budge a millimetre. She heard his respiration, he was breathing fast.

'How the hell do you . . .'

'Wouldn't you like to know!' She was still pressing down on the bonnet, he'd ceased moving now, he was gasping like an exhausted dog with his face pressed against the engine block.

'I can explain all that . . .' he gurgled, 'it was an accident!'

'Oh no it wasn't!'

'She had a knife, for Christ's sake!'

Suddenly he made a gargantuan effort and the bonnet rose, Eva slipped off and landed in the grass, but she was clutching the knife, she saw his hands, the ones that had killed Maja, saw them clench.

'I've got one too!'

She jumped to her feet and threw herself over the car once more, he collapsed, the first stab got him in the side, and the knife slipped in fairly easily as into a fresh loaf. The bonnet was holding him like a mouse in a trap. She withdrew the knife, something warm gushed over her glove, but he didn't cry out, just a small, amazed groan. He was getting ready for another effort and wrenched one arm free, when the second stab penetrated the small of his back, she felt the blade meeting resistance, as if she'd struck bone, she had to yank hard to get it out again, and just then his knees buckled. He sank part of the way to the ground but still hung there and now she couldn't stop, because he was still moving and she had to silence him, prevent him from making that awful groaning. After a while she worked the knife rhythmically, she thrust and thrust, stabbing him in the back and sides and sometimes hitting the metal of the car, the grille, the fender, until she realised at last that he was no longer moving, but hanging there still, completely butchered, like a stuck pig on a hook.

Something frigid and raw gripped Eva with terrific force. She had fallen forward and lay on her stomach in the grass. The river rushed onward as before, completely indifferent. All was quiet. With amazement she registered a paralysis spreading slowly through her entire body, she couldn't move a muscle, not even her fingers. She hoped someone would find them soon. The ground was wet and chilly and soon she began to feel cold.

Chapter 31

She raised her head and found herself staring directly at a blue and white trainer, then further up his leg, and wondered why he hadn't fallen. He looked ludicrous. As if he'd fallen asleep while inspecting the engine. But it was strange nothing had happened. People hadn't come rushing up, there were no wailing sirens. Just the two of them, alone in the darkness.

No one had seen them. No one knew where they were, maybe not even that they were together.

She struggled to her feet, swaying slightly, and feeling sticky and wet. The distance from the car to the water might be ten or twelve metres and he wasn't inordinately large, maybe seventy kilos. She weighed sixty, it should be possible. If he was carried by the current a bit before he was found, down towards the town, and if she moved the car, they wouldn't locate the spot where he was killed, and where she'd certainly have left clues. She considered a while, surprised by her own clear logic, and approached the car. Carefully, she raised the bonnet and propped it up again. He remained suspended. She would have to touch him now, touch the slippery leather jacket with its large blotches of blood. Automatically closing her nostrils to any smell, she grasped his shoulders and tugged. He slid backwards and fell like a sack across her feet. She pulled them from under him. He was lying on his back now. She bent over him, and all at once she had the idea of stealing his wallet from his jacket pocket. As if that would hamper them in establishing his identity. It was risible. Then she put a hand under each of his shoulders, turned, looked down at the bank and began to haul.

He was heavier than she'd imagined, but the grass was wet, and he slid along in short spurts, his legs akimbo. She heaved twice and rested, twice and rested, and slowly she approached the water. After a while she halted and stared down at the pale crown of his head, before continuing. At last he was resting with his face in the water. She let go of him and tentatively dipped a foot in the water. It was shallow. She took another couple of steps, almost slipping on the slimy stones, but was still able to wade. Eventually the water rose above her boots and gushed icily down over her feet. Still she went a few steps further, stopping when the water reached to just above her knees, then returned to the bank. She grasped him once more and started dragging him into the strong current, and soon he began to float and lighten. She kept moving out into the river until she felt the current pressing dangerously against her legs, then she turned him round on to his stomach. The water rocked and lapped at him, and then he began to drift. The current carried him quickly. The back of his head was a light patch on the dark water. She stood with the water almost to her thighs and watched him, as if spellbound, and then suddenly something strange happened. One of his feet rose and his head disappeared beneath the water. It almost looked as if he'd dived. A slight bubbling could be heard over the steady rush, then he was gone.

She went on watching fixedly, expecting him to resurface, but the river flowed on and vanished into the darkness. Slowly she waded ashore, turned and had to look again. Then she went over to the car. Carefully she lowered the bonnet. She retrieved the torch and the wallet, opened the boot. It was tidy and organised inside, she caught sight of a green beaver nylon boiler suit. She pulled it on. She was still wearing gloves, she'd had them on the whole time, and now she slipped into the driver's seat. But she jumped out again, and began searching the grass. She found the sheath just in front of the car and stuffed it into her pocket. She heard a couple of cars on the road, so she waited before switching on the lights. When they'd passed, she put the car in gear and drove slowly through the small clump of trees. She put the heater on full and turned on to the road. Her feet were like two lumps of dead meat. Perhaps they'd find him as soon as it got light. Or perhaps, she thought, he'd got caught on something and been dragged under. It had certainly looked like that. As if his clothing or perhaps an arm had snagged something that was sticking up from the bottom, a tree, for example, that had toppled and fallen into the river, or something else, anything, and maybe he'd lie there billowing with the current until his bones were scoured clean by the water and the fish.

The car handled well, she thought, and she kept a steady speed towards the town. Each time she met an oncoming car she held her breath, as if they could see through the windscreen at what had happened. When she'd crossed the bridge, she turned on to the motorway and drove towards Hovland and the rubbish dump. She would abandon the car there. They'd find it quickly, maybe even the following day, there was no point in trying to hide it forever. But this way they'd search the dump and waste time, search through the rubbish. And perhaps he'd float a long way, perhaps right out to sea and come ashore somewhere else, in some other town, and there'd be further searches in the wrong place, and time would pass and settle like dust over everything.

Chapter 32

Sejer rose and walked to the window.

It was late at night. He searched for stars, but could see none, the sky was too light. At this time of year he often felt that they'd disappeared for good, that they'd left and gone to shine over another planet. The thought saddened him. Without the stars he didn't have the same feeling of security, it was as if the earth no longer had a roof over it. And the sky simply went on and on forever.

He shook his head at his own thoughts.

Eva took the last cigarette out of the packet, she looked collected, almost relieved. 'When did you know it was me?'

He shook his head again. 'I didn't know. I thought possibly there might be two of you, and that you'd been paid to keep your mouth shut. I really didn't know what you wanted with Einarsson.' He went on staring out of the window. 'But now I see,' he muttered.

Her face was calm and open, he'd never seen her like this before, despite the swollen lip and the cuts to her chin, she was beautiful.

'You didn't think I looked like a murderer?'

'No one looks like a murderer.' He sat down again.

'I didn't plan to kill him. I took the knife with me because I was scared. No one will believe that.'

'Well, you must give us the chance.'

'It was in self-defence,' she said. 'He would have killed me. You know that.'

He made no answer. Suddenly the words sounded so strangely familiar to her ears. 'This man who pulled you down the cellar steps, what did he look like?'

'Dark, foreign. Rather slight, almost thin, but he spoke Norwegian.'

'It sounds like Cordoba.'

Eva started. 'What did you say?'

'His name's Cordoba, Ms Durban's husband. Jean Lucas Cordoba. Quite a name, isn't it?'

Eva began to laugh, with her face hidden in her hands. 'Yes,' she spluttered, 'almost worth marrying just for the name, isn't it?' She wiped away some tears and drew on her cigarette. 'Maja got all sorts. Policemen, too, did you know that?'

Sejer couldn't stop himself, a reluctant smile spread across his face. 'Well yes, we're no different from other people. No better and no worse. I don't want to hear any names.'

'Can they see me through the cell door?' she asked all at once.

'Yes, they can.'

She sniffled and looked at her hands. She began using one fingernail to scrape the polish off the others.

She had nothing more to say. She was waiting for him now, for him to do what he had to. Then she could rest and relax and just do what she was told. That was really the way she wanted it.

Markus Larsgård floundered beneath the blanket on the sofa. If it was someone he knew, it would ring for a long time. Someone who knew he was old and slow, that he kept the phone in his workroom, and would have to cross the full width of the living room on his swollen legs. If it was a stranger, he'd never get to it in time.

Not many strangers phoned Markus Larsgård now. The occasional telesales person, the odd wrong number. Apart from that it was Eva. Finally he got himself into a sitting position; it was still ringing, so it was someone he knew. With a grunt he heaved himself up using the tabletop and got hold of his stick. He stumped across the floor thanking his lucky stars that someone could still be bothered to ring up and disturb him during his midday siesta. He limped along, struggled to get his stick to stand against the desk, but had to give up. It crashed to the floor. To his surprise he heard an unknown voice at the other end. A solicitor. Acting for Eva Marie, he said. Could he come to the station. She was in custody.

Larsgård fumbled with the chair, he had to sit down. Perhaps it was all nonsense, one of these practical jokers phoning to annoy him, he'd read about them in the paper. But he didn't sound like one, he was educated, almost affable in his manner. He listened and strained, asked him to repeat, trying unsuccessfully to understand what the man meant. It was obviously a misunderstanding, and they'd soon realise it. But even so, it was an awful experience for poor Eva, a terrible thing. Custody? He'd have to go immediately. Phone for a taxi.

'No, we'll send a car for you, Mr Larsgård, just sit and relax until it arrives.'

Larsgård sat. He forgot to replace the phone. He ought to put on some clothes before the car arrived, but then he thought it didn't really matter. Whether he was cold or not. They had got hold of Eva and locked her up. Maybe he ought to try to find something for *her* instead, perhaps it was cold in there. For a time he tried to get his bearings in the room, to recall where his things were. It was his home help who did the tidying. Perhaps he should take a bottle of red wine along? But maybe that wasn't allowed. What about money? He had plenty of money in his jam jar, it seemed to be never-ending, as if it were breeding. He rejected that too, thought it unlikely there was a kiosk at the courthouse, he'd been there once, the autumn his moped had been stolen, and he couldn't remember seeing one there. Besides, they said she was in custody, and that meant she wouldn't be allowed out anywhere. He wanted to get up and go into the living room again, but his legs felt so feeble and strange. He had his good moments and his bad moments, he was used to that, but now he'd had a shock. He would have to sit for a while. Perhaps he ought to phone Jostein. He made another attempt, but fell back suddenly feeling faint. He often felt faint, it was caused by the hardening of the arteries at the back of his neck which prevented enough blood reaching his head, and this was because of his age, a perfectly normal situation, really, given the circumstances. But it was annoying, especially now because it wasn't subsiding. The ceiling began to get lower. The walls, too, began to close in, from each side, it all felt so cramped, and gradually it got darker. Eva had been arrested for murder, and she'd confessed. He took a firm grip of himself and pushed hard with his legs. The last thing he felt was his sharp knees striking his brow with great force.

Chapter 33

Sejer looked out of the window at the car park. At the flimsy gate through which the shadier street life constantly broke in, to vandalise or steal equipment, and the tufts of dry grass along the fence. Mrs Brenningen had planted petunias there once, now the weeds had won the battle. No one had time to weed. The report told him that the remand prisoner Eva Magnus hadn't slept at all, and that she'd refused all food and drink. It didn't look good. In addition, she'd been very troubled by the way they could look in on her through the window in the door, and at the light being left on all night.

He had to get up and give her the news, but he felt a huge reluctance, and so it was a relief when there was a knock at the door. A tiny postponement. Karlsen stuck his head in.

'You've had rather a night, I hear!' He sat down

heavily by the desk. 'We've had a missing-person report.'

'Ah!' said Sejer. A new case was just what he needed, something that would remind him that, after all, it was only a job he was paid to do, and that he could lock it away in his drawer at four o'clock, at least if he made an effort. 'I'll take anything provided it's not a child.'

Karlsen sighed. He, too, threw a glance at the police cars as if to make sure they were there. They were like a couple of old cowboys who'd found themselves a table in the saloon and were constantly on the lookout for horse thieves. 'Have you told Eva Magnus yet?'

He shook his head. 'I'm finding any excuse for postponing it.'

'Not much point, is there?'

'No, but I'm dreading it.'

'I could do it for you.'

'Thanks, but it's my job. Either I do it, or I should retire.' He glanced at his colleague. 'Well, who didn't come home last night?'

Karlsen pulled a sheet of paper from his inner pocket and unfolded it. He read it to himself, tugged at his moustache a couple of times and reluctantly cleared his throat: 'Six-year-old girl, Ragnhild Album. Slept over with a friend in the area last night and was supposed to walk home this morning. Walk of only about ten or twelve minutes. She was pushing a pink doll's pram with one of those crying dolls in it. Called Elise.'

'Elise?'

'One with a dummy in its mouth. When you pull it out it begins to cry. They're all the rage now, every little girl has one. But you've got a grandson, so you won't have seen them. But I have. They wail just like a real baby. Sounds like something out of a Hitchcock film. Anyway. She also had a nightie in the pram and a small bag with a toothbrush and comb. No sign of any of it.'

'Missing since . . .?'

'Eight o'clock.'

'Eight?' Sejer glanced at the clock. It was eleven.

'Ragnhild wanted to return home just after they woke up this morning. The mother of her friend didn't ring Ragnhild's mother to say she was coming. She was still in bed herself. But she heard the girls getting up, and Ragnhild leaving at about eight. She went on her own, it wasn't far, and the mother knew no more about it till Ragnhild's mother rang at ten and asked her to send the girl home. They were going shopping. Now she's completely vanished.'

'She lives – where?'

'In Fagerlundsåsen, Lundeby. The new estate. They've just moved into the area.'

Sejer drummed on his map-of-the-world blotting pad. His hand covered the whole of the South American continent. 'You and I'd better get off there.'

'We've already sent a patrol car.'

'I'll talk to Magnus first. Then at least that'll be over.

Let the parents know we're on our way, but don't give them a time.'

'The mother. The father's away, they can't get hold of him.' Karlsen pushed back his chair and stood up.

'By the way, how did you get on with those tights for your wife?'

Karlsen looked startled.

'Pantyliners,' Sejer said by way of explanation.

'They weren't tights, Konrad. Pantyliners are things women wear at a certain time of the month.'

He left, and Sejer chewed his nail as he felt an incipient nervousness grow in his stomach.

He didn't like it when six-year-old girls failed to arrive home when expected. Even though he knew there could be lots of reasons for it. Everything from divorced fathers demonstrating proprietorial rights, to homeless puppies that needed coaxing back home, or thoughtless older children who took them out without letting anyone know. Sometimes the kids were asleep in some bush or other, thumb in mouth. Not so many six-year-olds perhaps, but it had certainly happened with two- and three-year-olds. Sometimes they simply got lost, and wandered around hour after hour. Some began to bawl immediately, and got picked up. Others kept walking, speechless with fear without attracting notice. At least the roads were quiet at eight o'clock in the morning, he thought, and felt easier.

He did up the top button of his shirt and rose. He

reached for his jacket, too, as if the fabric could protect him from what was to come. Then he walked down the corridor. The morning light gave it a greenish hue reminding him of the old swimming baths he'd used as a boy.

The remand cells were on the fifth floor. He took the lift and felt a trifle idiotic as he always did, standing there passive inside the small cage which travelled up and down the building. It was too fast, as well. Things ought to take their allotted time. He felt he arrived too soon. Suddenly he was standing in front of the cell door. For a moment he wanted to resist the temptation to peer in first, but he couldn't. When he looked through the window he could see her sitting on the bunk with the blanket around her. She was staring through the window where a small patch of grey sky was visible. She started when she heard the rattle of the lock.

'I can't bear this waiting!' she said.

He nodded as if he understood.

'I'm expecting Dad. They were going to fetch him. My solicitor rang, they're collecting him in a taxi. I don't know why it's taking such a long time, it's only half an hour's drive.'

Sejer remained standing. There wasn't anywhere to sit. Sitting on the bunk next to her was too intimate. 'You'll have to get used to the waiting, there'll be a lot of that in the future.'

'I'm not used to it. I'm used to doing things all the

time, I'm used to the day never being long enough and used to Emma always nagging and wanting something. It's so quiet here,' she said in despair.

'Take some good advice. Try to sleep at night. Try to eat something. Things will be too tough otherwise.'

'Why are you here anyway?' She looked at him, suddenly suspicious.

'There's something you ought to know.' He walked a few paces and prepared himself. 'As regards your case, and the sentence, it may not be that important. But in certain other respects it could be rather hard.'

'I don't understand what you . . .'

'We've received various reports from forensics.'

'Well?'

'Both about Maja Durban and Egil Einarsson. They've been conducting a number of tests. And they've discovered something, which for you, is rather unpleasant.'

'Well, tell me then!'

'Maja Durban was asphyxiated by the murderer pressing a pillow to her face.'

'Yes, that was what I said. I sat there watching.'

'But before that they had sex. And that gives us a number of very concrete clues as to the identity of the murderer. And the fact is,' he drew in his breath, 'that the man *wasn't* Einarsson.'

Eva sat staring at him. Her face was impassive. Then she smiled.

'Mrs Magnus,' he went on, 'the fact is you've killed the wrong man.'

She shook her head emphatically and spread her arms, the smile was still there, but it was slowly congealing. 'Excuse me, but I'm certain about that car. Jostein and I, we had one just like it!'

'Please, just forget the car for a moment. Maybe you're right about that. But in that case it wasn't Einarsson who was driving.'

A sudden doubt assailed her. 'He never lent it to anyone,' she stammered.

'He may have made an exception. Or someone may have borrowed it without his permission.'

'It's not true!'

'How much did you really witness? You were peering through a narrow crack in a door that was ajar. The room was in semi-darkness. Weren't you sitting with your hands in front of your face for much of the time?'

'I want you to go,' she sobbed.

'I'm sorry,' he said feebly.

'How long have you known this?'

'Some time.'

'Find out where Dad is!'

'They'll certainly be on their way. Try to rest a bit, you'll need it.' He waited there, feeling as if he wanted to rush out, but he controlled himself. 'The crime itself is the same,' he said.

'No!'

'Legally what matters is that you thought it was him.'

'No! I want you to be wrong.'

'Sometimes we are. But not this time.'

For a long time she sat with her face hidden, then she looked up at him. 'Once when we were thirteen . . .'

'Yes?' Sejer waited.

'D'you think it's possible to die of fright?'

He shrugged. 'I'd imagine so. But only if you were old and had a bad heart. Why?'

'No, nothing.'

There was silence for a while. She brushed her forehead with her hand and glanced quickly at her wrist, and only then remembered that they'd removed her watch.

'But if it wasn't Einarsson – who was it?'

'That's what I'm going to find out. Possibly one of Einarsson's acquaintances.'

'Find out what's happened to my father.'

'I'll do that.' He went to the door, opened it and turned. 'You mustn't worry so much about us looking at you through the window. It's only to make sure that you're all right. We're not peeping Toms.'

'It feels like it.'

'Pull the blanket over your head. Try to remember that you're only one of many in here. You're not as special as you feel. It's only outside these walls that you become an object of interest, isn't it?'

'You can say that again.'

'You'll be hearing from me.'

He closed the door and locked it.

Rosenkrantzgate 16 was newly painted and greener than ever.

He parked by the garage, and was just stepping out of the car when he caught sight of Jan Henry over by the swings. For a moment the boy waited a little shyly, then he came padding across.

'I didn't think you'd come again.'

'I said I would. How's it going?'

'Not too bad.' He shrugged his thin shoulders and twined his legs.

'Is Mum at home?'

'Yes.'

'Have you had any good rides? On the motorbike?'

'Yes. But your car was better. The wind is so strong,' he added.

'Wait out here for me, Jan Henry, I've got something for you.'

Sejer walked towards the entrance, and the boy sat down on the swing again. Jorun Einarsson answered the door, she was wearing nothing except long johns, or perhaps they passed for tights, he thought, with a roomy sweater over them. Her hair was lighter than ever.

'Oh, it's you, is it?'

He nodded politely. She immediately stood back and let him in. He halted in the living room, drew breath and looked at her earnestly.

'Right now I've got just one question. I'll put it to you and leave again straight away. Think carefully before you answer, it's important.'

She nodded.

'I know that your husband was extremely particular about his car. He took great care of it and kept it in thoroughly good condition. And that he was very unwilling to lend it to anyone. Is that correct?'

'I'll say! He was really possessive about that car. Sometimes they'd even tease him about it at work.'

'But even so, on rare occasions, did he ever lend it to anyone? Do you ever remember him doing it? Even if it was only the once?'

She hesitated: 'Yes, he did occasionally. But only very rarely. To one of his mates who he hung out with quite a lot, someone from the brewery. He hadn't got a car himself.'

'D'you know his name?'

'Er, well I feel a bit funny about mentioning his name here,' she said, as if she sensed a danger she didn't fully understand. 'But he lent it to Peddik now and again. Peter Fredrik.'

'Ahron?'

'Yes.'

Sejer nodded slowly. He took another look at the

wedding photo of Einarsson and noted his fair hair. 'I'll be back,' he said softly. 'You'll have to forgive me, but cases like these take a lot of time and there are still some things we need to clear up.'

Mrs Einarsson nodded and showed him out. Jan Henry jumped up and came running towards him, keener now.

'That didn't take long.'

'No,' Sejer said thoughtfully. 'There's a man I've got to find, and quickly too. Come over to the car with me.'

He opened the boot and took out a carrier bag from Fina. 'A mechanic's suit. For you. I know it's too large, but you'll grow into it.'

'Wow!' His eyes were sparkling. 'Loads of pockets! It'll fit me soon, and I can turn it up.'

'That's right.'

'When are you coming back?'

'I won't be long.'

'No. I expect you've got lots to do.'

'Well, yes. But I'm also off duty sometimes. Perhaps we could take another drive sometime, if you want to?'

Jan Henry made no reply. He was staring down the road, to where the roar of a large motorbike had broken the silence. A BMW.

'There's Peddik.'

Jan Henry gave him a lukewarm wave. Sejer turned and stared at the man in the black leather suit as he nosed in by the cycle stand, stopped and took off his helmet. A man with longish fair hair and a small pony-tail at his neck. Now he was opening the zip of his leathers so that an incipient beer belly came into view. In reality he wasn't that unlike Einarsson. In poor light one might not be able to tell the difference.

Sejer stared at him until he began to squirm on the seat of the motorbike. Then he smiled, gave a brief nod and went to his car.

Chapter 34

'Where have you been?'

Karlsen was waiting in reception. He had been looking out for Sejer's car for some time now, minutes were passing and no one had phoned with the glad tidings that little Ragnhild had come home long ago and was fit and well. She was still lost. Karlsen was stressed.

'With Jorun Einarsson.' Sejer was tense and excited, which was unusual. 'Come on, I've got to talk to you.'

They nodded to Mrs Brenningen and retreated down the corridor.

'We need to bring in a bloke for questioning,' Sejer said, 'straight away. Peter Fredrik Ahron. The only person in Einarsson's circle who occasionally was allowed to borrow his Manta. Very occasionally. He works at the brewery, and now he's chasing after Jorun. He's been interviewed before, when Einarsson went missing. I've just met him outside the house in Rosenkrantzgate, and d'you know what? They look pretty similar. In poor light it would be hard to tell them apart. See what I mean?'

'Where is he now?'

'Still at the house, I hope. Album will have to wait, we've got people on that anyway. Take Skarre and bring him in straight away, I'll wait here.'

Karlsen nodded and turned to go. Then he stopped. 'By the way, I've got a message for you from Eva's solicitor.'

'Yes?'

'Larsgård's dead.'

'What do you mean?'

'The taxi driver found him.'

'Does she know yet?'

'I've sent one of the girls in to her.'

Sejer shut his eyes and shook his head. He walked up the stairs digesting the news as best he could, just now he hadn't time to think more carefully about what it would mean for the remand prisoner on the fifth floor. He shut himself in his office, opened the window and let in some fresh air. Tidied the desk a bit. Went quickly to the sink and washed his hands, drank some water from a paper cup. Opened the file drawer and took out a cassette, it was 360 minutes long and contained Eva Magnus's confession. He loaded it in the cassette player on the desk, and began fast-forwarding it. He stopped it now and then, fast-forwarded a bit more and found the episode he was searching for at last, he paused the tape and adjusted the volume. Then he settled down to wait and his thoughts began to wander. Perhaps Ahron had made a run for it, he mused, in which case he might already be a long way off on that fast motorbike of his. But he hadn't. He was sitting reading the newspaper on Jorun's sofa, a pouch of tobacco at his side. She was in the middle of the room with an ironing board and a pile of freshly laundered clothes. She looked uncertainly at the two policemen and then at the man on the sofa, who contented himself with raising a single eyebrow, as if they were taking him in at a most inconvenient moment. He rose from the sofa with apparent resignation and followed them out. Jan Henry watched them as they walked to the car. He said nothing. It mattered little to him what they were going to do with Peddik.

'Your name is Peter Fredrik Ahron?'

'Yes.' He rolled a cigarette without asking permission.

'Born seventh of March 1956?'

'Why ask when you know all this?'

Sejer glanced up. 'I'd advise you to tread carefully.'

'Are you threatening me?'

Now he was smiling disarmingly. 'Certainly not. We don't threaten here, we simply advise. Address?'

'Tollbugata 4. Born and raised in Tromsø, youngest of four, National Service: yes. I don't mind helping you out, but the fact is I've said everything I have to say.'

'In that case we'll go through it again.'

He wrote on, unperturbed, Ahron smoked furiously, but he kept control of himself. Kept control for the moment. He leant across the desk with a resigned expression. 'Give me one good reason why I should go round killing my best friend!'

Sejer dropped his pen and looked at him in astonishment. 'My dear Mr Ahron, is there anyone who thinks you did? That's not why you're here. Did you think that was the reason?' He studied him acutely and noticed how the germ of a suspicion grew in Ahron's pale blue iris.

'It's hardly surprising I thought that,' he said hesitantly, 'the last time you turned up it was because of Egil.'

'Then you're on the wrong track completely,' Sejer said. 'This is about something quite different.'

Silence. The smoke from Ahron's roll-up curled in thick white spirals towards the ceiling. Sejer waited.

'Well? So?'

'So what? What do you mean?'

Sejer folded his arms on the desk top and never relinquished Ahron's eyes. 'I mean, aren't you going to ask what it's about? As it *isn't* about Einarsson?'

'I haven't got the faintest idea what it's about.'

'No, exactly. That's why I thought you might want to ask. I would have done,' he said frankly, 'if I'd been hauled in while I was buried in the sports pages. But perhaps you're not the inquisitive type. So I'll enlighten you a bit. Little by little at all events. Just one tiny question first: what's your attitude to women, Mr Ahron?'

'You'll have to ask them that,' he said sullenly.

'Yes, you're right there. Who do you think I should ask? Have there been lots of them?'

He made no reply. All his energies were directed at keeping his composure.

'Maybe I should ask Maja Durban. Would that be a good idea?'

'You've got a sick sense of humour.'

'Possibly. She didn't have much to say when we found her on her bed. But she had something to give us all the same. The murderer left his visiting card. Know what I mean?'

Ahron's head trembled. He licked his lips.

'And I'm not talking about the sort you order in batches from the stationer's. I'm talking about a unique personal genetic code. Every one of the earth's four billion inhabitants has a different code. Just let that figure sink in, Mr Ahron. When we magnify it, it resembles a mad piece of modern art. Black and white. But of course you know all this, you read the papers.'

'You're just guessing. You've got to have a court order

before you can start testing me, if that's what you plan to do. And you won't get it. I'm no fool. And anyway I want a solicitor. I'm not saying another word without a solicitor, not a thing!'

'Fine.' Sejer leant back. 'I can continue the conversation alone. But I ought to tell you that a court order for blood tests is the least of my problems.'

Ahron pursed his lips and kept smoking.

'First of October. You were at the King's Arms with several mates, including Arvesen and Einarsson.'

'I've never denied it.'

'When did you leave the pub?'

'I assume you know that already, as it was you lot that came and picked me up!'

'I mean before that. When you took Einarsson's car and went off. About half past seven, would that be?'

'Einarsson's car? Are you joking? No one was allowed to borrow Einarsson's car. Complete rubbish. And I'd been drinking.'

'That never stopped you before. You've got a conviction for drink-driving. And according to Jorun you were the only person who was allowed to borrow the car. You were an exception. You were a good friend and you didn't have a car.'

He took two deep drags on his cigarette and blew the smoke out. 'I didn't go anywhere, I just sat there drinking all evening.'

'Undoubtedly. You were totally intoxicated, according

to the cook. Don't forget that he was at work and sober and that he keeps an eye on people. Who comes and who goes. And when they come and go.'

He was silent.

'So you went out, maybe you took a look at the street life and finished your little trip at Durban's, where you parked Einarsson's car on the pavement and rang the bell at exactly eight o'clock. Two short rings, wasn't it?'

Silence.

'You paid, and demanded the goods you'd paid for. And after that' – Sejer nodded slightly and stared at him – 'you began to argue with her.'

Sejer had lowered his voice, Ahron had lowered his head. As if he had something interesting lying in his lap.

'You've got a dangerous streak, Mr Ahron. Before you knew what had happened, you'd killed her. You raced back to the pub, hoping it would serve as an alibi and that no one would notice that you'd actually been away for a time. And then you began to drink.'

Ahron shook his head disparagingly.

'Through the haze of alcohol you realised just what you'd done. You made a clean breast of it to Einarsson. You thought he might be able to help you with an alibi. He was a friend, after all. You boys looked out for one another. And it had been an accident, hadn't it? You were just some poor devil who was having a bad time, and of course Egil would understand, so you took the chance and told him. He was sober as well, perhaps the only one of the group who was, he would have been believed.'

Ahron missed the ashtray, probably on purpose.

'But then, clearly, things got on top of you. You were foolish, you made a real spectacle of yourself. Late at night the landlord contacted us and requested you be taken in drunk and disorderly. Einarsson followed you in his car. Perhaps he was scared you'd talk while you were in the van, or in the cells. He wasn't only trying to save you from the holding cells, but also from a murder conviction. And the amazing thing was, he managed it! It probably didn't strike you just how incredible this was until the next day, but then I imagine you shuddered at the thought of just what a close call it had been.'

Ahron lit another cigarette.

'It must have been strange for you when Einarsson vanished. Have you thought at all about why he died? I mean, really thought it through. It was actually a genuine misunderstanding, just as you said.'

Ahron gathered himself and lay back in his chair.

'And then you began to visit Jorun. You knew that we were questioning her. Perhaps you were frightened that Egil had managed to talk?'

'You've obviously been working on this tale a long time.'

'But listen to this. I just happen to have an interesting piece of news for you. You were seen. A witness saw you, and by that I don't mean saw you as you left the scene of the crime in Einarsson's Opel. A witness saw you kill Maja Durban.'

This statement was so extraordinary that it made Ahron smile.

'Sometimes people are frightened to come forward. Sometimes they have good reasons for not doing so, so it took some time. But she came in the end. She was sitting on a stool in the adjoining room and was looking at you through the door that was open a crack. She's just made a statement.'

Peddik's eyes wavered slightly, then he smiled again.

'Quite a claim, isn't it?' continued Sejer. 'I agree. But you see, this time it isn't a bluff. You killed her, and you were seen. It was a gross and totally unnecessary murder. Totally unfair. She was a woman' – Sejer got up from his chair and took a few paces – 'and a small woman at that, with only a fraction of your musculature. According to the pathologist's report she was one metre fifty-five tall and weighed fifty-four kilos. She was naked. You were sitting over her. In other words' – he lowered himself into his chair again – 'she was utterly defenceless.'

'She wasn't fucking defenceless, she had a knife!'

His shout reverberated round the room, then there came a sob.

Ahron hid his face in his hands and attempted to keep his body calm. It had begun to shake violently. 'I want that solicitor now!'

'He's on his way, he's on his way.'

'Right this bloody moment!'

Sejer leant over to the cassette player and switched on the tape. The voice of Eva Magnus was crisp and clear, even slightly monotonous, she'd been tired by that time, but there could be no mistaking her.

'"You tarts are fucking greedy. I've laid out a thousand for a five-minute job, d'you know how long it takes me to earn that much at the brewery?"'

'Now perhaps you see why Egil died? You looked quite similar. Easy to make a mistake in that dim light.'

'The solicitor!' he cried hoarsely.

Chapter 35

Jan Henry was skulking in the garage. He was struggling to turn up the legs of his mechanic's suit, and when he'd finished, he tried to look at himself in an old, cracked windowpane that was leaning against the wall.

Emma Magnus was in her father's guest room where she had her bed, looking about with a bewildered expression. 'I'd rather sleep with you two,' she wheedled.

'There wouldn't be room for your bed in there,' her father said miserably.

'I could sleep in the bed with both of you,' she sniffed. 'I don't mind lying in the gap.'

Markus Larsgård was taken to hospital in an ambulance. The crew looked quickly through his house, in case there was a dog or cat that was in danger of being shut in. They looked in every room, even in the cellar, which only contained a load of old junk, a broken

Karin Fossum

washing machine, rotten apples and a clutch of old paint tins.

Eva Magnus had pulled the blanket over her head. Beneath the blanket it was dark, and quite soon it got hot. Nothing was happening inside her head.

Karlsen and Sejer strolled down the corridor in silence. They continued into the rear lot where the cars were parked. Karlsen aimed for a Ford Mondeo.

'What will Magnus be sent down for, d'you think?' He glanced at Sejer.

'Culpable homicide, I'm afraid.'

Sejer sighed heavily. He felt a knot in his stomach. Children got up to some funny things, they forgot about time, they had no sense of responsibility and anything was possible. Nothing untoward might have happened, it was probably just a small incident. That was what they were hoping, as they walked towards the car. But instinctively, as if at some given signal, they both quickened their steps.